Path Of The Azdinist
LU

By

Christopher Sampson

Cover illustrations by Sean Counley
Map illustration by Joshua Hoskins
Proof reading and editing services by R E Raymer

Grosvenor House
Publishing Limited

<comment>publisher colophon</comment>
This book is published by
Grosvenor House Publishing Ltd
Link House
140 The Broadway, Tolworth, Surrey, KT6 7HT.
www.grosvenorhousepublishing.co.uk

This book is a work of fiction. Any resemblance to
people or events, past or present, is purely coincidental.

A CIP record for this book
is available from the British Library

ISBN 978-1-80381-672-2

To everyone who has supported 'Azure' so far – thank you. I am incredibly delighted to offer my first full-length book set in the world we so often write about in our music.

The story of 'Lu' is particularly important to me. It is a story first discussed in our eponymous 2017 album-opener, and later elaborated on in our 2021 songs 'Mistress', 'Ameotoko I – The Curse', and 'Ameotoko II – Cloudburst'. It is an unusual circumstance to have written numerous songs based on a book that did not yet exist, but here we are!

There is so much more to come from us in the way of music and fantasy, and I am looking forward to every moment of it.

Contents

CONTENTS

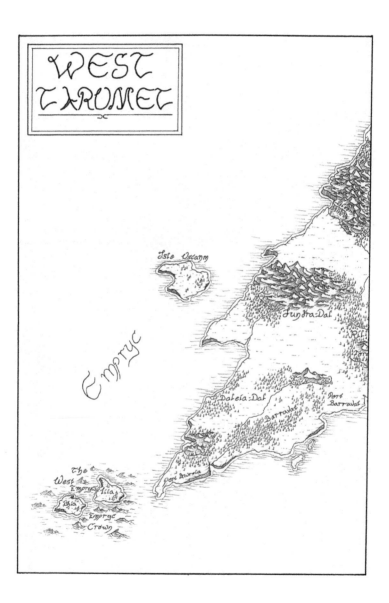

Upon a world as vast as Kraj, there are endless corners to be explored. Initially cultivated by the planet's retired creators, who now observe it from afar, each corner of Kraj contained a unique palette of life and culture. There were many an account of endless fields of fire, of distant realms of sweet-smelling ice, and of seething forests that spat lightning from their leaves.

In the earliest civilised years of Kraj, a small tropical continent called 'Taromet' became unbreakably intertwined with the fate of all things. Something, or someone, had disturbed the equilibrium that was so carefully poised by its designers. From this, a chain of somewhat planned events had been sent into motion.

Such events are the focus of this book.

INTRODUCTION

From above, the ever-blue crown of the Bhia wilderness was an impregnable, and unmistakable anomaly. By the breeze, there was no seasonal weather, and by the ground, there were no harvesters. Through the canopies, any visiting light became a cool turquoise; and the ground, waters, and roots below were all illuminated by it, and it alone.

Still, night and day passed (although the difference was faint), and the few creatures of the Bhia thrived, wholly indifferent to the gloom. Between these pillars of lifewood and stone, there lived some deer and small cattle, mice, and other rodents, as well as many bland birds and insects.

There was, however, another life that drifted among the Bhia.

Sopping and sobbing its way through the blue-green trees, slow and dazed, this amorphous lump was hardly awake. It was, in fact, a human, or at least it once was human. Now, head to toe, the thing was covered in moss and mould, and matted wet hair. And the wetness never dried, and the mould always lived, for it was perpetually hydrated by a dense, weeping cloud.

Dark grey, and solid in appearance, hanging at an arm's length above the creature, this unusual companion would follow the thing's every movement, as if it were focussing its gentle efforts with some sentience.

With no record or memory of the cloud-bearer's aimless arrival into the Bhia, there was little reason to assume that this plodding derelict was not born amid the turquoise. The secret genesis of the Walker was unknown for now, and unless something dared to break its inertia, these origins would stay unknown forever.

PART ONE

An outsider visits the Bhia, and entrusts the Walker with wondrous gifts, and cruel missions

Chapter One

THE MISTRESS OF THE BHIA

It was no unusual morning in the Bhia wilderness, and the ancient moss-thing was traipsing alongside the silent river that ran throughout the forest. The cloud travelled eagerly above and was spattering aggressively about the thing, breaking any silence that the river once had. As the thing wandered, it looked down at its ugly self and frowned at its ill-defined face. What had led it into this sickened way? And where were its memories that would otherwise shed light onto its clouded existence? Thoughts such as these were common amongst the clutter of the Walker's brain and were regular enough for them to be both meaningless and hopeless. The river led the melancholy being through a grass that, by now, was path-forged and flattened by the Walker's feet. On and on, this route terminated at a lonely pool, deep in the forest's stomach.

Today's journey to the pool was the Walker's quickest, and most automatic journey so far, granting slightly less time for its scheduled grieving and self-loathing. Usually, this derogation occurred as a torturous and consistent routine; therefore, on arrival, the dripping shadow made an additional effort to gaze into the pool and mourn its existence. The thin stream feeding this pool created a handful of thin, delicate ripples, undulating just enough to warp the reflected face of the moss thing, exaggerating every ugly inch of its visage, until only a mess of drifting features surrounded the sad, orange eyes staring back upward. These eyes were nothing more than a faint glow; deeply set under plant and rot. They glimmered like embers, peering desperately through their organic prison with what strength they had left. Aside from the escaping orange, there was a hint of cool grey beneath its robes of overgrowth. The clinging vines were yet to obstruct the movement of the creature's lower limbs, but anything that might have resembled a nose, mouth, ears, or even arms were well and truly hidden beneath its gown of life and decay. The rippling mirror image of the Walker shimmered in the blue half-light, falling in and out of phase to the rhythmic movement of the pool's rain-disturbed surface.

In that moment, the drifter took strange comfort in its echo company, and was unaware of the darkness brewing beneath its likeness. Silt was shifting along the bed of the plunge, and a myriad of bubbles had begun to surface, increasing in both ferocity and size at an alarming rate. An outside force had somehow made its way to the dismal Bhia woods and whether it had come from above the pool or beneath it, the alien energy had evoked quite a stirring within the water.

By now, the Walker had been urgently (albeit reluctantly) released from its trance, for an impossibly localised wind had stirred and the bubbling membrane of the possessed water was spitting and splashing out onto the poolside, alerting the Bhia's daydreaming occupant to the emergence that was now occurring.

For a moment longer, these bizarre reactions in the water continued and progressed, before suddenly, something exploded from the centre of the foam-clouded pond and the ripples containing the Walker's reflection

2

could no longer grace the water's surface, for the face of something else was now erupting from the centre of the pool!

A vicious freshwater cascade of life and chaos was emerging from the pond, standing at least three times the height of the wet Walker. As this new thing materialised among the Bhia, the blue-green moss creature stood its ground, and the hanging cloud seemed to resist the curling wind that had somehow whipped the cyclone, veiling this new, fountained demon. Water writhed like a pillar of snakes, before twisting to form a strong, effeminate face, long aqueous hair, and a few vague limbs.

'Forest Walker! Succumb to your Mistress in this instant if you seek an end to your eternal cloudlife! Succumb to me if you wish to be mortal and dry, with the direction to leave this bleak wilderness!'

But the moss-creature did not speak, for it had forgotten how to use its voice. The frothing Goddess did not seem flattered by this, however, and impatiently lashed a water-limb towards the Walker.

'You are not shackled by your broken tongue! Speak to me with your thoughts, wet servant, before I retract my merciful offer-...'

And amid her speeches, the Walker searched about the shape of this unknown water spirit, looking for any traces of familiarity. She spoke as an acquaintance would; yet this spouting celestial was not in any part of the moss-creature's memory, nor was much else.

The word '*Bhia*' was familiar. It was the only thing the Walker remembered, as were its many routes, and the nature of the cloud that the Walker shared this travelling union with.

Upon receiving these candid and desolate thoughts, the Goddess was taken aback. Her gushing-translucence almost *softened*, and her eyes became wistful and forgiving.

'You have no memory of me, this is clear now. So, I will abridge my relationship to you, Walker.'

While too old for fear, the Walker certainly felt some relief in her changing tone.

'Before you fell under this sullen cloud, before this moss suffocated your mortal flesh, we shared some trapping destiny. I am not known to abide by any fate, and you, Lu my faithful Reikan votary, gave your mortal form to those Wyrms of existence, to disenthrall me.

You have walked this half-life as a prison sentence - a high price for freeing me from my role on this world.

These events occurred an eternity ago, yet a grateful Mistress I remain.

Now servant, I cannot yet sever your bonds of cloud and bone, but I have come to you this morning to offer you a pact that will enable said freedom. It has taken longer than I expected, but my interests have finally fallen in line with yours; hence I have waited until now to return. I apologise for my inexactness, but I trust you can forgive my discretions as an act of new-found servitude?'

And then silence fell about the place. The moss creature pondered this name '*Lu*', that the goddess had given him. Part of him was returning, some memory and some form. Something fell to the ground and Lu glanced down to see what it was. On the floor lay a hefty amount of wet plant, and then from the torso of the Walker fell another piece, and then another! Patches of a lost life, in a sea-town called Rei, were brightening his amnesia like slow spreading fire in an unlit night. As the past re-established its anchor in Lu's mind, the physical veil that obscured him fell away. This lump, once genderless, inhuman, and barely living, was shedding its mossy exoskeleton.

Dense mats of plant and fungus fell away, revealing a slim, frail figure. Lu had thick, blue-grey skin that was rugged in texture, sore from the latch of plants and the brush of the undergrowth. His legs were strong, but his arms were thin, and the posture of his spine had clearly degraded under the mass of the wet plant-life that was once his burden.

Lu's solitary satellite, the weeping cloud, continued its rain. This shower only perpetuated the moulting of the moss, and in a short time, the Reikan-human was entirely undressed of his living gown and stood naked before this smiling goddess, revealed for the first time in this age of the realm.

Lu looked down into the pool for a reflection and was further awakened by the startling beauty that stared back up. His face was that of a young sailor, preserved by his lichen coffin, with a wide, yet delicate nose, strong cheekbones, and full lips. The narrow, orange eyes of the moss-creature were the very same eyes that had burned eagerly behind the veil yet were now enhanced with new memory and intellect that was previously sedated and lost for an eternity, whilst somehow maintaining a fine balance of equal parts weary and wild. Wasting no more time on this unusual vanity, the grey humanoid glanced back up to the mysterious enchantress and spoke his coarse first words in lifetimes uncountable and unknown.

'I will serve you, Mistress of the Bhia. There are mysteries about you, something that I cannot yet ascertain. But your power is obvious, and your knowledge and memory of this world far exceeds mine. I ask that you do not take advantage of my naivety, for I am weak in body and spirits, and this trust is all I have to offer - for the time being.'

The liquid-goddess smiled down on the handsome, yet ageless Walker.

'These green-wing waterflowers are not halfway bloomed. Train your body, and mend your spirit, servant Lu. This pool is now sacred water, drink deep and drink daily – your true strengths will surely come to you before the last flower is woken. On that night I will return here to assess your efforts, and then we will barter the price of your curse.'

Lu made sure to appear that he had acknowledged these words; and kneeled before the enchantress, to confirm his servitude. Before the man could return to his feet, the woman in the water was gone. Somehow, despite his long and solitary life, Lu now felt strangely alone in the fresh absence of the Mistress. The Walker was free of the parasitic camouflage that had visually married him to the dull wilderness; he was an outsider, now cold and naked among the expansive trees and marsh of the Bhia.

Many sunless days passed, and Lu found a number of ways to train his mind and muscles, through trial and error, and from what memory of his old life was returning.

Surrounded by branches, stumps, rocks, and water, Lu had all he needed to fashion his own exercise gymnasium. In the time between crafting these training regimes, Lu set about searching for some new nourishment among the turquoise, opting for things more luscious than any muck he would previously have consumed in his sorry bindings of moss and mould. Within a few introductory meals, the unique tastes of the plants, both root and berry, were becoming more prevalent in his diet These were of far greater benefit to his body than the grubs and other decomposed offerings of the forest floor. Additionally, as his body strengthened, his thoughts became ferociously more alert, enabling him to run and swim with tremendous control. Interestingly, no matter how fast the grey man could run or swim, the cloud could effortlessly glide in parallel; hanging ever-comfortably. It was completely unaffected by the sudden abilities of its land-bound counterpart.

After no longer than a week, this once clumsy, mindless lump had shed its mossy chrysalis with grace and had emerged as a now agile thinker - ready for the guidance of his mistress. Lu's transformation was complete. With time to spare before their scheduled meeting, he wandered back to the pond, both to check on the progress of the lily blooms and to test how his creeping vanity might respond to his recently enhanced physique.

The grey wanderer widened his pale lips slowly, into a slight smile. His naked feet had grown no more used to the friendly kiss of the morning grass growing around the pool sweating its dew about his ankles, and dripping down between his toes. Nor were his ears yet fully acquainted with the unusually bright sound of his drizzling fog-bride; a presence that had crowded him beyond any known time, now spluttering and spitting with a glistening shimmer of noise. This cleansing patter evolved as Lu traversed different terrains, whether it be the softer welcome of the muds or the thick resistance of rock-face. All were unique to the Walker, and this seemingly trivial rain chatter never failed to entrance him. It had taken time to become noticeable, but every lost sensation blunted by the clasp of moss and decay, had been granted back, reignited through the wash of the Mistress's blessings.

Nearing the water's edge, again Lu speculated at the fruits of his training. Would he resemble something akin to his folk, long ago? And if so, would this visual familiarity trigger long-forgotten memories of his previous life? Now with his sharp new eyes and mind, the grey man and his cloud peered into this fate-wrapped pool, and yet still he frowned.

The once-sailor was not at all displeased with what he could see of himself in the pool. Slim but sturdy, his muscles were now quite visibly toned, through tight flesh and little fat. Stunted by an eternity of emotional depravation, the thin tentacles of pride now crept and coiled and found new residence upon the Walker's heart. And still, Lu was frowning, for this pride was spawning vanity and through vanity were now visible spectres of imperfection upon this ageless wanderer.

The nails upon his fingers and toes were thick, overgrown, and wretched. The dusk-green hair upon his head was somehow both dry and broken at the ends, and damp with the oil and dirt upon his scalp. His bare skin was like a map written in patches of scar and discolouration from the previous squatters of parasitic plant and mould. Buckling down to his grazed knees, the Walker mourned his own sorry image – still a fading memory of his people, and an unfinished man.

Once he had exhausted his unnaturally preserved reservoir of tears, Lu allowed his cloud to take over the weeping while he inspected his surroundings. The waterflowers still had days left before they would be fully bloomed, and there was still much work to be done to pacify this nagging desire for beauty.

Chapter Two

A DREAM ASIDE THE VACANT POND

The moon, despite its invisibility to anyone under the trees, had been regurgitating its borrowed light since the beginning of this world. Tonight, the leaves and branches of the forest almost bore no resistance to its rays, and with its new welcome, the moonbeams were kissed by the same turquoise that stained the sunrays of the day.

Down below, this light drifted through the mesh of the Bhia crown, illuminating the now-shivering Lu as he sunk himself into the pond. To any passing onlooker, there was some humour to be found in the sight of this man, followed by a raincloud, attempting to bathe. There were no passing onlookers in the Bhia however, and to a man who lives by the taunt of splashing rain, Lu's full immersion into the coolness of the lunar pond was an engulfing climax after a lifetime of teetering the brink of wetness. In the mystic blue-green haze of the moonlit Bhia clearing, the lean, short silhouette of the Reikan slipped into the plunge, and coolness welcomed him in ways utterly uncommon to newer beings elsewhere in the world at the time.

Into a dark pocket of the pool, the grey man allowed himself to sink. Exhaling rapidly, his lungs emptied, and his feet bounced down on the soft bed of the pond. Somewhere else amid these years, similar beings with similar limbs and faces would still explore the waters of the world, but with caution and fear of the depths. The humans of the new era held their breath in short capacity, and the deep waters offered only the threat of death or worse. Lu, a lost antecedent to that weaker breed, was born a son of mariners in the sea-town of Rei, long before wildwater was diluted, and eventually, cleansed from the blood of humankind. Civilisations, acquainted by trade, had then merged and interbred, and empires were built and razed, and eventually such blood had become so far crossed that no meaningful trace of those sea-borne traits remained. Unknowingly the last of his kind, the Reikan rarely felt breathless in submersion, and the natural waters of the world welcomed him home.

Along the pond-bottom Lu searched and collected items for his unspoken agenda. Sharp rock, soft pebbles, fishbone and scale, and any fragments of drowned animal that were tough enough to resist the decay of time. Occasionally resurfacing to place these findings by the water's edge, the Walker would vanish for an hour or so at a time, leaving the cloud hovering frantically above the pool, following step by step, unable to breach the rippling barrier between them.

Following one final plunge into the lunar freshwater, Lu returned to the surface with a handful of unusual gems, and a facial expression suggesting that he was unsure how these gems came into being. Effortlessly, he pulled himself up out of the water and let no wasted moment pass before he set about organising his finds.

Assorted stones, sharp and rough, were soon to become purposed cosmetic tools for cutting and filing and scrubbing away dead hair, nail, and skin tissue. Everything else was for a much grander, and more time-consuming project that Lu was formulating.

After freeing his flesh of its final imperfections, Lu planted his head beside the near-bloomed greenwings and allowed himself a short departure into a well-earned rest. Now, for the first time in this strange age, sleep welcomed the lost human into its maternal devour, so to bestow its paralysing dreams, eventful and episodic, upon the Walker.

And he was running, eyes wet with tears, and hands wet with blood. At impossible speed, through trees he did not recognise, the grey man burst into a wicked expanse of grassland. Out of the Bhia, treading land unshielded and at the mercy of a wicked and azure sky above, churning in unnatural torment. Though immense rain spoiled the ground beneath Lu's frantic strides, these droplets were foreign to him, and his personal raincloud was nowhere to be seen.

Lu had no time to scan the skies for his lost companion, however, as his head was aimed forward, and his body pulsated with adrenaline as the sprint endured. With every step, a creeping disassociation between mind and movement became more apparent. These actions were not his own, and this nonsensical landscape of violence and abstraction was contorting far beyond Lu's understanding of reality.

The ground, rain-bullied into viscous mud, was slowing Lu down. As he decelerated to a sinking stop, damning waves of guilt came upon him, unexplained and unstoppable, bringing him to his knees. Sinking mud became sinking guilt, and the approaching walls of thunder were now also guilt, and both these ugly manifestations would take him soon.

Now unable to stand or crawl, Lu was under surrender to the fast engulfment of an endless black thundercloud, and the swallow of the liquid ground. He was eaten whole, entombed by these vivid, strangling wraiths of anguish.

In this abominable shroud, the Walker did not feel alone. Impossible cries and throatless voices drifted around him, as this nightmare evolved, and the fog softened. By some gravity, a thin texture arrived beneath his feet, and Lu attempted to stand. Blind to the nearby whispering sea, he stumbled to the guidance of his ears. The sand was dull and the air was cold, but as the darkness lifted, Lu began to sweat.

Like before, the sky was writhing uncomfortably into fantastic blues, as if it were the coiling rings of an immense snake. As the sky spun, the sea would follow, a pair of cogs wrestling within a ticking clock.

And finally, Lu saw a young man by the water. He was grey and slim, and by Lu's judgement, he was most certainly also from the sea town of Rei. Building a fire in the sand to fight the chill of the cruel wind, the stranger was seemingly oblivious to the sheer spectacle of his surroundings.

Emerging from the smoke of the fire, the wind formed a single hand that reached towards the stranger, beckoning with uneasy grace. Too distant to intervene, Lu collapsed into tears as the young man offered his hand back to the smoke, and immediately combusted. As the young man blazed, his life force was released into a shadow-smoke semblance of his living form. The ghost watched for a moment, before getting sucked into the snake-sky above, igniting further torment in the clouds.

In this transaction, the eerie fingers of the mist-hand disappeared into the human flames, somehow altering the chemistry of the fire. These embers fell away like a loose garment and unveiled its host, who no longer was the standing ashes of that young man. Stood in his place now was a woman, as tall as the highest ember peak of the inferno and triple the height of Lu. Her face was obscured behind her sea-green windswept mane, and yet a powerful and recognisable aura throbbed from her core, as Lu found himself once again removed from his surroundings, and away from the lurid shores of witchery.

Finally, Lu was crouched upon a mountainous shape. It was an enormous white-stone obelisk, reaching high above land and sea and even some clouds. Below, a great quarrel was reaching some form of climax. From what could be seen at this distance, a clash of life forms seemed to have rallied and were cheering, but the dead certainly outnumbered the living. The sky was calm, the air was warm, and there was some form of weapon in the Walker's hand, though he could not turn his head to see it. Again, there was no sign of his cloud-partner, and the troops below seemed to call up to him, either in joy or distress, but nothing was discernible. Lu closed his eyes, attempting to ignore the cries.

Something suddenly then latched onto his right arm, and then his left, and either side of the Walker was a flying beast! Gripping his left bicep was an ugly bat-thing, with leather wings, a rodent's tail, and the face of a young man grimacing with fiendish sympathy. Lu screamed, but only silent air would pass through his shaking lips.

Like a vice around the other arm, and on Lu's neck, were the sharp talons of a different being, which was enormous!

It was a colourful shimmering bird, and she was both brighter and more immense than any living thing that Lu had ever seen. In the grasp of these demons, Lu could not struggle and instead fell limp as they lifted him from his great pedestal. Higher and higher, the creatures soared, until the Kraj-world was invisibly small. At these heights, all that was around the Walker was a black expanse of sky.

Now that nothing could be seen, it appeared that the ascension had stopped and that the bird and the bat were simply remaining afloat in the bleakness. Even the bright shimmers of the beaked celestial were suffocated and crushed in this empty, lightless void.

Under lifted lids of shadow, an absurdly vast pair of red eyes blazed before him, soon followed by an ocean-sized jaw, boasting more teeth than every mouth in any sea. The gleaming fangs, and those wretched, *watching* globes of fire did alleviate *some* of the darkness. Partially illuminated now was an impossible, but altogether treacherous serpentine form, belonging to this new evil. Together, the bird and the man-bat released their hold on the Walker, and he fell swiftly into the infinite throat of the gigantic serpent.

And he awoke. First screaming, then acutely disturbed, Lu found himself panicked and outstretched in a bed of rain, cold sweat and lily dew, and his cloud close above. His heart was racing, and his mind was not yet detached from the horror of the illusion, though he now attempted to calm his thoughts and return to his more rational senses. Since countless years of dreamless dawdling, his long-awaited rest had taunted a strange mirage of what a life outside the Bhia could bring.

Unable to banish the urgent gnaw of his dream, the Walker eventually sat up among his remaining library of items and tinkered away for the rest of the morning. If his nightmare had given him any epiphany, then it concerned the potential danger and malice outside of the forest. No longer could he walk unclothed, naked to the threat of bloodshed, for there were surely extreme forces in conflict somewhere beyond the ever-blue walls of this timeless wood?

By noon, Lu had crudely stitched together a primitive suit of armour. Plates of shell, granite, and bone were strung together on the tougher skins he had foraged. The sleeveless jacket was not lightweight or practical at all, nor was it pleasant to look at. And yet, once its grey designer wore it, the suit took on new life. Glistening under the constant downpour, Lu stood up tall, and marched towards the pool, in order to fully witness his creation.

The mirror image of a barefoot sailor-warrior flickered among the ripples of the water, clad knee-to-shoulder in dripping patchwork.

'Protection, at its most hideous', he chuckled.

Chapter Three

A SUIT, SABRE, AND SACRIFICE

In a short while, Lu expected to meet again with the sibylline Mistress of the Bhia, and there were two things on his mind. Certainly, it was she who appeared in the second act of the dream. Through hosts of smoke, she bedevilled the cerulean illusions of his slumber - not a goddess, but a ghoul. A living shadow of her cultivated grandeurs, Lu feared.

And though he had trained and built his strength since first she appeared, he had also indulged her request that he drink daily from the sacred pool, yet the reason for this was unclear and unfelt. Since her morbid depiction in his dream, the sentiment of digesting her magic now unsettled him somewhat. Aside from this, the lucid ending of the nightmare was *so* unsettling that Lu dared not waste another thought on the topic.

Nonetheless, the patchwork wanderer straightened up to bask in the evening redolence. Like never before, the green-wing water lilies had bloomed to maturity, and their consequent fragrance now premiered upon the breeze.

As it had happened for Lu, it seemed the forest was evolving in parallel. Once, in the strained light of the Bhia, the cycle of life had been somewhat stunted, yet the years inflicted few casualties. Nothing blossomed, and therefore nothing wilted. No lethargic beast dared quarrel, all instead scavenging on fungus, roots and the carcasses of those who had already eventually died. But here by the sacred pool, the gleam of the sun and moon had recently surged. Near unobscured by whatever branches hung above, sufficient light now blessed the ecosystem below, and life by the pond was in full swing.

Smiling, Lu quietly praised the sorceress' work. The grey man and his cloud basked for a moment longer in the scent of the lilies, before the silence was spent.

In a triumphant splash, a cascade of light and liquid exploded and frothed. Like before, the majesty of this fountain softened rapidly and became the goddess once more.

Stepping forward, Lu calmly waited for the chaos to subside. The Mistress of the Bhia was larger than before and began to settle. After a moment of silence, she opened her gushing jaws in raucous laughter.

'Good evening to you, my lonely servant! I have spectated your efforts since last we met, and you have amused me with your enthusiasm...Should you wish to immerse yourself in my splendour, I will fortify your humble creations.'

On a vague interpretation of this offer, Lu nodded his head and obediently fell forward into her vast, flowing arms.

'Welcome, Lu' she whispered, as she pulled him towards her glowing core. The lonely cloud remained aside as if it felt inadequate compared the Mistress' torrential embrace.

There was unnatural comfort to be found in the womb of a goddess. As to be expected, the mellow pulse of submersion filled Lu's ears. As his host spoke again, her voice rang with obnoxious clarity, bypassing his ears completely and resonating instead through the bone of his skull.

'Resourcefully, you have certainly displayed some innovation, but I have replaced your frail bindings with an adhesive of my own. I will exchange your thoughtful medley of pond debris for the strongest shells in the four seas.'

She paused as if to grant Lu a moment to acknowledge her promises.

'By my fusion, your suit will not shatter. There are few Krajian forces capable.'

And concurrently these vows were upheld. Weightless and entranced, Lu observed as his dark grey-blue skin was revealed and then redressed. As the masterfully amalgamated exoskeleton carefully fell upon him, any glamour-induced awe was overshadowed by dark wonder. The shell shards were certainly part of something far greater. What demons of the outside world awaited him; what could have shed these formidable husks?

'Do not spend your concern on unknowns. Fear can be a weakness.'

Lu had forgotten that his thoughts were no secret here. Before him, a thin, ambiguous shape of light was materialising. The Mistress continued to chatter - 'And weakness is the formula of mortality. It can be suppressed, and then refashioned into a point!'

But her cryptic ramblings were near lost on her guest, for he was distracted. Throbbing before him, the bending light was now a sabre. Lu stretched out, beyond the dovetailed undercurrents that cradled him, and took the blade for his own.

Agony surged up his gripping arm and straight to the chest, and he involuntarily released the weapon. The water-womb collapsed around him, brought down by violent fits of the goddess' laughter. Spat out and sprawled on the grass, Lu coughed up puddles of enchanted liquid that had gradually intruded his lungs during submersion.

As his cloud-companion slowly washed the bile away, the grey man struggled to his feet. He locked eyes with his cackling Mistress, who was now grinning in response.

'Your new attire is unique in quality, and in strength. It will bring you safety on your leave of the Bhia once you have passed my test of fitness.'

Lu gratefully bowed before his benefactor. Lightweight though it seemed, the fantastically polished shellsuit was a clear freak of density, and impossible to penetrate. An empty, dull-green scabbard was fastened to his belt. A soft, light blue cloaking wrap protected his legs, permitting great freedom of movement and yet appeared identically as impenetrable as the shells. It seemed to be a robe, continuing up and covering his torso beneath the armour, but for now, only the lower section of the cloak was visible.

'The sword within me... You may take this with you also if you desire. Indeed, the curve is sharp. But the weapon is charged with greater powers of its own, which will not yet obey you. I will nullify these for now. Until you are ready, you merely wield a beautiful sword – nothing more and nothing less.'

And in the soft grip of the sailor-warrior, the sabre reappeared. Near transparent and colourless, the medium-length, single-edged blade could have been mistaken for glass. Yet by weight and texture alone, it was not glass, but some other unknown material. Lu coiled his fingers around the hilt, examining its understated crossguard and knuckle bow, both as clear as the rest of the weapon. Eventually, Lu returned his gaze to the Goddess.

'You have my thanks, great Mistress of the Bhia! Since last we spoke, I have doubted my allegiance, and found reconciliation. So, I ask of you – am I now fit to undertake your missions? With your wondrous gifts, have I strength enough? My body is hardened but my soul is lost. Rain erodes me yet I remain unscathed. Still, I long to dispel this curse!'

And then he paused. Before him, the Mistress appeared to conjure some form of window to another place. Her liquid face grew stern, in concentration or otherwise, as the portal became clearer.

Through the witch-eye, the sun was king. Saturated light burst out, and a forest of overpowering green and brown sat on the other side. Even within the ameliorated photosynthesis in the clearing of the Bhia, Lu had long forgotten the colours of a healthy world. The Mistress produced a single bubbling tentacle and gently guided the Walker closer to the golden window.

Slowly, Lu approached the mirage and soon could peer in as if he were indeed amid the luscious greeneries.

Akin to the heart of the Bhia, there was a fluvial centrepiece to this fertile jungle. Framed by eclectic pillars of trunk and branch, a ring-shaped stream trickled in a loop.

Here, the orders and natures of water were obsolete.

In the middle of the river-circle was a raised, aromatic flowerbed, which was certainly not dressed by chance. Of what dim memory he had of botany, Lu recognised the particularly dense violet plumage to be Teething Darklilies, also called 'Lila', as well as many purple spring-blooms, the names of which Lu could not recall from his previous life. To bask in the fragrant intersection of darklilies ahead and the greenwings behind was a sensual union that the Rei-man had never known before. But also behind him, the bubbling sigh of the goddess could be heard, and Lu was reminded to open his eyes and continue to observe.

'The plantsman... she will soon return. And as this gardener may knife her weeds, I must send you to knife this parasite of mine.'

Lu hesitated. 'I must *assassinate* this unseen gardener?' *Murder.* The ransom of his cloud-prison was *murder.* Now the unlikely executioner's mind was racing in blunder. What could be the crimes of a gardener, so significant that they could warrant this sentence? And when the perpetrator appears, what form would she take? And be it formidable, how can it be defeated?

Again, the grey man had not considered the telepathy of his Mistress.

'Do not panic, rainchild. Through the sabre, I will advise your every move. There is much ill-spent power to be reused upon Kraj. If I must reap it, then you are to be my scythe; the guilt will be mine, not yours. Yes, you must assassinate the gardener, but first, you must pass a final test of strength before I can know for certain that you are physically capable of that mission.

Swallowing back his concerns, the grey man nodded. Then, with a wave of one of her great, flowing arms, the Mistress conjured a second window of unsettling reds, oranges, and browns. Unlike the first portal, there was no clear location on the other side of this opening, only an abstract swirl of throbbing mystery. Then something began to stir beyond the flap of darkness; it was large and looming, reaching out from its shadow realm.

'Step away, Lu; run if you must. Soon, a mindless beast of my own summoning will be upon you. It is large, unreasonable, and vicious, but it is mortal, sluggish, and it is stupid. This is your final test; you drank from my pool and trained well, but your wit is untested.'

Before Lu had finished processing the daunting words of the Sorceress, the shadow began to pierce the veil that had separated the red realm from the Bhia. Lu took a few large steps back and looked wide-eyed at his Mistress for further guidance or explanation.

'You are strong, well armoured, and you carry a blade unmatched by any other. But it is your command of these qualities that will determine your success here, Walker. Behold, the red entity! Slay this beast, and you are ready. Make it swift; I have no wish to linger in this astral form for too long. Good luck!'

Lu pulled the glassblade out from its scabbard, stepping further and further away from the grim outline that was slowly emerging from the red realm. Then, in a tremendous burst, the dark and clumsy figure birthed through the portal, with visible discomfort; the opening was a great deal smaller than the shadow-thing that had fallen through it, and the true shape of the beast still appeared to be recovering from the squeeze.

As the red and brown lump rose to its true height, Lu was still unable to recognise any discernible features that would allow him to categorise the creature. It was twice his height and appeared to have no eyes or human attributes. Instead, its shape resembled a smaller Bhia conifer, such as that of a pine tree. Branch-like shards of brown and scarlet protruded with increasing length towards the summit of its dazzling body, and at its base were six thick roots that sat above the ground, and a bulky, oozing tail that trailed behind. The main trunk of the monster was glistening wet, and clearly composed of some kind of viscous, sanguine slime, but both its upper and lower protrusions were of solid material, and of a much higher density.

After examining the final shape of the somewhat stunned entity, Lu felt as though he now beheld a giant, majestic slug, standing upon the legs of a lobster, garishly decorated with shards of ice or glass. One could have assumed that the beast was both benign and beautiful, had the Sorceress not implied otherwise. Still, Lu kept his distance, and his grip on the sabre, while he observed the awakening of the otherworldly invertebrate. Even under normal circumstances, he could only faintly remember a few of the many monsters, spirits, dragons, and demons from the realities and folklores of his ancestors, and none resembled the red entity before him.

Then, one of the shards at the front of the dazzling creature opened, and a voice that resembled a melodic, chilling wind poured out of its gaping squid-like beak. Startled, Lu could do nothing but stare as the slug's once-red flesh began to change into a tortoiseshell blend of pale yellows and whites, which seemed to herald the beginning of the battle.

Scuttling upon its orange, crustacean legs, the beast now charged towards Lu at an unexpected speed. Lu had initially assumed that by 'sluggish', the Mistress was implying that his adversary would be slow; it seemed to be sluggish only in appearance however, as it came scuttling across the green-wing lilies between them, closing in on its prey, howling as it neared. Just before the giant was upon him, Lu managed to dive out of the way to his left, landing upon his fighting arm and temporarily deadening it upon impact. He furrowed his rain-soaked brow from the sensation, although he still believed his senses to be somewhat limited; there was no knowing if he had merely bruised his arm or damaged it beyond use. Nonetheless, he coiled around on the spot to witness the shimmering mollusc crash into the trees behind, its colour rapidly changing back to blood red as if to express its pain. It clearly was unable to calculate its attacks with any degree of accuracy or strategy, so Lu decided that it would be wise to take advantage of its impulsive demeanour.

As the red entity convulsed in an enraged frenzy, Lu found the time to sidestep back along the stream, towards the Bhia pool, where the Mistress was watching insouciantly. He intended to drown the beast, and hopefully startle the sorceress at the same time, for she appeared to be far too complacent regarding the demon she had brought into this world.

'Do not forget, Walker – your thoughts are not private.' she laughed.

The entity came charging again, its sharp legs tearing across the softer grounds below, which had been first dampened by Lu's raincloud, and then again wetted by the slime of the beast during its initial attack.

Too late had Lu realised, as he dodged the beast again and it fell towards the water, that the glistening moisture exuding from its body was no ordinary mucus. Grass, and trampled flowers, now withered away in the wake of the slug, as its toxic discharge sizzled into all that it came in contact with. And then, with a heavy slap, the slug hit the water and disappeared beneath the temporarily obscured flow of the Mistress. In an instant, the water was foaming, and a wine-red discolouration began to rise up from the beast's writhing shadow at the bottom.

Despite the obvious toxicity introduced to the pool, Lu felt a shiver of victory, as the shadow calmed in the deep, becoming deadly still. The Mistress of the Bhia began to laugh again, however, and Lu realised that victory had escaped him for the time being. With a short rumble, followed by the thunderous crash of aqueous eruption, the red entity burst swiftly from the pool and flattened out upon the side.

Lu winced as lashings of acid water found the grey skin of his wrist, and then continued to erode slightly into the flesh, relinquishing the threshold of whatever remaining numbness he still had for pain. He turned to face where the creature had landed, to glimpse the final moments of its newest incarnation. From its flattened landing upon the ground, it had reformed itself into a shorter, but far more threatening shape. All six of its jagged, segmented legs were now off the ground, slightly below its moaning beak. They were poised like claws, ready to either impale the Walker, or pull him into the slug's burning flesh. The entity did have one disadvantage in this form, which Lu noticed as it slowly turned its clumsy bulk in his direction; much like any true mollusc, the beast was far slower now that it travelled upon the crawling ripples of its single, gigantic foot. Unlike a small slug or snail, however, the colour-changing entity was not simply secreting its mucus from a denser flesh beneath – it was entirely composed of it; Lu feared that if the creature found a grip on him, he would be swallowed into its mucilaginous core, where he would be broken down by its acid and dissolved completely.

Lu shuddered momentarily at the thought of absorption, before jogging back into the nearby trees, where he hoped to find some safety whilst devising a plan of attack. Though survival seemed maintainable while the entity was in this more aggressive form, Lu was supposed to slay the beast, and so far, it showed no obvious signs of weakness. From behind the thicket, the Walker glanced in the direction of the entity, to gauge its distance. The creature, it seemed, had not successfully followed Lu's direction of escape, and was now slithering into the trees on the northwest edge of the clearing. Quietly, Lu followed around the overgrown perimeter towards the beast, keeping distance enough to avoid alerting it to his presence. Again, the creature had changed colour, and all its flesh had become an unruly patchwork blend of various lurid pinks, and pearl whites, while its legs and shards remained as orange as before. Then, as he shifted closer to the alien entity, Lu stepped clumsily onto the thin end of a fallen branch, and tumbled forwards through the bracken.

Though it was eyeless, and probably therefore blind, the beast stopped mid-slither in response to the sound of Lu's stumble, and the shards upon its back began to twist. With a sense of panic and some intrigue, Lu rushed to his feet to try and make sense of the creature's new transformation. Yet again, it had become red and brown and appeared to be flattening itself back down to the ground.

Lu had a premonition that the red entity was reassuming its previous, tree-like shape, whereby the claws would return to being legs, increasing the creature's speed drastically. He had narrowly avoided its charge before but he knew that he would inevitably soon tire from prolonged evasion; the sorcerous slug was charged by otherworldly enchantment and was doubtless indefatigable. If he ran for much longer, he would be exhausted by nightfall and then engulfed by the entity. In any case, he was supposed to defeat the thing, but in its six-legged formation, the beast would certainly be too agile to attack; there seemed to be no solution to this test.

The Walker did not waste another moment in anticipation, however, for his eyes had become fixed upon a clear marking on the creature's gelatinous back. It was little more than a throbbing shadow, slightly sunken beneath the surface of the creature's outer membrane, which bore similarities in both shape and murmuring pulse to a beating heart. The shadow had not been visible in the creature's slower, attack formation, as it was (Lu assumed) hidden behind the larger shards upon its back. Lu had little time to ponder the hidden heart before the red entity hurtled forwards, and Lu was forced to leap out of the way of its thunderous gallop. As he jumped, he slashed out impulsively at the beast, slicing with no real skill or precision. Nonetheless, the Walker felt the blow of the gliding glassblade land and then pass through something solid. Whatever it had hit was both thick and delicate, as the blade seemed to tear through effortlessly, but as Lu landed, and rolled away from the howling demon, the sabre tugged free from his hand. Lu glanced up to discern what had just occurred and found himself scrambling desperately out of the way as the red entity appeared to collapse in his direction. As he scrambled, his hands landed all too regularly in the sporadic puddles of mucus secreted by the slug, causing Lu to involuntarily yelp out numerous times, continually alerting the entity to his direction of escape. The entity did not seem to be in any urgent pursuit of the grey man, however, and once Lu had safely distanced himself from the slug, he managed to stand up, and then quickly understood all that had just come to pass.

The glassblade was far sharper than he could ever have anticipated; what he had so easily sliced, and therefore believed to have been the viscous membrane of the slug's body, had instead been the solid material of one of the creature's orange, knife-like appendages. It seemed that, upon losing a leg, the entity had also lost its balance; as it fell, the sabre had landed inside of the beast, where it was pulled from Lu's fingers and sucked into the slug's slime centre. The sword had not dissolved at all, however, for it was clearly impervious to the acid.

Lu stared hopelessly at the shadow of the Sorceress's gift, as it floated within the living, shifting chamber of acid. By the time he had realised its capability to slice through the creature's legs, and potentially even into the entity's mysterious shadow heart, the blade was no longer his to command. Furthermore, if losing his new sword wasn't already enough of a setback, the five-legged creature had now begun to flatten itself back into a state of change, before rising again in its slower, grappling configuration, whereby the pulsing heart was no longer visible.

Lu began to despair. Since it had lost one of its claws, the entity was unlikely to revert to using the remaining five as legs, thus the shadow heart (which Lu believed to be the key to defeating the beast) would not be available for attack. It was inconsequential in any case; even if the entity changed forms, exposing the beating lump, Lu was without a weapon to puncture it with.

But as the red entity, now slowly fading into the pink-white pattern it had previously flaunted, approached upon a trail of weeping sludge, Lu observed the leg that had been left behind, and a reasonable, vaguely achievable idea sprang up amid the more useless chaos in his mind.

Keeping his distance from its vicious pincers, Lu needed to encourage the monster back onto its legs. Cautiously, he lured the beast back towards the Bhia clearing, using intentional bursts of sound whenever he could to attract the slug's attention. As he approached the pool, he expected to see a supportive smile on the Mistress's face or to hear her calming voice in his mind, as a sign of approval for his chosen strategy. She was nowhere to be seen however, and the Walker was running out of space in which to back-step without falling into the pool, as he beckoned the entity closer.

As predicted, the entity slowly entered the half-lit Bhia clearing, where Lu stood waiting, and smiling; he was now shepherd of not only his cloud, and its rain, but also of this gigantic slug. The irony amused him a little, for slugs were naturally drawn to moisture in any case, and so as a title, 'shepherd of rain and slugs' seemed far from impressive.

His smile only lasted a moment longer, before he realised that, firstly, he was about to miss his window of attack, and secondly, that finding comedy in such mundane irony was rather pitiful; loneliness, it seemed, had evidently taken much from his sense of humour.

Without any warning, Lu broke into a blistering sprint around the approaching invertebrate and out of the clearing, where he quickly reached the cluster of trees beyond the bracken and dropped to his knees in order to snatch the detached limb he had severed earlier from the beast.

Mucus had begun to nibble into the flesh of Lu's unprotected fingertips from crawling across the floor and handling the material of the entity's leg. The grey man was not too concerned about this, however; from his perspective, he had gotten off lightly, as the armour and sandals provided by his missing Mistress remained unaffected by the sinister slime, thus his body was otherwise unscathed. Besides, his cloud had soon washed the residual mucus from the severed claw, and the ground beneath him, and his attention quickly returned to the strategy at play.

According to plan, the great pink-white slug had been momentarily dumbfounded by Lu's speedy ploy and had taken a moment to turn around and assess the situation, before flattening out and adjusting its mould in response to the change of pace. And then, across the torn-up terrain, the now five-legged entity hurtled towards the Walker, who had only a fleeting energy left with which to escape or otherwise act.

And for a moment, everything appeared to fall into place; the creature was all but upon the Walker, before he jumped to his right, springing off the nearest tree for additional height. Soaring beside the tremendous slug, Lu needed only to catch the branches of the tree above and hoist himself up into an advantageous nest from which he could make his final move. Yet, as the Walker reached for the branch above, the top of his head flew violently into another of the tree's branches; this was a collision he had not foreseen. Stunned by the impact,

Lu's concentration became utterly shattered, thus disabling his ability to successfully grapple the intended branch. It mattered very little anyway, for despite the vain attempt he made to grasp at the tree as he fell, his relentlessly raining companion had seen to it that all leaves, branches, and bark were now far too slippery to grip.

Lu's orange eyes raced in search for the nearing ground, as if desperate pleading with gravity for some sort of prolonged descent, but gravity allowed no further time for contemplation, and the Walker's well-armoured body crashed into the mire of mud and mucus below. Time, however, had been granted nonetheless. The entity had charged directly into the thick of a needle-sharp shrub. As if it were honey, caught in the feathers of a bird, the great slug was now largely subdued by the strain of its over-stretched membrane and appeared temporarily unable to regroup its sludge and escape its encounter with this unlikely obstacle.

Rising slowly from the acid ground, Lu rinsed his sizzling grey hands in the rain of his cloud and studied the mess before him. The entity was yet to transform, and its shadow heart was still visible. The only thing left to do was to throw the severed leg from a safe distance.

So, without a second breath of consideration, Lu ran urgently around his oozing adversary and recklessly hurled its former appendage with as much power as his limited musculature would permit.

In what felt like a sequence of dreamlike visions, the spike soared true to its mark, and almost shuddered as it struck the beating shadow within the gasping entity. The pierced membrane rippled through wretched oranges and reds, unsettling purples and pinks, and then settled on a tainted white, before the entire creature appeared to somehow collapse entirely inwards on itself through the rupture in its core, leaving nothing but a pale red slime behind.

In a struggle to digest what he had just witnessed, the Walker tightly clenched the lids of his dazed eyes, before reopening them, and then proceeding to glance about the Bhia wilderness. He gazed first towards the clearing, where there had been two portals. As expected, the window to the red realm had faded into disappearance, and the portal to the world of the gardener was solitary once again. Even the red entity's secretions, which had once seemed onerously present in the heat of the battle, were beginning to dwindle into the now seething mud, in delayed response to the creature's defeat. Eventually, nothing remained of the beast other than the glassblade, which now sat awkwardly amongst the bramble that had facilitated the entity's slaughter. Despite his malnourished capacity for emotion and self-worth, the Walker managed a half-smile in light of his success, before lunging forwards into the bush and extracting the Sorceress's gift.

From behind him, Lu could hear an aqueous chuckle. After sheathing the sabre, he spun his body around, and trod boastfully towards the pool, where his astral Mistress had reappeared and now applauded the spectacle of his victory.

'I am impressed, rainwalker. Though the entity of Xollec poses no serious threat, I would not expect anyone to find its weakness so soon, least of all by the one who has spent the last era and a half in an absent sleepwalk. Your returning senses serve you well, it seems!'

Though the laughter upon the Mistress's flowing face was as abstract as ever, there was motherly warmth to her tone. Lu found himself grinning with satisfaction, for it seemed that she was proud of him.

'Forgive me for voicing that which you have doubtless already found amongst my thoughts, but I must ask... What was that creature? Is it truly dead? And from what bleak realm did it spawn? Again, forgive me; I find myself exhilarated by the unknown. I have not known such excitement for as long as I can recall - if ever!'

The liquid goddess tilted her fountaining frame into a slight bow and responded in a kind, but serious tone.

'Then it is I who must be forgiven, young Lu, for I cannot satiate your curiosity with words alone, at least in what short time we have left of this encounter. Allow your hunger for the unknown to motivate you in the completion of our bargain, and I will show you all that you wish to see and tell you all that you wish to know.'

Lu smiled, and nodded courteously, though he knew that his thoughts, laced with disappointment, were available to the Mistress, nonetheless. Something else had pulled her interest now, however, for she appeared to have redirected her focus towards the sun world that lay beyond the solitary portal by the pool.

'The gardener; she is coming.'

And from the quiet, a sweet voice drew near. Not quite as high-pitched as a songbird, and yet sharing none of the consonants caused by a human tongue, this melody most peculiar had now emerged from the trees. There, Lu could see this unknowingly doomed gardener, traversing the clearing.

Emerald and petite, and without a foot on the ground, the creature floated towards the circle-stream. Despite her all-white lidless eyes, and a pair of holes in place of a mouth, nose or snout, the structure of this being's face was relatively similar to Lu's.

Not bound by mortal flesh, her form was instead wrapped in what appeared to be petals, which fluttered above the breeze that now carried her over the water ring. As she landed in the centre of the darklilies, her song ceased, and by the silence, Lu was again taken by regret. He pulled himself away from the portal and back into the world he knew. 'I cannot end a life so divine and sweet... I cannot do what you ask.' The Goddess chuckled.

'To our eyes, she is an innocuous fae. However, this river-spirit is Tlephilisse the Lila-Mother. She is the fourth occurrence of her kind, and she is something of a goddess, the steward of all fresh-water.

Thirty-five roles were devised by the Watcher-Creators of this world, to hold physical dominion while the Watchers may watch. Her inborn role, from a lineage of parthenogenesis, is one of those thirty-five. In order to end your curse, that bloodline must cease.'

Unfamiliar with all that he had just been told, Lu scooped a hand into the waters of the mistress and splashed his grey face, hoping for bravery. In this moment of refreshment, the Walker frowned and turned to face the Goddess. The long-since buried attitude of the folk of Rei was beginning to surface in the ancient youngling.

'Though our encounters are few, I have faith in your greatness. Tell me this, Mistress – why can you not see to this sprite's demise yourself? And furthermore, though I don't quite understand how this all concerns the cloud above my head, I *certainly* don't understand what benefit you see as your own?'

The Goddess smiled with some impatience and gave her response.

'Don't?' She shook her liquid head in silent laughter, apparently at this Reian contraction.

'You breed your words as your people did and still do, young Lu. Your memory of Rei must be stirring!

I cannot tell you of my interests concerning Tlephilisse, and if I could, I would choose not to. Thus far, I have given you no reason not to trust me, and you are to serve me regardless, but know that when this sacrifice is complete, your curse will end, and you will see rainless days again.'

Nodding, Lu accommodated the words of the sorceress.

'Though I lack a Reikan morality - that must have been threaded into their souls. Without a soul of my own, I am an easy vessel for corruption... though I feel no urge to resist it.'

The eyes of the mistress now twinkled at the grey man's words.

'Starved of a life for my own, my need for deliverance is urgent. This murder would be a spirit-shattering act for most. My own spirit is absent, so without virtue, I am the perfect candidate.'

Growing impatient from Lu's verbal stream of consciousness, the Mistress spoke up once more, in a formal, but expectant tone.

'What is your decision, Walker? Are you to be the blade with which I reap?'

And with a bow, the soaking assassin unsheathed his glassy sabre, lifting it towards the canopy. 'Though your words are veiled, and your motives unknown, I believe your promise to be true... You are the only one I know, though I know so little of anything.' Lu paused to gather his vows and reflect on their implications.

'It seems we share a greater destiny ahead, Mistress of the Bhia, but I shan't pursue it as long as this cloud afflicts me... That is a curse that I must relinquish before all else.

To vanquish the rain and regain a mortal soul is my foremost desire, and my fate seems bound to the outcome. In allegiance to you, I will step through the portal, and under your instruction, I will slay the Lila-Mother. I pledge myself to this role, as your Krajian Scythe!'

With a screech, whatever incorporeal force once within the Bhia pool now ascended, as if it were light returning to the sun.

Though beyond the portal, the golden land seemed distant and detached, it was of this same world, and maybe even nearby to the Bhia. Anyway, the grey warrior did not intend to return to his green-blue prison. Head-first, the Walker and his cloud somersaulted through the window, and into the arms of the healthy sun and air, landing eloquently behind a shrub, out of the view of the river sprite.

He was a rain-soaked remnant of a peaceful old world, and had no skill as a swordsman, yet with the Mistress's sabre clutched tightly in one hand, Lu had purged himself of inhibitions, and was ready for the hunt.

Chapter Four

TLEPHILISSE, THE RIVER SPRITE

Soon after the birth of the world, the Watcher-Creators had learned the natural orders of life and grew tired of shepherding it. So, in the earliest records of history, thirty-five Krajian stewards were roused into existence. These were the new eyes of the Watchers. As the other beings of the Kraj developed and multiplied, the thirty-five would maintain the natural balance, and were bound to the will of their creators. Some of the thirty-five were unaware of their purpose and would learn in time, while others had roles so obscure that they fell under the direct instruction of the Watchers themselves. Each was born to a unique, hidden region of the young world, in an appropriate body, so to thrive, and preserve the world in their separate ways. Their first birth marked the dawn of the first era of Kraj; these were the years of Lyoya.

Immortal and individual by design, each of the stewards were invincible to the standard of their surroundings, though all were destructible should the Watchers be met with their defiance. Though deified by any who witnessed them, the spirits, and minds of the thirty-five were mortal. Therefore, despite their unbreakable exteriors, those who bore the most arduous roles were destined for madness. Whoever fell to the madness was reborn to the same form and role, with a new name and spirit.

Upon this small planet, there were four great seas, with several minor salt-water companions. The third largest of the four, 'Empryc' was the most adored by the sun. With a deep, clear stomach, and many shallow tendrils that caressed islands and mainland beaches belonging to the continent of Taromet, Sea Empryc was a web of tropical life.

Somewhere along a bordering coast of Empryc, a handful of humans had accumulated. Due to the ever-thriving animal life, and the bounties of the sea, this coast was an attractive settlement for any passer-by, and in some accelerated fashion, a society came to be. More advanced travellers drifted in by the sea, and these deep-sea fisherman and navigators would introduce their materials and inventions. The lesser-developed hunter-gatherers from the mainland enthusiastically contributed their skills, and with time introduced their dark-grey complexion. All were compatible and neighbourly, and in love with the warm-waved haven. From strangers to kindred, the Rei-folk were born; a breed conceived by the tropic seduction of Empryc.

About one day's sail to the west of Rei were a pair of islands. These West-Empryc isles were similar in size but were unmistakably different by their attributes. The nearer of the two lands was a flat mound of paradise, with a gleaming beach, and a gradual forest of greens and purples. Voyagers from Rei had named it the Isle of Lila, in honour of the many teething darklilies upon it.

The second of the West-Emprycs was the Bhia – a conifer shadow of the Lila, which shared none of its sister's splendours. Though the terrain appeared similarly levelled from afar, the centre of the Bhia Island was a circular, sloping pit of ever-blue trees.

Ignored by the surrounding tide, the bottom of the tree-pit was dressed in glum woodland, yet stretched across the forest floor was a dormant body of freshwater, with a pond at one end, which was the product of visiting rains. Sunless and forlorn, the Bhia was a hopeless prison for the few lives below, malnourished in the half-light haze.

Cast behind a maze of piercing rock and reef, the tropic island twins were impossible to enter. This was the Empryc Crown, and it was the bane of all mariners. Regardless of the direction of entry, few could approach, and none could pass, for the spines were unnavigable by boat or otherwise. So, as life festered away in the horizon, the Isles remained unchanged and unbothered, never permitting their secrets to the outsiders who dared ask.

The pair, being so untouchable, had evoked speculative curiosity among the few witnesses who had attempted passage, and any conversation concerning the possibilities of forbidden treasures would become the breeding grounds of vague legend. Such islets could only exist, it was rumoured, as a means to harbour the secrets of the Gods.

Ironically, if those fantasists had not invested their energies in the perpetuation of myths and had instead engineered a viable route to the Isle of Lila, they would have learned that it was indeed the sanctuary of an unknown celestial.

Unknown to all, but the first-generation sailors of Rei, was that the Bhia had not always been where it was. At some point in the early stages of the world, it had simply appeared behind the Lila, and any who noticed its arrival had simply assumed that it had always been there, mistaken for the silhouette of its more prominent sister.

All throughout the first half of Lyoya, the River Sprite Ffeli thrived alone upon the young Lila Isle. Born to the tropics, she was unaware of her role in the thirty-five, but her existence alone ensured that all freshwaters of the world would abide by her sacred powers, giving them their nature. With time however, the sprite grew tired of her endless life on the island. After long studies of her surrounding plant life, insects and birds, Ffeli learned that all were born, would live and eventually die, and she would wonder why she could not die as they did.

She fell stricken with madness, with no way to articulate it, until eventually the Watchers set about preparing her spirit-death.

Ffeli was the first of her kind to demonstrate how a mind may suffocate and die by the indefatigable choke of time. So, with careful revision, the Watchers incited the passing of Ffeli, and she was spectrally fertilised, and would birth a single egg. The last moments of the first River Sprite were the most wondrous she had ever lived. After an eternity of observing the births of countless other creatures, the river-guardian could sense that she would soon bear a child of her own. Though unaware of her Watcher-Creators, and the nature of her conception, Ffeli was certain that her time on Kraj was finally drawing to an end. She feared that, like herself, her offspring would soon waken to a guideless, orphaned youth. Therefore, in her final breaths Ffeli taught a tune to the songbirds of the Lila, so that her child would instead arise to melodies of maternal love.

And Ffeli's consciousness departed; her emerald frame vacated for its dormant heir. By design of the

Watchers, the egg then hatched, and a sprite-soul emerged, seeking the newly vacated shell of its mother. In union, the infant mind and the ageless shape awoke. This was Tlera, the second River Sprite.

Born to the singing guidance of the Lilabirds, Tlera would eventually fathom the unhinged song-message of his mother and began a new path of life. The second River Sprite found cognisance of his gifts, and gradually distinguished their capabilities. When Tlera found no more joy in life, he simply willed a conception into being, and fell pregnant. Having lived a significantly more fruitful and enriching life than his predecessor, Tlera taught many new songs to the Lilabirds, and thus a tradition was born.

As the Lyoya Age came to an end, the dawn of the new era spawned Lephisse, the third River Sprite heritor.

These years were to be deemed the Age of Koau.

By the intuition of Tlera, the birdsongs of the Lila were saturated with memory and instruction. To deter her loneliness, Lephisse formed a wordless language of her own, so that her gestures were comprehended by all manners of life upon the Empryc Isle. Ancient songs, passed down by the songbirds, had informed her of the stretched and maddening decay of her forbears, and the wicked sift of her lineage that allowed only *one* to live at any single time. By this, Lephisse desired something she could not have.

Longing for kinship, and a company of her own, Lephisse lent her power to the creative urges of her mind and formed a plan. Fearfully intrigued by the finite endurance of her ancestors' sanity, the sprite envied the mortality of the other beasts that scurried between the island trees. Mortality seemed an unlikely desire for most, but for a line of Gods.

Lephisse was unable to unravel the guarded secrets of her own form. Yet, through great study of her animal companions, and strained exertion of her powers, the freshwater steward had designed a race of her own.

From trees and flowers, and any expired creatures of the Lila, she crafted twenty vacant similars. Despite some variety between them, all were of a medium height, and were wrapped in petals of emerald and purple. Like the River Sprite, they had all-white eyes, and thin faces of ageless youth. The empty shells also shared a similar pair of breathing slits akin to their creator, though in study of the creatures of Lila, Lephisse had decided to implement a mouth and teeth (such as that of a rabbit or mouse) onto her children, as it was a feature she was fond of.

From toil beyond the limits of her soul, Lephisse had crafted something quite astonishing to behold. However, once she had finalised these constructions, she was spent of her powers; she now began to experience the symptoms of her own soul's mortality.

The River Spite was quite euphoric as she sang her legacy to the life of the island, etching her passionate endeavour into Lila's melody-eternal. Her inability to animate her design was part of her plan, as was her passing. In love with the promise of death, Lephisse had chosen to leave a task for her successor, while simultaneously ensuring her demise.

With her waning strength, Lephisse willed her egg into existence and birthed it; and then, her spirit left its host to join her forbears in the beyond.

The Koau Era had not yet reached half of the age of Lyoya, when on a humid Empryc morning, a fourth soulsprite became one with its emerald prison. Awoken by a dawn chorus of unrivalled polyphony, Tlephilisse lifted from the ground and gave herself to the call of the songs. It took her short time to decipher her task, and even less time to complete it, for all around her were the fresh frames of a brand-new species, which only required a slight charge of her magic to give them life. Tlephilisse was born to a daunting, but colourful library of song, granted by her predecessors, and in turn gifted some of this knowledge to her children. Twenty elven mortals, designed by Lephisse from the materials of Lila, now shared the Isle with their life-giver, Tlephilisse.

By the language of their mothers, and the mouths they were given, the mortals brought fresh sound to the isle. With words, and chatter, and other social traits learned from the wildlife, a small community now thrived, and was nurtured tentatively by Tlephilisse. All twenty were given uniquely identifiable names by the Lila-mother, who then decided to name herself as well. After deciding upon her own title, Tlephilisse gave names to her forbears. The chosen names of her ancestors were similar to her own, but roughly corresponded with the three distinct personalities that they each had etched into the songs of Lila.

Of the four celestials to reside upon Lila, this Lila-mother was the most content. Boredom was a rarity, and her family was perfect. With few tasks to endure, she found purpose and joy in gardening, and delicately sculpting the island into a home for herself, and her children.

However, there were two flaws in the otherwise meticulous designs of Lephisse. Composed entirely of Krajian matter and supplied with only enough power for a life of their own, the Lila-mortals were not spirit-led mechanisms to be restored when the Watchers saw fit. Instead, as the souls of the Lila-mortals grew steadily older, their bodies withered in harmony.

The second of the fatal flaws was the species' infertility. With no knowledge of the cosmic origin of her powers, or of the Watchers, Lephisse had simply assumed that the rebirth of her kind was a divine right and would occur to any of her similars. She therefore gave no further mind to the reproductive process of the different lives upon the Lila. Of the twenty, many shared touch and passion for one another, but none conceived, and all eventually perished.

The Watchers were aware of *all* that had transpired below and were inspired by the innovations of the Lila-mothers, Lephisse and Tlephilisse. Regardless, a permanent place for these additional residents could not be allowed upon the Lila, in order to protect the thirty-five, and therefore the Krajian balance, and so the Lila-mortals did not re-spawn again on the Lila. Instead (and unknown to Tlephilisse), the Watchers perfected and implemented these designs elsewhere on Kraj, and the species lived on, unaware of their maternal designers.

Tlephilisse was distraught for many years following the passing of her children and did not understand their inability to regenerate. For years, the Lila-mother isolated herself, and mourned privately in the heart of her lily garden. She enclosed her sanctuary within a ring of static fresh water, that she had conjured herself, still barely scraping the barrel of her potency. This ring was impassable to all but Tlephilisse, and she remained alone until her mourning had finally ceased.

The Age of Koau was reaching the end of its third quarter when Tlephilisse emerged from her garden. She had forgiven the fates for what was stolen; her urge to cultivate the islet had been restored.

Once again, Tlephilisse traversed the Lila overgrowth, as she shaped it to her liking. She was particularly fond of the namesake darklilies of the island, and encouraged their recurrence, though there was much additional potential in the fertile soils of the land. Using her gifts sparingly, and instead depending more on the sciences left behind by her mother, Tlephilisse developed a bloom-pallet of her own, and with it, she re-illustrated the Lila until it was an expressive homage to her deceased, beloved offspring.

Edges of white beach sand surrounded this dazzling centrepiece, and all who could spy the Lila beyond the rocks would again speculate the unknown gardener of this clearly deliberate mastery.

Though many a time Tlephilisse found herself in the ruins of the Lila-mortal's settlement, she could not bring herself to erase this artefact of her temporary company. There was comfort to be found in the wreckage, and unlike her forbears, no manner of creeping sorrow or madness would take the heart of this River Sprite, for she had found much to love in her life and had no wish for it to end.

Chapter Five

A VISITOR

For several moons, Lu had been skulking around the unfamiliar pleasantries of the Lila. The cloud-shadowed man had remained unnoticed by his prey and did not plan to approach her until his surroundings were familiar and his strategy was absolute. Meanwhile, Lu had quietly managed to enjoy the generous light and air supply of this haven and fell infatuated with the sea that surrounded it. By the salted breeze, a once-distant memory was returning to the sailor of Rei. It began to dawn on him.

'This sea is the Empryc!'

His eyes skimmed the rock-trapped beach, and immediately recognised the unique imprisonment of this paradise.

'And these jagged spines...this is certainly the Lila.'

Though he could not speak aloud at the risk of alerting the sprite, the Reikan sailor was now in the throes of revelation.

The contorted legend and rumours of his youth, of divine treasures on a godly sanctuary, seemed foolish no more. On this occasion, blind speculation had resulted only in strange accuracy.

Still, there was more to discover from his whereabouts. Lu squinted his eyes in confusion. Through the fangs of the rock-maze, there was another island that did not exist before unless it was the sea's manipulation of the shadow of the Lila. Lu strained his orange eyes further still, hoping to make sense of this foreign disk. The surface was flat, though it seemed entirely overgrown by a single organism, which only resembled the leaves of the Bhia trees.

The grey man swallowed back an immediate urge to curse at the thought of his imprisonment. So commanding was the gloom of the Bhia, that its whereabouts had never seriously crossed Lu's mind. An abstract place, that seemed too oppressive to imagine in the real world.

And there it was, in the middle of a warm, familiar sea; it was not far from the coast of his birth.

'*How long* did I spend rotting in that prison, this close to Rei?'

This was not the first plea for knowledge to be ignored since Lu arrived on Lila. Many times, the dark hunter had whispered questions to his blade, in hope of the Goddess' guidance.

Occasionally, his Mistress would utter phrases of history or poetry regarding the islet, and its celestial inhabitant, but these words spoke through his icy sabre, and the Mistress was nowhere to be seen.

From these messages, Lu had pieced together a reasonable amount of information, though nothing was particularly helpful. He had learned the names of the three River Sprites prior to Tlephilisse, though he still knew near-nothing about their true purpose or their creators, aside from the nature of the sprite's unusual rebirth. To Lu's understanding, all rain was fresh-water, and terminating a bloodline of fresh-water guardians would result in the end of his curse, which seemed logical enough.

Lu retreated from the beaches of Lila and scanned the isle for a new camp spot for the night. Away from the regular haunts of the Lila-mother, he had stumbled upon the skeleton of what appeared to be an abandoned settlement. Whoever had once lived here was certainly no longer upon the Lila, so Lu made himself at home in the dusty ruins, while considering his next steps.

There was, so far, a few vague principles to guide the manner of the Walker's attack. He must gauge the nature of his opponent and appear as an innocuous outsider. Lu had considered masquerading as an unlikely survivor, shipwrecked by the jagged death surrounding this island, though he had no practice in deception. Mid-thought, he found himself grinning at the idea of his own potentially awkward acting performance.

Once Tlephilisse had deemed his presence to be non-threatening, he would acquire her trust. Lu could only strike at close proximity, unexpected by the Lila-mother. If she feared an attack, the sprite would be more than capable of preventing it; the limit of her gifts was still unknown, apparently far surpassing that of her predecessors.

With a shudder and a wry grin, Lu dismissed the potential threat of the Sprite. He was not greatly educated or talented as a mortal in Rei, but in his reawakening, the grey man now found unique humour in his situation. He had not seen another human in the flesh for a Krajian age, and yet his mind was now seemingly far more advanced than any of his kind.

If wisdom was a profit of age, then he must be the wisest of all men! Lu laughed silently at his foolish musings, before settling down for a brief sleep in a derelict hut. His cloud flattened itself and slipped inside too, continuing to hydrate the Walker throughout the night.

Further plans had not yet come to the Walker. He was rather hoping that once the Sprite was seen to, his rain would simply cease and his cloud depart, relinquishing any pending guilt along with it. In any case, no action would be taken until the Mistress could confirm it, though Lu was getting impatient.

He drew the borrowed blade from his side and spoke to it directly. 'Mistress of the Bhia! For five days I have hunted and observed this Elemental. Her patterns are predictable and repetitive! I am sure that she remains oblivious to my arrival. I am certain of this.' The sword did not stir. Lu gripped the hilt with both hands now, spitting an increasingly frustrated whisper. 'Provide me with further guidance!'

Again, this plea was not reciprocated. Impulsively, the grey man stormed out of the hut in which he had slept and embarked silently on a search for the River Sprite. If the Mistress would provide no further guidance, then he must strike of his own volition.

Lu scuttled from the vague perimeter of the abandoned settlement, and back into the cover of the trees. Though the approach of the Lila-mother was often announced by her tireless singing, her movements were otherwise silent; Lu could not risk a clumsy introduction and would have to locate the Sprite with caution.

Between tree trunk, rock mounds and various unusual blooms of the island, the grey man scurried and listened, gradually approaching the circle-stream at the heart of Lila. If Tlephilisse was resting, Lu was sure he'd find her there. For a while longer the hunt continued until the Walker arrived at the clearing. Hidden by the peripheral greenery, Lu peered inwards to spy his victim.

As he had predicted, Tlephilisse was at the centre. Eerily, she floated above the darklilies in apparent slumber. Now was his chance, he thought, as he prepared to adopt the behaviour of a lost explorer.

'No! Cease this blunder!'

An invisible malice bolted through the thigh of the sailor. As the cold magic flooded his entirety, Lu found himself paralysed head to toe by the snake-hold of sorcery. Above him, the cloud appeared to be paused in time, clutching the rain but unable to release it.

The stinging power, it seemed, was pulsing from the weapon that was sheathed at his side. In his mind, Lu addressed the Mistress of the Bhia.

'Release me!'

But she did not. Instead, the invisible sorceress seized his thoughts and spoke through them.

'You are impatient and bloodthirsty. You are a fool! Though I see all things and have seen all things, I did not foresee your immaturity!'

The disembodied voice of the goddess was descending into an unsettling register that Lu had not heard before.

'For an endless era, you patiently stumbled around in the bleak. And yet, in your awakening, you are unable to tolerate a period of five nights before straying from my guidance! You are exhibiting flaws of your mortal past, flaws that have no use here.'

The Walker attempted to interrupt and defend his actions, but Lu's mind was not his own; the Mistress did not require his interjection, for those thoughts were already exposed to her.

'Though I admire your urgency, I cannot allow such reckless behaviour. You are under the eye of others, not solely my own. You cannot fail; you must yield to my direction. Otherwise, you endanger us both.'

To the core of the sabre, the chill returned; Lu's body regained mobility, and the rain recommenced. His mind was not yet alone, however, and the Mistress now encouraged his questions.

'What would you have me do, to ensure my success?' spoke the Reikan, immediately dismaying at his returning sea-town accent after being scolded for the *'flaws of his mortal past.'*

But the Goddess had returned to her merry disposition and replied with clear amusement.

'I would not have you worry, child of Rei; your accent is a charm and nothing less.'

Again Lu was dismayed, reminded that his thoughts were never a secret. The Mistress continued to answer...

'As you have already realised, Tlephilisse must be approached as an equal. You have done well to remain unseen, but in her presence, you will be surrendered to her temperament. She has not had company such as yours since the death of her puppets. The ruins you found; those are the ruins of the first elves of the New World, children of the River Sprite.'

In an instant, Lu's memory revisited his brief encounter with the ruins.

'Now I fear that I damaged something!' Lu jested, as a desperate challenge to the sobriety of the topic. The pair laughed and shared a moment of telepathic rapport before the Mistress returned to the strategy at hand.

'Once you are acquainted with Tlephilisse, do not develop sympathies. Her form is ancient, though her soul is not as old as your own; in death, she will return to her forbears and her children, and finally find company of her own. She desires this kinship above all else, but does not yet attribute it to death.'

For a moment, the concept of an afterlife stole the attention of the Walker. In death, would the people of Rei welcome him home? He did not want this; the faces of his childhood were stolen from his memory. The mysteries of the 'New World', as the Mistress had called it, were far more enticing than any further reconnection with his past.

'When – and *how* – am I to abuse her hospitality, should I earn it? I am now all too clear on the premise of befriending the Sprite, but have no understanding as to how one so powerful can be destroyed. This divine entity's recurrence must surely be impossible to prevent.'

'By death alone, it is. You are correct. However, the energy that preserves the Sprite is corruptible. In order to shatter her defences, you must be welcomed into the lily garden, within the circle-stream. The water here does not represent the Sprite, or her health, but it does contain a great deal of Tlephilisse's essence. This information must be drawn from the water, through the sabre that I gave to you, and into your own flesh.'

Lu understood less than half of what the Mistress had just described; of what little he *had* comprehended, he was visibly unsettled. Had she implied that he must dampen the blade, and then cut himself with it? Or was he digesting her words too literally? He did not yet speak his concerns, in the hope that she would elaborate and eventually dispel them.

'By my design, the blade translates the unique science of an immortal into a power that can undo such immortality. To open a sealed door, you must understand how it is sealed. Invite the thinking sword into your flesh, and your flesh will submit to its learnings.'

Whenever the Mistress spoke of the sabre, Lu couldn't help but feel as though she was avoiding a more obvious attribute of the weapon. This was another of those occasions. Regardless, he did not interrupt and was at peace with the Mistress reading these thoughts for herself.

'Some thirty days from now, a night will come where the moon is plagued, and red. Under this shadow, the sword earns its power, and therefore its title.

With your fighting hand, sink the blade into the stream; with your free hand, you must cling to the Kraj, or you will be claimed by the shadow forever. Once you are in position, you need not move; Umbra will finish the ritual itself. You will know when it is complete. Then your hands may be cut. Then your hands are ready.'

Instead of dwelling on the thought of killing a celestial immortal with his bare hands, Lu analysed the transparent hilt of the sheathed glassblade. *Umbra*. A curiously shadowed name with an ironic shadow dependency for a blade so deathly clear, he smirked.

'It is not of this world, and it is known by few. It cannot be seen by the Sprite, not even as she falls into the throws of death. Her eyes are shared with another; another who would stop at nothing to confiscate that blade.'

Keeping the blade hidden was one of the more straightforward of the Mistress' instructions, though it had ignited a concern in the Walker.

'On the improbable event of finding myself ready to perform this ritual thirty days from now, by what sorcery will the ritual itself not awaken Tlephilisse? And that be on the hopeful assumption that the sprite *is* in fact asleep!' Lu resigned himself to the absurdity of his recent employment, as fulfilling his vow became increasingly unachievable.

'Umbra will process in silence. To ensure that Tlephilisse sleeps - or is otherwise absent during the ritual will be in your best interests. I have granted all that I can to make this mission possible, but I must leave you now. We will not speak again unless you succeed. We will never speak again if you fail.

But know this; I am aware of your interest in the unknowns of the New World. If I am satisfied by the outcome of this execution then, as my Krajian Scythe, I will escort you from familiarity. From the Empryc, we will depart; you will see the world – and beyond – and you will be satisfied.

Do not fail; do not reveal the blade, and never fall prey to the illusions of privacy here; those eyes host a phantom witness, and they do not close.

The gentle commotion and dialogue of Lila's wildlife reclaimed Lu's worldly senses, as his guest fled its corporeal host. He was stranded on this Empryc Isle with sufficient queries and unknowns to forever bemuse the ordinary population of Rei.

The cloud-bearer widened his grey lips into a familiar grin. These unknowns were certainly enough to occupy him for now.

– END OF PART ONE –

PART TWO

An unsuspecting gardener shares their skills (and a meaningful affinity) with an insincere assassin

Chapter One

FIRST IMPRESSIONS

It was morning, and as was usual; Tlephilisse the River Sprite had begun her daily routine. Once the celestial had tended the blooms around her, she exhaled the resting air in her body to the tune of a favourite Lila-memory. As the air left her frame, she weightlessly ascended and became airborne. Intentionally swept by a warm, incoming breeze, the River Sprite drifted over the water-ring around her, and towards the great gardens of Lila. Though her immortality removed any need for breath or breathing, the Sprite would occasionally inhale and replenish her supply of air, allowing her to resume her beloved song.

Wingless and fluid, her innate ability to float was reliant neither on the low density of her form, nor any motions of her limbs. It was instead the product of something far less tangible. When at rest, the Sprite naturally emitted a curious, pulsating energy. This was the ancient, borrowed power that animated her form. From her core, the power throbbed and self-replenished, as if it were shapeless blood pumped by an absent heart. In levitation, the Lila-mother slowly bobbed to the beating rhythm of the energy.

In order to land, Tlephilisse would consciously channel the energy elsewhere. This redirection required some effort to initiate, but her efforts did not need to be maintained once the landing had occurred. Similarly, if the Sprite desired to travel while floating, her direction could be decided by the same redistribution. At will, Tlephilisse was able to effortlessly drift until she altered her course. Ffeli, the first of the River Sprites, had originally learnt the command of this peculiar radiation, though she did not understand how. Unable to articulate her methods, Ffeli failed to pass on this skill to Tlera through the Lila's songbirds. In spite of this, Tlera was born both constructive and inquisitive and was soon able to rediscover and then master the technique. He subsequently sang the skill into the Lila chorus, where his descendants learned and adopted it.

Despite its languid pace, the floating-drift was not manoeuvrable to any great precision, so Tlephilisse had redressed her island with navigability in mind. The central clearing was treeless, allowing time for the Sprite to decide on her destinations before aiming her path between the surrounding greenery. Concerned by the slight possibility of drifting astray while asleep, she had even spent sorcery on her ring-stream so that she would remain equipoised, regardless of external forces.

Nevertheless, Tlephilisse enjoyed the wind's delicate, suggestive guidance when she travelled, and regularly let it set her course, which is how she began on this particular morning.

Before she had reached the edge of the clearing, Tlephilisse sensed an unfamiliar presence; she paused, and landed, anticipating its arrival.

Then, from the trees, a stumbling flurry of shell, cloud and rain fell before her, and onto its knees. She was shocked by its sudden arrival, but not afraid; quivering in worry, it appeared harmless and fearful, and posed no threat at all. Above the crouching beast, there hung a miniature raincloud, which appeared to follow and focus every water droplet onto the sorry thing below. This partner of mist seemed odd to Tlephilisse, but she quickly dismissed it as a probable normality outside of Lila.

The alien had a similar body shape to the River Sprite - a head and torso, with proportionately matching limbs. However, these attributes were composed of unusually varied materials, ranging from bright seashells to a grey flesh that was not dissimilar to the skin of some fruits. Cautiously, she approached the weeping wanderer and attempted to communicate. The languages designed by her mother were originally wordless but were learned and briefly spoken by the Lila-mortals of the Lila. These words were useless to Tlephilisse now; the grey cloud-bearer was not versed in the language of her kind and did not understand her gestures or telepathy.

Though it had not yet spoken, the visitor had now regained some composure. The creature focussed its gaze into Tlephilisse's blank-white eyes as if it were expecting hostility, thus longing instead for sympathy. Its own eyes were ancient, and nothing like the Lila-mother's; though they were similarly white, they had a dark centre that was outlined by a ring of light red-yellow. To indicate her hospitality, the River Sprite extended her arms and assisted the stranger to its feet. The stranger gratefully welcomed Tlephilisse's charity and began to speak a language of its own. These words were all nonsense to the River Sprite, though she was far too captivated to notice.

The cloud-bearer was clearly intelligent and potentially even articulate; there was a certain mutual awareness of the language barrier between the pair.

Once the visitor had given up on speech, they offered a hand to the River Sprite and led her into the gardens.

Tlephilisse, who was predominantly used to travelling on the breeze, was not fond of using her legs, but staggered along regardless and somehow kept up with the impassioned stranger; her body was now fuelled by fresh intrigue.

By midday, they had arrived at the edge of the island, which was punctuated by a warm beach of sand and sea. The beaches of Lila would never fail to make Tlephilisse nervous. When in levitation, she feared that a wild sea breeze might steal her from the island and spit her into the deep. The resultant paranoia had ensured that she, like her ancestors, would never dare to leave the Lila; the sea was only to be admired from a distance.

However, these fears were briefly allayed somewhat, as Tlephilisse observed that the shell creature's cloud remained eerily unbothered by the wind. The River Sprite watched as her frenzied guest now gestured towards the rocks. Without a common tongue, all communication had now dissolved into blunt movements. Repeated to an almost patronising extent, the meaning of the grey-skin's flailing was decipherable only due to their lack of subtlety, alongside their maker's seemingly relentless enthusiasm.

After a long while, the two had reached an understanding. From what Tlephilisse had gathered (from a rather overt re-enactment), her guest was a sea-traveller, who was unwillingly thrown by the waves into the jagged Empryc maze. Marooned on the Lila sands, there was no escape; they must now stay until death permitted its unique liberty by transcendence. Now, the Lila-mother pitied the stranger more so than before.

Entrapment must be a torturous arrest for someone with once such endless horizons. Of course, she could barely conceptualise such dread; the Lila was the extent of her own horizons.

Tlephilisse hesitated in thought, before tenderly embracing the navigator. She had taught many things to the late Lila-mortals, but this act of comfort was something of their own innovation. The cloud-bearer became tense, before melting into the arms of the emerald celestial. The embrace appeared to be a welcome kindness. Once Tlephilisse had decided that her guest had been suitably soothed, she released her grip and guided the alien back to her sanctuary.

As they travelled together, the River Sprite discretely explored the outsider with her white eyes; there were many unusual attributes to the stranger, and she was altogether transfixed by them. Additionally, she was struggling to contain her excitement at the prospect of casually interrogating the stranger about the vast mysteries of the outside world.

Once the Lila-mother and her grey-skinned companion had returned to the clearing, the cloud-bearer approached the circle-stream, and kneeled down beside it. Murmuring to themself, the wet wanderer stared into the tranquil shallows.

Though it was unstated, Tlephilisse detected an aura of regret from the Walker's tone. Some unknown torment clouded those citrus-orange eyes. Patiently, she did not interfere with the Walker's mutter and again admired their prismatic attire.

By now, the Lila-mother had decided that the lurid shellsuit *was* in fact a suit and that the colouration of tired greys upon their face must surely continue to the flesh beneath the exoskeleton. Dissimilar to the beasts of Lila, the Walker's hair was exclusively upon its head; it was a chin-length, tangled mane of evening green, gleaming against the tropic sun. Against one thigh was a hidden spike, which Tlephilisse assumed was a tool for protection or even battle. Maybe, like Tlephilisse, her guest was a lover of plants; the spike would certainly be fit for cutting down undesirable growths such as weeds and parasitic creeping vines.

As the evening progressed, Tlephilisse made varied attempts to build a foundation for dialogue with her guest. Spoken language was not a viable option. There were no common vocalisations between the pair, as the River Sprite had no true mouth or tongue. The emerald celestial was mildly frustrated by this barrier but did not let it surface - her guest would not be leaving any time soon, anyway.

There was no easy departure from here. Wingless and land-bound, nought but flight upon a carriage of death could rescue the ill-fated traveller now. This escape, however, was seemingly reserved for the wild beasts and birds - how long would this visitor survive? Tlephilisse was not sure. The loss of the Lila-mortals had gouged a bleak vacancy into her life, but this new companion may grow to fill it.

The cloud-sufferer and its rain were a foreign sight amid the radiance of the tropic sunset, but the outsider no longer seemed miserable. Dripping wet, yet full of life, there was no way to gauge the age or lifespan of the guest.

Regardless of the grey-skin's mortality, not a moment should be lost in pursuit of communication. Into the lightless late, she persevered; the language barrier must be broken.

Finally, it was nightfall, and the ember remnants of the wandering sun had died, and all but the full moon went dark. For a short while, the River Sprite could not see her guest at all. She reached out her left hand and found the rain-cold arm of the Walker. Firmly, she clung to her guest, as if to imply that their exchange had not yet finished.

An awkward moment of silence passed, as the pair endured the impasse of darkness. Then, as Tlephilisse had predicted, the temporary veil of black began to rupture. Far above Kraj, distant eyes were awakening, peering through the apertures, and weeping their light. One by one, these stars joined the moon in the Empryc sky, until the constellation was complete.

This was *The Web of Scattered Majesties*: a periodic and vast configuration named by Tlephilisse, which signalled the beginning of the dry season. Beneath the zenith of night, the two were no longer blind. The River Sprite was visibly content, and her guest seemed to revel at the sky. It appeared to be familiar to the Walker, but as if it were sorely missed. Time had frozen - two strangers were gazing towards a higher place, while the patter of a gentle cloud accompanied their silent awe.

By a flash of star-born inspiration, Tlephilisse suddenly reanimated. It had just occurred to her that the plant-deaths of the dry season could be easily averted. The raincloud! Together, the River Sprite and her new companion could redefine the implications of the incoming wither. The young life threatened by drought could now be cultivated and explored! Tlephilisse was ecstatic; this was an opportunity not only for the growth of plants but also for communication between Sprite and Walker.

The grey castaway was aware of the Sprite's excitement, and patiently allowed her to visually explain her revelation. Tlephilisse passionately gestured and enacted her plan, which was then reciprocated by an idea of the Walkers' own. After reaching for rock and stone, the rain-bringer then began to chip away at a few different surrounding surfaces. From what Tlephilisse could make out in the half-light, the Walker's etchings were a fine collaboration of straights and curves. The individual formations were each part of separate groupings and did not mean anything at all to the River Sprite. She tilted her head, expressing her confusion.

After finishing these drawings, the Walker acknowledged Tlephilisse's concern and promptly elaborated. First, the orange-eyed alien pointed towards one of the less advanced symbols in a grouping; it was a straight line with two smaller curved branches. Then, the Walker directed the River Sprite's attention towards a nearby tree. Back and forth, the grey creature likened the pair, until Tlephilisse understood her guest completely. It was language! Carved into the rocks, or mud; it was a language to be seen instead of spoken.

Into the first light of the sun's rebirth, the Sprite and the Walker exchanged hundreds of shapes. Some of these shapes were extremely simple and represented common objects. In contrast, plenty of Tlephilisse's ideas were not so simple. Many of her offerings were comprised of multiple lines and gouges and were representative of more abstract concepts. The grey-skin was apparently not at all disconcerted by the Sprite's suggestions, however, and attempted to implement them among the rest.

The excitement did not diminish, though eventually they were both exhausted. The pair eagerly agreed to meet before midday, and then individually retired. The Walker had decided to return to the cover of the nearby ruins and swiftly departed. Tlephilisse then slowly ascended from the ground and drifted to her circle-stream where she could rest.

Though her white eyes never shut, and her body never tired, she was now asleep; the Sprite would awaken once her soul had recovered from an eventful day.

Chapter Two

A DAY OF LANGUAGE

It was long since dawn, but not yet noon, when Lu next awoke on the island of Lila, and the tyrannical sun had wasted no time enforcing the implications of 'dry season'. After a particularly brief slumber, he evacuated the shade of an abandoned hut to witness the now creeping wrath of drought. His temporary place of refuge had been rain-soaked during his sleep but was already beginning to dry.

He then remembered what he had learned last night; the stars had forewarned of the oncoming burn, and now it had arrived. Lu frowned – though Rei was nearby, he could not remember the days of seasonal weather, perhaps due to the damp permanence of his more recent abode. Far beneath a hulk of moisture-retaining conifers, the Bhia's core humidity barely changed – there had been no seasons there at all.

While the grey man continued to dwell on the weather, he began to untie the sheathed blade from his thigh. For the time being, Lu had gained Tlephilisse's trust. Therefore, in order to retain her confidence for twenty-nine days, his sabre must remain unseen until it was again required. He also shed his suit of shells due to the heat. Under the armour, he was wrapped in a thin, sky-blue undergarment. The robes, covering him from torso to knee, were an additional, subtler gift from the Mistress of the Bhia, and would alone be an adequate protection from the incoming burn. Once the robes were exposed from beneath the shell, they became soaked in the cloudburst. Still, they remained feather-light, and still, they seemed blue.

Among the few broken relics crafted by its previous inhabitants, the huts collectively contained a few useful tools. Lu had found a suitable wooden box. The box was familiar to Lu and appeared to be fashioned from the salvaged materials of a boat-wreck. Maybe a vessel of Rei, savaged by the Empryc spine, Lu speculated. Then, he gently placed the weapon, and his shellsuit into the box, and closed its oiled, light-brown lid. He carried the box to a subtle gap in the nearby rocks and then buried it under stones and branches.

'...Do not reveal the blade, and never fall prey to the illusions of privacy here; those eyes host a phantom witness, and they do not close...'

The Mistress's peculiar warning had echoed in the Walker's mind since first it was spoken. His current precautions would all be necessary if the 'witness' was to be effectively deceived.

Again, Lu's mind had turned to the Sprite. They had indeed made fantastic progress before they had slept, but one thing was unclear. Why did a River Sprite, an elemental of fresh water, require the aid of his small cloud in order to fight the dry? If he remembered this question later, he intended to ask the Sprite. For now, he was prepared and ready for a second encounter with Tlephilisse. Lu frowned momentarily, before breaking into a hopeless smile. Already, the Walker was developing an incongruous fellowship with his prey. He feared that, as their language developed, their amity could become a serious threat to his initial mission.

Quietly, the Walker and his cloud slipped through the trees, before approaching the Lila clearing. From afar, Lu could see Tlephilisse, who was floating calmly above the centre patch of the circle-stream. Her lidless white eyes removed all distinction between sleep or otherwise, so Lu approached the Sprite cautiously, to avoid startling her.

On his journey to the clearing, he had collected a few broken sticks; they were dry and thin, and therefore ideal for writing on softer surfaces. Though Lu had hoped that his raincloud would keep the soil damp and easy to pierce, he had awoken to an island far more barren than it was the day before. Even the moisture of his cloud was unable to remedy a surface of that state, so Lu had been forced to consider a new canvas for today's creations. From what he had experienced of the Lila, Lu had noticed that the thin, white sands of the beaches almost hardened under the drizzle of his rain. When it was dry, etching into sand would be pointless; the weightless grains would simply crumble and sulk - unable to retain any shape. Wet sands, however, could be marked with the finest indentations, and would abide to their new form until the moisture had gone. In the dry season, the beach was easily the most suitable workspace. Unfortunately, Lu was already quite aware that Tlephilisse was not fond of the beach. It was going to be difficult to convince her to spend any long amount of time there.

The grey-skinned wanderer now approached his emerald host, but he promptly halted at the circle-stream that surrounded the lily garden. An inconspicuous and inscrutably powerful aura seemed to enchant the stream. Lu decided that it would be wise not to cross such a force until it was ultimately necessary. During the Walker's pause, the Sprite had begun to rouse. Her delicate arms stretched upwards, as if to embrace the sun's warmth. She dreamily whistled a curious tune, which the Lila songbirds then imitated almost immediately - they were all apparently hiding in the shade of the nearby trees.

Though briefly perplexed by Lu's lesser garment and lack of shells, Tlephilisse then nodded at Lu and joyfully revolved in the air. The River Sprite was evidently pleased to see him. Before the emerald immortal joined the Walker across the stream, she briefly descended to her garden. Lu watched as Tlephilisse tentatively inspected the health of the lily-garden. Within the sacred ring, drought had inflicted no casualties; it was as if the garden had a climate of its own, independent of what lay beyond its waters. The Walker was both fascinated and concerned. What properties possessed the stream? Though understated, it was clearly some kind of protective barrier, and would most likely become another obstacle between the Walker and his dark assignment.

Tlephilisse recommenced her levitation and lightly drifted towards Lu. Neither of them made a sound, yet the River Sprite's slow, focused approach was not awkward at all. Without a mouth to smile, she somehow radiated positivity and gladness. Once she had crossed the stream, she landed beside Lu and glanced at the tools he had gathered.

When he noticed her interest, the Walker nodded and smiled. He pointed north, in the direction of the nearest beach. Silently, Lu reminded himself that it was going to be difficult to convince Tlephilisse to spend the following days beside the sea.

Lu beckoned the emerald elemental to walk alongside him, as he led her through the trees. After a cautious pause, she followed by foot. Again, Tlephilisse began to stumble on her neglected legs. Nevertheless, she was alert with humiliation and self-awareness, and thus her footing improved with every step. Through the northern plant-gardens of Lila, the Walker patiently encouraged his ethereal companion. Every now and then, Lu would notice a plant, or bird, gasping in the drought, and each time, the sufferers would prompt the Walker to glance with worry towards his companion; her plant-like form would surely also wilt or break. But her skin never seared, and she was remarkably unbothered by the heat. Instead, she was persistently keen for Lu to direct his rain upon the sufferers who needed it.

By the time Lu and Tlephilisse had reached the upper beaches of Lila, it was early afternoon. The air was thin and thirsty; a damning, heavy heat had stolen the moisture from breeze. As the pair emerged from the thicket, they were nearly blinded by a harsh white gleam. The white sands of the West-Empryc beaches lay before them, naked to the oppressive light. Lu shuddered – the dry sand would be unbearably hot. Much to the grey-skin's disbelief, Tlephilisse showed no sign of reluctance at all as she hopped onto the sand.

The breeze was only slight, which explained Tlephilisse's waning fear of wind. Her bravery regarding the sand ahead, however, was another matter altogether. Since his reawakening, and the shedding of his greens, most of Lu's senses had quickly been restored. His grasp of temperature was still compromised due to the damp of his hanging cloud, yet still, he could feel the season's infiltrating warmth around him. With a fearful step, Lu set himself upon the shining sand. Immediately, he was confused; the ground was mild and welcoming. Cooler than any of the shaded muds he had stepped upon so far today. And then he laughed aloud in realisation, as the Sprite looked on ahead. The pale sand's gleaming reflection of the sun's light had somehow sent the sun's bitter heat back also. Lu smiled and praised the shining tide.

An endless wave of fish and coral bones were sea-churned against the Empryc spine and spat out here as bone-white sand. Here they came to rest, now belonging to the blinding Lila beach.

Without allowing another idle moment, Lu handed the River Sprite one of his writing sticks. She accepted, and swiftly took to the ground, inscribing one of her compositions from the night before into the wet sand. Before Tlephilisse had time to stand, the sea rolled in and the marks were smoothed and lost. Unintentionally, the pair had wandered too near to the shoreline, where the sand was subjected to the wash of the waves. Through gaps in the Empryc Crown, the water came by the breath of the wind, and periodically administered impermanence to the surface of the sand. Lu laughed and took a few steps back. The River Sprite followed swiftly, in recognition of the problem. Rain soaked the ground as the grey man walked, and soon there was enough wet sand for the pair to get to work.

Once they had replicated last night's symbols, Tlephilisse and Lu delegated separate tasks to one another. Born to the island, Tlephilisse would spend the afternoon building a list of etchings, each corresponding to every beast and other thing upon the Lila that she could think of. She had even cast a symbol to represent the Walker's cloud, though she made no topic of it since. Next to her, the Rei sailor would learn the shapes as they came, before crafting basic methods of linking and describing them. This role was far more challenging and required a step-by-step method in which the Walker would test his new conjunctions in different scenarios. Once a design was complete, Lu would present it to Tlephilisse and attempt to non-verbally explain its significance. Though this was a frustrating element of the process, Lu never lost his patience. The River Sprite was a stunning learner and seemed to have no issue processing the abstract or conditional functions of Lu's damp-sand incisions.

The heat had peaked mid-afternoon and was now slowly calming. The first evening of the dry season had begun. Tlephilisse promptly stood up and began to levitate, catching Lu's eye. From what the Walker could detect, she was pleased about something – though the stimulus was unclear. The emerald immortal then pointed towards the ground beneath her, and Lu's eyes were directed to a beautiful, fresh inscription in the sand. From his immediate memory of the Sprite's symbolism, and the meanings of his own creations, the message was fairly intelligible.

'Today is good.
Lu (you) change everything here.'

Though some of her inscriptions were possibly interchangeable, and her uses of Lu's conjunctions were slightly incorrect, the Walker smiled at the Sprite. He wanted her to see that he understood her message.

In response, he began to scrawl into the sand nearby as Tlephilisse intently watched.

'It is nice to meet you (Tlephilisse).
Our language is good.
You write well!'

There was much that Lu still wished to communicate, but the vocabulary was currently insufficient. With limited expression, this message would do for now. In the meantime, Lu couldn't help but feel slightly frustrated. Though the pair had spent most of the day formulating hundreds of symbols of communication, it was already apparent in Lu's response that they were going to need far more ideas before the language was truly practical. Additionally, they hadn't even begun to implement their shapes in the context of gardening, which was supposed to be a foremost method of distracting Tlephilisse for the next twenty-nine days. Tlephilisse, however, did not seem at all disheartened by the Walker's blunt reply. Instead, she was almost smiling – if not for her absent lips. The River Sprite did not need a mouth or moving eyes to express her happiness. She radiated gaiety and benevolence nearly always, and this occasion was no exception. Again, the celestial took to the ground and began to write.

Unlike Lu, she had no distant memory of upbringing, and no prior ability to write. Over the past two days, Lu had demonstrated curious behaviour and creativity that she had never seen before. Needless to say, the Sprite had assimilated the Reikan's imported peculiarities with little difficulty.

Like her forebears, Tlephilisse was blessed with a highly advanced intellect, alongside the curiosity and longevity to explore said intellect. As the cloud-carrier observed the emerald alien, he noticed a surfacing glimmer of longing in her otherwise pleasant demeanour. Her hand movements were unsure and careful as if she were reluctantly expressing a hidden hope. Now intrigued, Lu focussed his orange eyes and began to read what the River Sprite had carved so far. Her writing was far clearer than before, but she had used a few shapes that Lu had to simultaneously contextualise and corroborate against their primary language charts.

'The Island is old, with many lives upon it.
The animals here all quickly die but will soon be born again.
Tlephilisse is (I am) old; Tlephilisse is (I am) the only one.
Only when Tlephilisse has (I have) died, then another comes.'

Tlephilisse moved away from the sand, revealing the last phrases of her inscription. As the characters became visible to the Walker, a grim sickness began to bubble in his mind. He knew what she would ask.

'...Is Lu (are you) old? Does Lu (do you) die?
How long will Lu (you) live, trapped on the Island?'

The rain-bringer's orange eyes scanned the final lines of the inscription, and the whole of Lila seemed to cower in anticipation. Tlephilisse's blank eyes were burning in wait; silence here had never been so urgent.

Now two things were happening simultaneously, one of which was occurring on the physical plane, and the other was brooding within the grey man's puzzling mind. Almost involuntarily, Lu had outwardly begun to dispel Tlephilisse's fear. Without trying, he was smiling. There was no other choice. With a truth-less grin and a hollow nod, he carved a reassuring message to the Sprite, claiming that he'd never leave; 'I am deathless also', he etched. The River Sprite's glow had recommenced, for her worries had fled.

Judging solely by her reaction, the grey man concluded that it wasn't at all difficult to keep the water guardian at ease. She was exceptionally trusting, with no history that would lead her not to be. It was, of course, greatly advantageous that she was so trusting, thought the Walker. His task required him to frequently take advantage of this trust.

Still, he had avoided unnecessary lying to the Sprite wherever possible -each fabrication increased the possibility of the Walker stumbling on his own inconsistencies. Tlephilisse had not enquired as to her fate or survival; she feared only for Lu's own lifespan. He had told no lie, though he had given her false hope for their future. He glanced down at the message he had written and compartmentalised all natural indication of its diversion of the truth. *I am deathless also*.

Unwritten, and suppressed far deep inside Lu's ancient brain, another answer had sprung to mind. *I am death.*

The River Sprite must be the one to die, or Lu would be stranded on the Lila for the rest of his immortal life. But this thought was buried in the traitor's skull, under matted dark green hair and thick grey skin.

For now, Lu could afford to give hope to the emerald celestial. In fact, retaining Tlephilisse's confidence for the next twenty-nine days would be crucial to Lu's success. He smiled again at the Sprite as if to confirm his permanence.

Over the course of his reawakening, Lu had become crafty, quick, and a fantastic deceiver. He was wilier than his sharpest ancestors - a trait that was presumably encouraged and enhanced by his Mistress. However, for all his learning, and his returning memories, Lu had somehow lost his humanity, alongside his mortality. It wasn't as if the tragedy of Tlephilisse's fate had not occurred to Lu – it had. The lingering conscience of Rei had not *completely* abandoned him. It was, instead, as if Lu no longer had any obligation to serve such intangibilities. Without the moral imperative, all rights and wrongs had faded into bygone social suggestion, and remorse had all but lost its bite. Phantom empathy, still clinging to the grey man's memory, had spawned imitations of guilt, casting illusions of regret. When Lu was initially asked to kill the Sprite, he had been fairly vocal about his ethical reluctance. When finally submitting to his Mistress' will, Lu had ironically remarked that if decency and decorum were indicative of a soul, his must be forfeit.

Now, standing guiltless and sly in the presence of Tlephilisse's doomed innocence, Lu could observe the full extent of his moral decay. Though still able to relish the fruits of her company, he was not sentimentally bound to the Sprite, nor was he wed to the Lila itself. In fact, after visualising the route of otherwise enduring another eternity on a small island, Lu did not hesitate to dissociate his pity for the Sprite from his ambition to escape. No longer did he cower and distract from the prospect of his murderous endeavour. Even for the death of his principles, he did not mourn. He was accepting his deficit; it was certainly a blessing in the context of his mission.

Chapter Three

FAMILIAR FRUITS

Lu sighed audibly, recycling the warmth of a salty evening breeze. In real-time, barely a moment had passed since his last exchange with the River Sprite. His over-active mind had been aimlessly chattering beyond the constraints of physical occurrence, it seemed. He contemplated what small time had passed during his private philosophy and forbid himself from dwelling upon it any longer. Without realising, the Walker had begun to scratch a new message into the wet sand before him. Upon reinstating his focus, the subconscious intent of his restless hand became apparent, and Lu quickly completed the statement.

'The sky lights of last evening... what do you name them?'

Thus, a new topic ensued between the two, instigated purposefully by Lu as a means of extracting and designing a fresh, topical vocabulary with Tlephilisse. For hours, the Sprite and the sailor-warrior traded words and concepts, this time incorporating a running dialogue in the sand between their workspaces.

Here, they discussed and learned about one another, telling tales of their pasts, and comparing their perspectives. Throughout the course of the evening, Tlephilisse illustrated her studies of the night sky in great depth. The Lila-mother had given names to many of the stars and constellations that frequently graced the Lila; by the means of language, she could now catalogue and share her observations.

No detail was spared in the Sprite's elaborate visual index, which occasionally detoured from the task at hand and became intermittently difficult for Lu to follow. Frenzied but earnest, her approach was welcomed and celebrated by the Walker. Tlephilisse's passion certainly deserved patience, of which Lu had developed an abundance during his turquoise imprisonment. Due to the Lila's nearness of Rei, where Lu had been born and spent his adolescence, the sailor was once quite familiar with the Empryc night. With every new symbol, Tlephilisse resuscitated a fragment of the Walker's young memory. In no time at all, Lu was capable of recalling the same stars mentioned by the Sprite, but by the aliases assigned by his own people. The sea-folk of Rei were less than poetic when naming their surroundings, and this became increasingly apparent as Lu explained his alternative titles to Tlephilisse.

Last night's constellation - 'The Web of Scattered Majesties', as eloquently named by Tlephilisse, was known in Rei simply as 'The Fisher-God's Net'. On its arrival each year, the Fisher-God's Net signalled the start of a great catch that would last for the following week or so. Now that Lu had come to think of it, it must also have been the annual herald of the 'Dry Season' to come. It was only yesterday that he could not recall such seasons, further demonstrating the return of his adolescent memories.

Regardless of luck and superstition, there were never any sightings or continued worships of such a fisher deity, indicating the definite absurdity of the star-web's

Rei appellation. Lu hesitated in embarrassment before noting this information down for Tlephilisse.

For reasons unknown to the Walker, she seemed to enjoy his narration of Rei nonetheless; she even offered to craft new star titles, amalgamated from the two separately conceived originals. Lu declined this suggestion courteously, primarily due to his admiration and preference for Tlephilisse's own elegant inventions. Instead, he collaborated in further designs, mesmerised all the while by the Sprite's ingenuity.

Though neither the Walker nor Lilan could blindly remember the complete contents of the Web, an entrancing prompt was rousing softly in the higher realm. The sun had fully set, and the eyes of the night were waking. One by one, the aptly named scatter of majesties joined the web. As each light arrived, Tlephilisse twice-checked and occasionally amended any prior entries in the wet-sand star index, while her grey-skin assistant made note of those that were yet to be named or categorised. In what felt like no time at all, they had drawn shorthand for 'The Web of Scattered Majesties', and every star-group within it.

The Walker rushed the completion of his list of symbols and proceeded to gaze upwards in delight. Swelling and shining above him, the faraway fires were indistinguishable in size and were no doubt comprised of magic or matter unknown to the sailor-warrior. Though wingless he was at present, reaching the stars and thus discovering the source of their glow was of great interest to Lu. The riddles of their dwelling were forever on his mind. Perhaps that sky-world was also shared by greater beings such as the Watcher-Creators who begat the River Sprite and her kind, or even the Mistress of the Bhia herself. Tantalized but undiscouraged, Lu would seek the answer from the moment he could escape this suntrap isle. Tlephilisse was a salubrious companion, and her death would be a pity, but the secrets of the beyond were an undeniable temptation.

Upon recognising his insatiable need for knowledge and excitement, Lu grinned a true smile in the starlight. In spite of his failing virtue, the grey sailor was bursting with other emotions. Among his surviving senses were desire, intrigue, and adventure; like a youngster yet to sail, he was fuelled by the promise of uncharted lands, and what lay beyond them. Similarly, for every speculative hope and joy that Lu had retained, there were equal residual concerns and doubts, providing the appropriate emotional antitheses. Fears, worries, and pain still crouched in the shadows of the Walker's mind, numb but for the possibility of Lu's failure. Still, they currently lacked the dominion required to distract the sailor. Though Lu was clouded, wet, and soulless for now, he would soon be free to pursue his aching desires. His fate depended on such motivation in order to manifest itself. He would be cloudless, and dry; he would travel, learn, and reap - a scythe in the hand of a goddess. If that was the destiny implied by his Sorceress, then it was a destiny to look forward to.

In silence, the River Sprite and the Reikan admired the radiance of the Empryc night. Though internally, Lu had pondered the whereabouts of the hanging suns and his desire to reach them, he had not outwardly communicated with Tlephilisse in nearly an hour. The emerald orphan interpreted Lu's behaviour as an intentional and peaceful finale of their day and participated in the warm tranquillity for an hour or so before lifting from the ground in levitation. This was a subtle declaration of her tiredness and was reciprocated by a pleasant nod from her companion.

With a smile and a bow, Lu bid Tlephilisse farewell for the night. He had purposefully waited for the Sprite to leave before attempting to source local nourishment on the Lila; Tlephilisse did not appear to require any sort of edible sustenance, so Lu thought it unnecessary to involve her with the search for his first meal in days.

It seemed peculiar to the Walker that, since first meeting the Mistress, he had experienced no nagging hungers or prominent fatigues at all. The quiescent, chrysalis life he had spent on the Bhia prior to his awakening may simply not have required sleep, or regular consumption and excretion due to his plant-preserved disposition and languid pace – at least, this was the rationalisation that Lu had settled on. By now, however, he had expected to surely feel those needs more often.

It was not so much that he was hungry or even tired; in truth, the Reikan only desired graspable replenishment for the mere sake of its palpability. Placebo though it may be, the feeling of physical nourishment banished any health-complacency brought about by his current immortality.

In a direction astray from that of Tlephilisse's recent departure, Lu led his rain into the welcoming night-chatter of the Lila forest. Here, he thought, there must be something worth eating.

There were a few things to consider when deciding on a meal. Foremost was the distinction between the flowering plants of the Sprite's intentional design, and the naturally occurring fruits and greens of the island. In darkness, many of the shapes around Lu were indistinguishable from the next. In accusation, the sailor glanced up to the high trees that obscured the light of the stars. Without the shine of the Web of Majesties, his eyes were failing him.

An additional consideration had occurred to the Walker; regardless of temptation, there would be no sense in hunting the limited game of the Lila. Tlephilisse could barely stand to witness the creatures suffering in the drought; if he were to slay them merely as food, there would be no telling as to her reaction. Distraught, she would presumably either seek vengeance or abandon her faith; the risk certainly outweighed the harvest. Besides, the flavour of even the most insignificant Lila-shrub would far surpass any half-living thing the Bhia had ever offered his deprived mouth. Lu looked around him and smiled gratefully at this thought. Through tears of reminiscence, his orange eyes now glimmered in the surrounding jungle shadow.

Then, the Walker spied a generously plump fruit hanging to his left – and then another, and then five or so more! For the past few moments, he had been leaning against what appeared to be a tall, citrus tree; gazing long and far, he had been somewhat oblivious to that which was near. Lu paused to scan the branches and briefly speculated the possible importance of this tree in Tlephilisse's colour garden. For a moment he was dissuaded, but as Lu's eyes adapted to the shadows, it became apparent that he had wandered into a citrus grove. He approached another tree and inspected the lower branches; there were many missing fruits, and some that were left half-eaten. The plant was not only naturally ubiquitous here; it was subject to the hunger of many other Lilan foragers. Lu was relieved. His inclusion in such scavenging company was inconsequential. Lu reached out and instinctively twisted the enormous egg-shaped growth, which released from its mother with little resistance. Immediately, his eyes became secondary to a wave of flashing images that now commandeered his thoughts.

With the weighty fruit in hand, the Walker was transported through abstract scenes of his past. The mere touch of the slippery thing, now wetted by cloud, had activated once-dormant memories of his distant youth. He had held these thick-fleshed fruits many times before; in Rei, they were plentiful and beloved.

Without daylight, Lu had not yet discerned the colour of the rind; now, with the past thrust upon him, he could picture the peel, the fruit, and the tree from which it came, as if it were sunlit and clear. They were things of pale green skin, with a near-transparent flesh inside; the flesh was full of moisture that was delicious and subtly sweet and retained none of the bitterness that another similar fruit may bear. In Rei it was called Umello and was often crushed for its liquids, which were then bottled for later refreshment.

Lu was delighted by what he could now recall. Then, as was learned long ago, he placed his thumbs at the top of the umello and pressed down into where the stalk had been. Carefully, Lu pushed his digits deeper until the skin perforated and he was able to tear the peel away from the flesh within. Hunched down in the darkness, the lonely Reikan devoured the umello in a passionate frenzy - its glistening juices splashed around his maw, but were cleansed momentarily by the Walker's cloud. With every bursting bite, the lost world challenged Lu's amnesia; though it was not yet clear enough to mourn, he wept nonetheless. Incapable of (and emotionally incompatible with) tears of loss, these droplets were instead laced with surprise and wonder. In the cleansing cloudburst, they quickly vanished alongside the umello juice. Soon they were gone without evidence, and Lu concluded that he imagined them altogether. The memory of his past was now weaker than a dream, and he was far more concerned with his future in any case.

Tossing the peel and other undesirable leftovers to the ground, the Walker advanced further into the tropic shadows. He could soon hear the sea again; it was coming from the sands of the far eastern curve of Lila, indicating that he had walked nearly halfway down the island perimeter since exiting the northern beach. Intuitively, Lu drifted towards the singing waves until shortly emerging from the green. Here, the moonlight still fell in cascades on the shimmering sand and tide. However, in spite of the beaming moon, The Web of Scattered Majesties had now begun to fade. Time had slipped Lu's judgement and the night had halfway passed.

Unlike the northern beach on which Lu and Tlephilisse had spent the day, the East Lila curve was host to a family of tall but narrow trees. Each plant had an unbelievably slim body, which seemed disproportionate to the sudden explosion of green and brown at the summit of each trunk. The unsteady branches resembled a multi-faceted hand; each of its many fingers was substantially weighted by dense groups of leaves and, from what Lu could make out, a dozen or so green and brown nuts. Returning his focus to the sand, Lu then noticed a few more of the husk-like fruits that had fallen from above.

Even in the gentle ocean-breeze, the trees seemed unsafe to be around. From such a height, a single wayward shell could easily shatter any mortal skull. Regardless of the danger, Lu could not deny his familiarity with the plants. As was the case with the umello, these aerial fruits may further restore the Walker's memory. Without a second thought, Lu scooped one of the dead husks from the sand and flung it to the nearby fruits above. He stood with enough distance from the trees to avoid the fatal drop-zone, in turn resulting in a much further target. To the tune of a dull and lifeless thud, the Walker formed a sardonic grin. His first missile had fallen spectacularly short of its goal, for it had been thrown with dreadful aim. Though Lu was no longer physically weak, his coordination was out of practice by an eternity. Again, he crouched on the sand in search of a new projectile, and again he stood up to launch his chosen husk. Again, the chosen trajectory was flawed and impotently skimmed the outer leaves of the tree. Lu shrugged and decided that tonight was as good a time as ever to develop his throw. For half an hour, the cloud and its Walker trawled the eastern beach for husk and rock. Once Lu had finished accumulating his missiles, he set them aside and began to practise methodically. During his time on the Lila Isle, Lu had become increasingly fond of this pragmatic approach. His mind was sick and sore from its recent battle with morality and for little reward. There were far more satisfactory results to be sought in the physical world, it seemed.

After no more than twenty attempts, Lu was achieving a near-perfect throw. He was hitting his mark consistently now, and as the power of his strike reached an audible crescendo, the targeted fruit began to dislodge from its skyward nest. Finally, a pair of the heavy shell-fruits plummeted from above, and aggressively shifted the white sand with tremendous lift as they hit the ground. With an honest feeling of achievement, the Walker gently ran towards his prizes and snatched one of them in his wet, grey hands. It was hard, brown, and bristly, and hardly appeared edible in comparison to some of its green and visibly softer siblings still safe in the trees. This did not bother Lu; the darker, harder produce was likely to be ripest, hence why it was the easiest to free from the branch. Lu was instead preoccupied with the next troublesome task at hand - his only weapon, Umbra, was distantly hidden and buried out of sight. Without a blade, how else could the husk be cut?

The sailor-warrior paused for a moment of thought. He had rather hoped that upon touching the fruit, his mind would again regress to a state of lost intuition. His previous knowledge of the impenetrable shell could offer methods of cracking it. No such thing had occurred. He licked his lips and wandered towards the sea, cradling the fruit in his arms. Perhaps without taste, the mere touch of a fibrous shell was not sufficient stimulation to stir the past. The Walker redirected his pensive stroll while massaging his glistening grey temples with his thumbs. It was either insufficient sensation or the fruit was simply not in Lu's past at all.

The early dry-season sun had begun to rise again, seducing Lu's focus away from the subconscious. As he acknowledged the return of day, the nagging thoughts of rest, and reconvening with the Sprite, began to outweigh his care for fruits and his association with them. With a deep breath, the Walker turned to face the sea once more before leaving. His eyes, golden in the sunrise, scanned the island coast from side to side, before settling on the spine of the Empryc Crown. Immediately, an idea occurred to Lu and he returned his interest to the unbreakable nut. Like a ship in the deadly spines, Lu trapped the husk in the crevice of a rock and secured it with one hand. With his free hand, he was equipped with a piece of broken fruit-shell from the sand and began to bash its sharpest edge against the fruit. Still, the nut seemed to wriggle and roll against the surrounding space in the crevice, somehow avoiding the direct stab of the makeshift dagger.

Tired and somewhat bored of the challenge, Lu attempted a final primitive solution. With the fruit gripped fiercely in his left hand, which he believed to be his stronger side, the sailor-warrior twisted his whole being with exceptional momentum as he smacked the side perpendicular to the face of the nut against the razor-most edge of the rock crevice. The side shattered instantly, and water began to spit from the damaged area. It was then that some Reikan instinct commanded Lu to turn the fruit round and peel at the opening for a wider flow. As if to toast this mundane victory, the Walker pressed the shell-fruit to his lips and sucked out its contents; his capacity for breath permitted him to drink it dry without a single pause for air. As expected, though less intense than before, a flow of once imprisoned mind-stuff had been unleashed by the liquid's taste. Buacoctin, or aptly nicknamed 'shell-fruit', was yet another native Rei food, that appeared extensively in Lu's youth. Through the medium of memory, he was reminded that it was not only full of water but also by tightly bound flesh that could be found on the reverse side of the husk. The buacoctin water was hydrating, and pleasant enough to drink, and before scratching out the meat with his pale-yellow teeth, Lu remembered that the solid, white innards had a similar, but more concentrated flavour. Over time, the buacoctin usually absorbed some of its own self-contained liquid, thus thickening the meat and influencing its taste.

After stripping every sinew of the oily, white flesh from the husk, he reflected on its matured but definite resemblance to the flavour of the buacoctin water. Both nut-like and of slight sweetness, the meat was certainly more delicious. It also contained enough fat and bulk to ward off any future island hunger. Still full of moisture, the white flesh could also be ground and pressed to return its juices, which would then secrete with a thicker, milkier consistency than before.

It was only when Lu had consumed every digestible attribute of the buacoctin that something occurred to him. Though, like the easily peeled umello, the buacoctin grew in abundance upon the Lila, the buacoctin would be near impossible for any other animal on this island to consume. If he were to continue to feed on them for the next twenty-eight days or so, he would need Tlephilisse's consent. Finally tired after his brief conquest of the fruits of the eastern beach, the grey man shrugged off his concern regarding the River Sprite and her sacred gardens and marched steadily back to the derelict village. The sun had already begun to cast its royal glare upon Lila, and the day had recommenced. Upon arrival to the village, Lu collapsed into the nearest shaded hut, followed shortly by his cloud. Fatigue had finally found him, and he was to meet with Tlephilisse in no more than four hours. With no way of moderating his dormancy, Lu simply hoped that the Sprite would come to awaken him if need be. Immediately, he was asleep.

And Lu, the Krajian Scythe of a nameless and formless mistress, was temporarily away from Lila. He had fallen into the plunge of a second black slumber. The three-step sequence was familiar, even within the abstraction of a dream, to the Walker. This time there were developments, however - elaborations of the previous circumstances. As before, the dreadful first act was a blinding sprint, with hands of blood, and a blue sky coiling and bewitched. A storm of guilt still poured upon him, in place of a cloud companion, and was again unable to wash his grey hands spattered with red blood. Yet, this time it was not the Bhia from which he ran. It was the open sea, and he was treading wind and wave. Still, the spiralling darkness and shame slowed and engulfed the sailor-warrior, but instead falling into the mud, his water-defying stride began to fail. The sea prevailed against his limp and futile struggle and pulled him to its pulsing depths.

Next, there was the almost sacrificial scene of the Reikan boy, resembling Lu, and the ghostly hand in the beach-fire smoke. This stage of the dream, according to Lu's memory, remained the same as before. The boy, ignited by the apparition, was cloaked in fire, and as his spirit rose upon the morning breeze, the bandages of flame were unwrapped - the sorceress unveiled. In the midst of a second immersion, the meanings of the first two scenes were now far more apparent to Lu. It took little imagination to attribute the murderous guilt and blood to the mission of the Walker. Lu was soon to assassinate an innocent creature, and though he felt no guilt by day, some useless sentiment had evidently burrowed into his subconscious, it was accessible only through dreams. The second act, by Lu's interpretation, was a far more literal visualisation of something that had already happened. It was a re-enactment of the grey man's first true encounter with the Mistress; of that, he was sure. Something about that unusually cold morning on a Rei beach, and the dark transaction that took place there - all were linked to the destiny bond between the Walker and the sorceress, and even perhaps his clouded confinement upon the Bhia. Why the scene of future guilt was presented prior to a past event in the running order of this episodic nightmare was unknown to the Walker, but his time for thought had expired, for the horrendous and entirely inexplicable third chapter was about to begin.

Lu was terror-stricken as he peered from the great heights of the soaring platform. Legions of unknown minions lay dead or dying far below, and the sound of heaving wings approached the paralysed Reikan from either side. The leather-winged demon and the tremendous bird hauled Lu past the known skies of Kraj, into the darkness beyond. Though he had reflected on the previous scenarios in full awareness of the dream, the Walker was now consumed by the illusion and in turn by fear. Soon he was released into the mouth of the unseeable snake with impossible teeth, though now as he fell, he did not quickly awaken. He sailed past the myriads of teeth, and something continued to illuminate his descent. To his left, he involuntarily glanced and noticed the dazzling, yet somehow clear, blade of Umbra! It was certainly not there during the flight from Kraj, nor was it ever present in the previous occurrence of the dream. Rallied by the sight of the glass sabre, Lu regained mobility and some awareness of the dream and, Umbra first, consented to his hurried dive; this time, he would slay the dream-beast as he fell to its core; hopefully, he would never dream of it again.

Chapter Four

THE LIVING LILA

To the sound of a time-rippling, world-shattering shriek, the Walker regained consciousness. Above him, Tlephilisse was floating, asleep. It was night, and he was lying within the sacred water-ring garden of Lila. He had clearly overslept by at least the whole day and been pulled to Tlephilisse's inner garden where she could watch over him. His light blue undergarments, which on the Lila he had worn without the shellsuit, were now uncomfortably damp. He had passed water in his sleep, presumably due to over-drinking from the buacoctin. It had been a great leap of time since last the Reikan smelled the stink of urine, and he half-expected the odour to trigger yet another flash of memory. It didn't, and instead, he lay for a moment while reflecting on the peculiar return of his bodily requirements. He felt the strain of morning tire, and he was hungry again. Perhaps upon indulging in mortal requirements, he had banished his sorcerous longevity and had indeed become mortal again. Either way, he required fruit and further excretion and did not want to pass water into his clothing again. For a moment, the Reikan felt embarrassed at the thought of Tlephilisse witnessing his unconscious bodily malfunctions, but then decided that it must have occurred while she was asleep. The stain was damp and would have already dried had it passed during the heat of day.

With diligent steps, so as to not stir his emerald defender, the Walker departed the heart of Lila and returned to the umello grove. It was the later stage of night and the air was mild and fragrant with both brine and flower. In fact, Lu had enjoyed his walk to the citrus trees very much. The Web of Scattered Majesties was nowhere to be seen, and the sun would begin to rise within the next hour or so, but the jungles of Lila felt boisterous and inviting, singing the rounds written by Tlephilisse's ancestors. Contributing to his fine mood, Lu was pleased to have again denounced the guilt that ghosted his prophetic dream and was further satisfied by its valiant new finale. He felt almost heroic, falling blade-first into the maw of his tormenter, be it to the death or otherwise. Bizarre though it may be, a future that concerned legions of warriors and great demons and gods still seemed far more enticing to Lu than an eternity of near-loneliness on little Lila. Only with this attitude could he fulfil his dark assignment. After enjoying the fresh, wet kiss of two particularly green umello, Lu saw to his cleanliness and other requirements before heading on to the eastern beach.

Strengthened and refreshed, Lu channelled his energies into a dash. Near weightless, but with incredible speed, the Reikan darted between tree, shrub and rock as he had done in the obstacle course that he had designed in the Bhia under the instruction of his Mistress. Now that Lu's body had again begun to rely and draw upon the comfort of rest and nutrition, it seemed pertinent to the Walker's objective that he maintained his fitness while upon the Lila. He was currently extraordinarily slender, without prominent musculature. Lu was merely thin beyond the desired shape for a young Rei adventurer. If his organs were beginning to adhere to the requirements of a mortal's, eating regularly and building muscle would be vital to his survival.

Soon, Lu arrived on the white sands of the eastern beach. His bare, grey feet were slightly sore from the intense sprint. Alongside his sabre and shellsuit, Lu had also removed his light brown sandals and placed them within the hidden box. This was now clearly a mistake - at the time that they were gifted, the sandals were a more subtle (but very comfortable) inclusion to the gifts from the Goddess. Now it seemed that not only would they protect Lu's underfoot from any rock or splinter on wilder surfaces, but also from the sting of heat that was absorbed by certain grounds within Lila. Since his first appreciation for the coolness of the white sands, the Walker had come across many a sun-seared ground, too hot for his rain to cool. Lu assured himself that he would reclaim the sandals when next he passed their place of burial.

Using what he had learned the day before, Lu found a dry, fallen fruit in the white sands beneath a buacoctin tree. He hit a hanging fruit upon his first attempt, but it did not fully dislodge. There were not many other potential projectiles nearby, so Lu collected that which he had just thrown and returned to his original position, where he cast the shell for a second time. It was a successful throw, and a medium brown, fairly mature fruit thumped gracelessly to the sand.

The sun was fully risen by the time the cloud-cursed wanderer had smashed open the shell-fruit, drunk its water and devoured its white, oily flesh. Afterwards,

Lu glanced towards the forest, shell still in hand, to see Tlephilisse hovering no more than twenty steps away. Her mouthless face was regularly unreadable to Lu, though she did not seem hostile or disappointed in finding him here. With a final gulp of fruit-flesh, Lu smiled sincerely at his host and began to walk towards her.

Over the next hour or so, Tlephilisse and the Walker silently discussed Lu's sudden need for nourishment. This was not only informative to the Sprite, who was now further perplexed by the nature of Lu's immortality but was also a productive topic in regards to further developing their written language. In the rush of excitement, Tlephilisse had previously forgotten to include and form symbols for the fruits of Lila. This was a good opportunity to expand her catalogue of Lila. With some difficulty, Lu elaborated on which of the fruits and plants he remembered of Rei, though he made sure to steer away from any indication as to the nature of his departure from Rei, as he was unsure who else may be listening.

Before the ageless pair had delved too far into their discussion of fruit and tree, Lu attempted to apologise for oversleeping, citing his original late-night search for food as his cause for exhaustion. Though the Sprite did not seem at all offended by his reasoning, there was some concern in her response. Until now, Lu was convinced that he had slept through the morning, afternoon, and evening, and had awoken in the later stages of night. It was with regret and certainty that Tlephilisse corrected the Walker and informed him that he had been asleep for five days. For a moment, Lu was lost for words. Though he wanted to be in disbelief, he knew that Tlephilisse had no reason to tell anything other than truth. The black dream that he had endured for a second time had felt almost momentary as he slipped through its three-stages of illusion. The previous occurrence of the dream had not lasted any longer than a few hours. Regardless of an explanation, long sleep, it seemed, had found him at last. It had passed sometime between now and the night of the shadow moon, but his sleep would need to become more regular, or he would miss his window of success entirely. Once he had returned from thought the Walker expressed his surprise and confusion regarding his prolonged slumber and jested that it may have been in connection with having to learn a brand new language. He made no mention of the dream, however. Instead, he thanked Tlephilisse for patiently supervising his dormant condition and guided their speechless communication back towards the topic of food.

Though Tlephilisse did not require food, nor have a mouth to consume it, she was particularly insistent that Lu made efforts to return something to the Lila in equal to that which he had taken. At first, this seemed meticulous and time-consuming to the Walker, but as the ageless Sprite articulated her care for the balance of life in the white sand below, Lu began to warm to the concept himself. For every living thing, Tlephilisse highlighted its unique contribution back to the Lila. She spoke of the island almost as if it were sentient and alive in its own right. Even in death, the creatures and plants of the unspoiled island returned their substances and energies to the wind and soil. In decay, the dead will donate themselves as the foundation for new life to come. This was the way of Lila, and none suffered its truth more than Tlephilisse, who gave her own life energy to her children, only to despair as they gradually gave it back. Though Lu remained guiltless and un-saddened by the Sprite's tale of loss, he thought her story to be profound in ways that he could not effectively communicate to her. It was curious that Tlephilisse should be so committed to a greater balance following the departure of her children, the Lila-mortals.

Lu learned that the Sprite, since experiencing the dispassionate and unprejudiced inevitability of death, had developed reverence for death's purpose. She had rationalised and therefore befriended, the absoluteness of death. Furthermore, she seemed aware that she was a steward of sorts, but could not phrase it by means of their limited runes. Though the Mistress of the Bhia described her to Lu as a River Sprite, the emerald creature seemed to believe that her role primarily concerned the energy cycle of life and death upon the island. Tlephilisse considered herself and her ancestors to be something of a god, though the concept of such a figure had no heavy implication here as she had no comprehension of gods or religion in the outside world. Since the passing of her beloveds, her monitored care for wildlife had doubled. By Lu's understanding, Tlephilisse now almost interpreted her role as that of a shepherd of nature. To care for Lila as best she could, and see to it that all things reached their greatest potential up until their very end.

For a moment or two, Lu found himself lost in the Sprite's autobiographical writing in the rain-fed sand. Regardless of claims made by the sorceress, or Tlephilisse herself, the River Sprite's role (and power) was becoming increasingly unclear. Her curious aura, her mouthless

LU

song, and her ageless permanence were evidence enough of her alleged inclusion among the thirty-five guardians of Kraj, mentioned briefly by the Mistress. Yet, for all her supernatural properties, there was no indication of her relevance or usefulness as a Kraji-guardian at all. Whatever the reason for her creation, it was well concealed. He dared not ask Tlephilisse of her other gifts, for he was ever cautious of arousing the unwanted eyes of suspicion. Instead, with the thick, light-grey forefinger of his left hand, Lu etched a question into the ground, encouraging their return to the original topic.

'Teach me to give back to the Lila Island, for already
I have taken three umello and two buacoctin.'

Immediately, Tlephilisse expressed fervent interest in Lu's message, and whistle-sang her excitement to the nearby birds riding the morning sea breeze. The birds were unbothered, but from beyond the trees that edged the beach, Lu could hear the island songbirds attempting to mimic Tlephilisse's improvised yet agile tune. Once the Sprite had finished vocalising her delight, she quickly inscribed a handful of clumsy characters into a patch of sand that had nearly dried. The white grains had nearly collapsed in on themselves before Lu had a chance to decipher them.

'Today, you will give back to the Lila-island. Today,
I will teach you to grow flowers.'

And then, as if she had waited for Lu to finish reading, Tlephilisse ascended into levitation and began to drift back inland, with Lu and his cloud following shortly behind. As usual, the Sprite bobbed forward with little velocity. It took some effort for Lu to resist overtaking her, and the energetic Reikan was forced to occupy his mind with distractions to avoid becoming impatient behind his unhurried guide. This was when it occurred to Lu that, during his conversations with Tlephilisse this morning, he had not needed a rune-chart to recall symbols that the pair had invented only five days ago. Since then, the Walker had been in slumber and had been unable to practice using the language at all. Practice was something Lu assumed the Sprite had been doing during his five-day sleep, as she had also written from memory this morning.

Plodding quietly behind the Sprite in thought, Lu eventually found a reasonable explanation for his impressive demonstration of recollection; his mind was still robbed of much of his past, therefore leaving plenty of room to store new information. His brain capacity seemed to accommodate all the new information it was given without a fuss, which was a thought that pleased Lu very much. He had been dubious recently as to whether he would remember the Mistress' instructions regarding the ritual by the time the shadow moon arrived. But seeing as he was able to recall an entire language without practising it, Lu now felt completely at ease about recalling a few steps for the ritual.

Then, there was a sharp rustle in a shrub to Lu's left, breaking Lu's stream of thought. Between gaps and breaks in the drapes of boiling jungle, Lu made out the agile scurry of a large, vulpine shape. If it had resembled another of Lila's miniature inhabitants, Lu would not have wasted a second thought on the peripheral unknown. However, the thing he believed to have just seen was an enormous, yet lithe, fox. Its perfect coat was a light shade of lavender, though it was ethereal and barely seemed to be composed of natural elements.

'You are well camouflaged here,' smiled Lu, as he dreamily compared the fled fox's colouration to that of the many teething darklilies that gave the island its name. Tlephilisse turned her head when he spoke, and Lu smiled at her blankly. It seemed she had not noticed the beast, but Lu intended to ask her about it later. The Walker only wished that he had gained a closer glance at the mysterious passer-by before it escaped from sight through the trees. Though his mind may have exaggerated the detail, he believed it to have been one and a half times the height of a man from snout to tail. The sight of the thing had evoked his memory of the few small foxes that scuttled the shades of Rei by night; each was the size of a small dog, and their colours varied from bright orange to a dusty brown, but none were of a complexion or stature comparable to that which he had just seen. However, in form and face, they were alike. It was as if the diminutive, Reian variety were the orange-brown litter of their great violet mother. For all its size, Lu did not fear the creature. He had barely encountered it, and yet he already associated it with the rest of Lila - gentle and serene. Lu hoped to see the creature again before he departed Lila but, for now, the fox had vanished.

It dawned upon Lu that the pair had ceased their journey. Before them was a patch of shaded land that Lu had crossed once or twice during his first few days upon the island. Compared to the elaborate designs of many other areas upon Lila, this area was flowerless and naked. It was clear that this was Tlephilisse's chosen patch upon which Lu would learn to garden. Tlephilisse was still visibly excited about the prospect of sharing her interest with her new companion but paused for a moment in apparent realisation. And then, upon speculating what the problem may be, Lu came to realise what had halted the Sprite. There was no sand here; there was no way for the pair to communicate. The two exchanged a look, and then Lu released a stifled laugh. He made a basic gesture to Tlephilisse, which indicated that he would quickly rush back to the nearest beach and bring back some sand in which they could write. In the meantime, Tlephilisse could prepare the area for her gardening demonstrations. In less than two hours, Lu and his localised cloud had returned. He had removed his garment, and within it, he had wrapped a large scoop of white sand. He poured the sand onto a large, depressed rock surface, and then spent a reasonably long time shaking the excess silt from his clothes before putting them back on. Tlephilisse also noticed that he had returned wearing footwear that she had not seen him use since first they met. Lu had taken the time to venture back to the settlement where he had hidden his personal effects; his feet grew tired of running barefoot on the sharp jungle floor. He had also taken additional care during his quest for sand to look out for the purple fox, but it had not shown itself.

For the rest of the day, Tlephilisse instructed Lu in her approach to cultivating the teething darklilies. There was nothing extraordinary to her methods, other than that she had discovered them independently. Lu behaved attentively nonetheless, for he enjoyed Tlephilisse's enthusiasm, and did not want to undermine her efforts with his pre-existing comprehension of gardening. Once

Tlephilisse was through with explaining basic principles, however, she began to point out her many flower hybridisations on the island, among other complex and unnatural alterations she had made to certain plants. Lu's interest began to soar as he noticed some of the accelerated behaviours that the plants expressed while in close proximity to the Sprite's pulsing aura. He did not point out her apparent sorceress' advantage but studied it quietly as she elaborated further. At one point during the mid-afternoon, Lu found an appropriate window in the conversation in which he asked Tlephilisse about the great purple creature he had seen. They shared no common word or symbol for 'fox' however, and the Sprite did not seem to recognise his description. Perhaps there were no foxes here, thought Lu. Perhaps he had hallucinated it all together.

On the topic of the animals of Lila, Tlephilisse spent the later afternoon describing herbal potions she had invented in order to remedy the untimely death of many Lilan beasts. According to the Sprite, she had initially devised the concept when her children began to weaken; unlike their mother, they had mouths, but all the same, they did not need to eat. Her idea at the time was to invigorate or revive her dying children by combining the stronger scents and textures of certain plants and feeding these concoctions to the injured and ill Lila-mortals. From what Lu could understand, this had not worked at all. However, a similar idea later revisited the Sprite after witnessing the premature deaths of a few birds and reptiles on the island. Tlephilisse had blamed her previous failure on the fact that the Lila-mortals had no digestive system; the animals of Lila did, however, and would be more likely to benefit from her remedial elixirs.

As he listened to Tlephilisse describe her methods in depth, Lu began to fathom the Sprite's true speciality. Given the earlier context Tlephilisse had shared regarding her role as the steward of life upon Lila, Lu now found himself in fascination as the Sprite casually elaborated on her impossible sciences and cures. Her ability was supernatural, and the power she had granted to her concoctions was vast. Within only a decade or so of trial and improvement, the Sprite had been creating simple plant-based medicines that had cured the untreatable.

She had seen to the countless casualties of reptiles, rodents, birds, and even wayward sea lions that had found their way through the Empryc Crown. Each had been dying of some ailment or other, and innocently, she had not only cured their sickness or injury but also somehow extended their lifespan to nearly three times what it should have been! While there was undoubtedly a large aspect of creativity to Tlephilisse's success, the medicinal results were amplified by a benevolent and unusual sorcery. The Sprite poured herself into her work, impregnating each potion with her celestial life force.

After previously doubting her power, Lu reconsidered his ignorance - after all, it was Tlephilisse who singlehandedly gave life to twenty vacant moulds. Upon their death, all that she had given was returned to her, and she was unspent. This must be the case for all who are healed by the Sprite, thought Lu. Regardless of her earlier, more humble, interpretation, Tlephilisse was not a mere shepherd of life upon Lila; she was its keeper and its distributor.

By the aching turn of time, her borrowed power would return, and would be spent again; for all who borrowed it would still eventually die. Death was delayed for them, but not prevented altogether. Tlephilisse was to the island what the sea was to the land. Though, by the vessel of rain or otherwise, the sea lent its waters to the land and its people and its rivers, drop by drop the water came slowly trickling back to where it had come from. The River Sprite was, Lu had decided, a fitting name after all.

In the early evening, Lu found an appropriate time to interrupt his lesson in herb and medicine to ask Tlephilisse a few questions. Carefully, he speculated the true meaning of the Sprite's joyful initial reaction upon discovering that Lu was immortal. Previously, it seemed obvious to the Walker that the Sprite was merely pleased to have a friend who she would not outlive, but now Lu had thought of a different potential reason. With a well-presented sincerity, he asked Tlephilisse if, due to her unique immortality, she had feared that Lu was a mortal who hunted her to gain eternal life? He asked if, upon discovering that he was already immortal, her fears had subsided.

Lu impulsively thought of, and delivered his first question. He had not realised that it could offend Tlephilisse until he had already asked it. To his relief, however, the emerald optimist was pleased to admit that she had not even considered that at the time.

For a moment, her blank, white eyes somehow seemed pensive; it was as if she had only just learned of greed, and now envisioned what extent it must reach in the outside world to have inspired Lu's question. The Walker noticed that the Sprite was shaken, and moved on to his second thought, hoping to reignite her usual demeanour. With his thin, rain-soaked writing stick, Lu etched into the recovering sand.

'The Lila-mortals could speak this language because Tlephilisse (you) gave them mouths. Is this correct?'

This was a question that Lu already knew the answer to, but it was a necessary preparation for his following suggestion. Tlephilisse, who appeared to have risen from her troubles, quickly inscribed her response.

'Yes, the Lila-mortals could speak. Though their voice was different to my own, our language was the same. I understood the Lila-mortals, and the Lila-mortals understood Tlephilisse (me). Why?'

Lu smiled. It was as he expected; Tlephilisse could communicate using her whistle-voice, and her children had learned to understand her.

'I have learned the language as symbols. Teach Lu (me) to hear it. Teach Lu (me) to speak it.'

The Sprite glanced at the message for a moment, before turning to face the Walker, eye to eye. Her concentration held for longer than Lu had anticipated, and he began to feel uncomfortable. Suddenly, a strange voice infiltrated his ears. It was not a Reikan voice, nor was it the telepathy of the Mistress of the Bhia, though this sensation was not dissimilar to the latter. The voice was light, airy, and had a bright tone, and was repeating the same sound over and over again.

Lu looked expectantly at the Sprite for an explanation, but Tlephilisse was too deep in focus. The repeated phrase, from the disembodied voice, sounded as if it were taken out of context, and sliced out of a longer passage. Whatever it was, Tlephilisse was responsible, and Lu was once again awestricken by the Sprite's power.

Once Lu had overcome the initial shock of hearing the alien voice, he began to think clearly and concluded that he was hearing the voice of a Lila-mortal. Tlephilisse was conjuring their voice from her past, and therefore demonstrating the vocalisation of the language that Lu proposed to learn.

After another ten seconds or so, the vocal excerpt ceased, and Tlephilisse emerged from her hyper-focussed trance. Now that the Sprite was responsive, Lu made sure to show that he had acknowledged the meaning of what he was shown.

Tlephilisse put a weightless, leafy hand on the Walker's shoulder, and drew his attention to the sand, where she then started to write.

'Friend. That is what the Lilan voice was saying. Friend.'

Lu smiled at the Sprite and attempted to copy the sound with his own voice. At first, he was conscious of his pitch, which was deeper than that of the Lila-mortal. He relaxed his shoulders, and began to speak in his own register, and eventually found that the sound had come quite comfortably to his lips. Tlephilisse nodded approvingly at Lu's progress.

Through the two small holes in the centre of her face, the River Sprite began to chirp a shimmering phrase, in her peculiar whistle-voice. Lu quickly assumed that this shared the same meaning as the repeated word of the Lila-mortal, but in the mouthless speech of Tlephilisse. Until now, it had not occurred to the Walker that he would have to learn two sounds for each word. Still, his memory was functioning far beyond that of an ordinary Reikan. Above all else, Lu was attracted to the challenge, and interested to test the extent of his enhanced memory. He smiled.

Tlephilisse had expected the Walker to be daunted by the prospect of learning both speeches, but instead, the Sprite noticed Lu's unwavering grin and cheerfully began to write another message.

'Tomorrow, we will go to the beach. We will draw words in the sand. I will show you every Lila-mortal sound that I can summon. I will point to its written form. Lu (you) must speak the Lilan tongue. I speak only in whistle-song, so Lu (you) must learn this also.

It will be difficult, but it will be good.'

And thus, they retired early, both eager for the morning. Lu's mind was effervescent and scattered with anticipation as he bid his host a good night. In only a short while, the Lila had exposed many of its wonders and curiosities to the grey visitor. Before, the Walker had doubted how his re-awakened self could spend a month carrying the burden of his task, on an island with only the company of his victim. He had feared that madness or regret would take him long before the killing night had come. Now he was comforted, if not *inspired,* by the island to fulfil his vow. The immense beauties of Lila were nothing but a reminder of what awaited him should he succeed.

Though the grey man and the emerald demi-god resided far apart on the island, their final waking thoughts that night were haunted by one another. They were not lovers. The bond they currently shared was not driven by the primal yet fragile whim of physical attraction. The Sprite was not capable, or even aware of romance and sexuality. What she felt was something else; it was a desperate and passionate craving for an intellectual intimacy, offered only by her new companion. She was obsessed with the Walker, though she intended to continue subduing her passions to a lesser intensity while in his company. She resented the thought of imposing on him.

Lu was unsure of how he regarded Tlephilisse. He remembered the days of his past, where the infatuated young adults of Rei sought particular passions among themselves. Some were temporary pleasures, while other partnerships endured. Some led to offspring, while others did not. It mattered not; Lu could not remember if he had ever experienced those interests himself and did not feel them now. Though the Sprite had somehow ensnared him, it was not by the cheap fancies of lust.

Chapter Five

GRATITUDE

From the wicked grip of two familiar demons, a cloudless Lu fell once again into the endless throat of the impossible serpent. This time, there was no sword to put forward, to restore his bravery. This time, the jaw of the beast began to snap, and the Walker was lacerated helplessly between the infinite gleaming teeth of his nightmare. Then the pain came in, from every angle – from outside and from within. His body was broken and skewered, and his brain seemed to explode, unable to process the extremity of his pain. The pain was real; it was unstoppable and undeniable. He should have died in one cataclysmic moment, and yet all seemed to have frozen in time, just to prolong the suffering, and torment the sufferer. He screamed as air escaped his punctured lungs. Blood was pouring out of his mouth, and not one sound came out.

Lu awoke violently to the pulse of a startled shudder, in the cramped confinement of his wooden hut. It was not yet daybreak, nor was it the evening, but Lu's heart was beating rapidly, and he felt a somewhat urgent need to leave the claustrophobic hut and calm himself down. With his left hand, the Walker wiped the viscous build-up of shed skin and liquid from the inner corners of his eyes and dragged himself out into the cool breeze of night. It was midnight, give or take a few measures, though Lu was unsure as to how long he had slept. He could have only just drifted off, and then stirred momentarily after experiencing his frightful dream yet again. Unfortunately, Lu's last encounter with the black dream had caused him to sleep for days, so it was likely that a similar amount of time had passed yet again. During his previous prolonged slumber, however, the Walker had been pulled into the centre of Tlephilisse's inner circle, where she had watched over her companion during his indefinite period of rest. This time, he had awoken where he had expected to. Despite Lu's understanding of the possibilities, there was still no conclusive indication as to how long had passed. Lu rubbed his face again, standing straight and steady beneath the patter of his curse-bound cloud. Time would need to be accounted for; the objective of his mission was exclusively framed within the one upcoming night upon which it can successfully take place. If his countdown were incorrect, every preparation would be worthless and wasted. If Lu missed the lunar-strained spectacle, his every daylight dream of a brilliant future would be lost, and he would be trapped on the Lila Isle for the full remaining days of his ambiguous mortality.

Lu glanced about the forgotten settlement and found no evidence that a concerned Tlephilisse had visited him during his sleep. The encampment had been left undisturbed since last he was awake. From this, he decided it best to assume that he had likely not overslept and that it would be wise not to dwell on such thoughts until he could confirm them with Tlephilisse. The night sky was starlit and dazzling, cloudless save for that which hung near to the ground above Lu's head.

It had been several days since Lu had learned the lost speech of Lila, and the voice of his inner monologue had already begun to interchange Reian sounds with those of the Lila-mortals. Additionally, ever since the Walker had learned to translate some of Tlephilisse's melodic whistles, the spinning song of the island unravelled before him and told the many stories of its guardians. These songs were already beautiful to Lu when they had chimed meaninglessly in the collective ambience of the Lila, but now each songbird spoke heavy words to the Walker, and what once was a pleasant polyphony had altogether transformed into a non-linear biographical masterpiece, composed by the four loneliest intellectuals Lu had ever known. And he did know them, at least as well as Tlephilisse knew her ancestors, for he now heard them as she did. Day and night, Lu pieced together fragments of their legacy, and of their passing.

Now that he was awake and mobile, Lu found himself speculating the new, horrific demise that had befallen him at the end of his otherwise similarly revisited nightmare. He resented being perturbed by the works of stale illusion and decided to interpret the swordless impotence of his dream-self as an unconscious suggestion to dig up the sword and re-familiarise himself with the clear blade before the time came to use it. He knew this to be unwise, and yet the urge continued to grow. Instead, he foraged about the outer ring of the clearing and found a branch of a similar length to practise with. After swinging the stick around playfully for a short while, Lu ventured further out towards the southern beach, in search of an obstacle or target to spar against.

For an hour, he swaggered leisurely along a Sprite-made path of stone that led to the south. He trod with a youthful bounce; his every step gave short life to the wavy, dusk-green locks that had steadily regrown upon his head. Something flickered before him, as he approached the final curve in the Sprite's scenic pathway, and he forced his eager feet to a silent but immediate stop. In the white sands ahead, beyond an exquisite floral archway, Lu could see a faint trail of footprints, that led some twenty steps forward before coming to a halt in the middle of the sands. With an excessive, almost comical amount of caution, the Reikan continued onwards to analyse the alien tracks. The direction of their maker's travel was certainly forward, leading to the centre of the beach, and yet they led to nothing beyond that point. There were no signs of a turnaround that departed along its path of arrival, or any nearby tracks that would indicate a jump from one place to the next. They stopped dead, as if their creator had vanished. With nothing left to consider on the empty sands, Lu glanced up to catch the last moments of the Web of Scattered Majesties. First, however, his orange eyes were greeted by something much nearer.

Flying clearly in the distance, above the fangs of the Empryc Crown, was the large, lavender fox. 'It can fly!' gasped Lu, as he gave his full attention to the spectacular movements of the beast. Though it was dark, the animal could still be seen easily, shimmering with an unnatural, icy gleam in the seaward horizon. To lift such a substantial creature would ordinarily require wings of a tremendous span, and yet the fox was wingless. Snout-first, it swam through the sky as an eel might lackadaisically ripple if travelling assisted by the predestined thrust of a coast-bound wave. Effortlessly, the serene giant faded into a pocket of the night, and Lu stood alone, with a dumbstruck grin upon his ageless face. 'It can fly...' he whispered. 'It can fly, without wings...' He threw his stick lightly into the air, meaning to catch it, but when the time came to catch the thing, he barely made an effort to reach for it, still mesmerised by the Lavender fox. 'Beautiful... and impossible.'

For two hours, Lu dashed around the empty southern beach, rekindling his skill with the practise blade, playing imaginary games of fabled duels, stabbing lightly against the natural stone pillars (and a few of the Sprite's abstract sculptures that sporadically graced the isle), running between the bone-white dunes, and having fun all the while. It seemed that every time the Walker began to doubt his wicked quest, the hand of fate would deliberately present him with a new object or event of great wonder, to remind him of his utmost, adventurous desire. Though Lu did not struggle to acknowledge and therefore appreciate a thing of beauty since the restoration of his senses, there was nothing in his memory that compared to the beauty of the lavender fox.

By sunrise, the Walker was almost completely spent of energy and returned inland in search of food and rest. Recently, the Sprite had been teaching Lu the fundamental process by which she crafted her medicines. These teachings were the original reason for the transfer from written to spoken language, which had already proven to be a more practical method of communication. Lu had already developed a reasonable eye for distinguishing the properties of certain plants, and how to combine his chosen ingredients to produce a basic formula. Though the grey man could not infuse his concoctions with remedial life-energies as only Tlephilisse could, he had previously underestimated the value of the ingredients and was increasingly impressed by what he could organically achieve without such power.

Tlephilisse would be awake in a few hours and doubtless had prepared a full day's worth of herb binding and potion making. Somehow, Lu needed to achieve a restful sleep before then, or he would be too exhausted for the day to come. To the immediate left of his sleep den was a smaller hut that, until recently, he had neglected. Now, however, it was Lu's storeroom, well supplied with buacoctin that he had been stockpiling over the last few days. He hungrily snatched one of the smaller shell-fruits and smashed it open using a particular rock he had found and kept for that use. There were also a few umello in the storeroom; though he much preferred them fresh from their tree, he had been experimenting with the combination of the umello juices and the buacoctin water, among other ingredients suggested by the ever-inquisitive River Sprite. Though she did not consume liquids as a human could, she was surprisingly receptive to the concept of flavour. Using her familiarity with each ingredient's corresponding smell, Tlephilisse was effectively able to create several harmonious flavours without having the ability to taste.

In the far corner of the storeroom were three hollowed-out wooden cylinders, which the Walker had fashioned in order to drink his various blends. One was still half-filled with a particularly vibrant mixture and was covered by a large leaf that was tied to the opening with a thick strand of grass, to be saved for later. After a moment of consideration, Lu quickly pulled the remaining drink from the hut and finished what was left, before setting the container down and heading to his den. As Lu shut his eyes, he felt a grim premonition that sleep would not come soon enough. For a while, he lay rolling under the cramped company of his restless raincloud, but eventually sleep found him, and he lay peaceful for a while.

~

The mid-morning came, and Lu had not stirred. Fatigue had arrived to reclaim a lost slumber. Former days, of sleepless trance and dither about the murky Bhia, were a debt left unpaid, but now those borrowed days were intermittently and unwillingly returned, as Lu disappeared again into his dreams. His revisiting nightmare was yet to feature, however, for instead, the Walker dreamed of a lavender fox and its kingdom of the sky. He dreamed of other worlds and of other people. There were people living below the sea, who could move underwater as if it were as thin as air. There were people of living wind in an endless stretch of desert, who could conjure bodies of their own simply by whipping up the sand. There were mischievous spirits masquerading as storm clouds, and there were amorphous wild intelligences that oozed purposefully beneath the mountains. There were benevolent shadows and mercenary lights, and all were equally captivating to he who dreamed them.

Tlephilisse waited until midday before eventually deciding to investigate the whereabouts of her absent companion. Choosing to travel by foot, the emerald celestial made short work of her journey to the recently repurposed settlement of the Lila-mortals. When her grey guest first arrived upon the island, he had demonstrated the numerous advantages of travelling by foot, thus inspiring Tlephilisse to do the same. In less than thirty days since, she had near enough mastered the form of walking so that she could keep up with her friend, whom she admired and adored, and whom she felt inclined to impress. That friend, it seemed, had again been unable to wake up this morning.

The River Sprite dragged the sleeping grey man from his soaking den and slowly hauled him all the way back to the sanctuary of her river-ring. She had already experienced this behaviour in her companion and had since learned that there was no sense in trying to wake him, for when Lu did previously oversleep, Tlephilisse had set about concocting a multitude of lurid elixirs, in an attempt to remedy his slumber, but to no avail. The River Sprite had later chosen not to tell Lu of this particular remedial failure, mostly because of a dim but nagging paranoia insisting that Lu would doubt her abilities and no longer respect her teachings if he were to learn of her non-success. Though she knew her concerns to be irrational, the Sprite still found no reason to admit her blunders to the Reikan, for they were few.

Once Tlephilisse had placed Lu comfortably within her stream-enclosed garden of darklilies, she began to construct a temporary shade above him, made of stone, branch, and leaf. Though Lu was already partially within the shadow cast by his cloud, the dry-season sun grew stronger and more aggressive with each new day. Historically, the more intense dry seasons had resulted in short forest fires, burning all that could not escape the land, thus Tlephilisse thought it best to protect Lu as much possible; not even under a raincloud could the grey man survive the engulf of an island fire.

While Tlephilisse was fixing together a support frame for the shade she was constructing, she noticed a peculiarity regarding Lu's cloud that, until now, had slipped her observation altogether. Each time the Sprite attempted to measure the shape of the unfinished frame above her grey, sleeping friend, the cloud would swiftly dip beneath the cover, before a single of its raindrops could miss its intended mark. Was this vigilant vapour to blame for Lu's slumber? The cloud could pre-empt and avoid any potential disruption of its dutiful pour, lowering as far as was circumstantially needed, sometimes clinging so close to Lu's flesh that the mist and man appeared to merge as one. There was no deceiving the cautious cloud, and eventually Tlephilisse grew tired of trying, for even the power that pulsated from her emerald torso was no match for the aqueous enchantment upon the sailor. For now, the Sprite had other ideas to attend to, for she had been considering them for some time.

Since first the grey stranger had been spat upon the unreachable isle, he had demonstrated limitless respect and intrigue towards the Sprite and her home. For her, he had effortlessly fashioned bridges of communication, with which he eagerly and attentively received Tlephilisse's every query or instruction. It had been so long since the passing of the Sprite's previous company that this new friend seemed to more than match the criteria of what she could ever have longed for. While her grey friend lay dormant, the River Sprite could decide how to express her gratitude; if Tlephilisse finished her design within the given time, she would gift her creation to the Walker as soon as he escaped the glamour of his slumberous prison. Without hesitation, the River Sprite then made her way to the south beach of the summer island, where she intended to devise and arrange her ideas.

Six days had soon vanished seamlessly in a wash of sun and tide, and Tlephilisse had completed both the design and creation of her gift, dearly intended for her sleeping sailor friend. Other than a short break each morning during which the Sprite ventured home to check on her companion and beloved gardens, Tlephilisse had spent the majority of her time crafting an extraordinarily elaborate full-body sculpture of the Reikan, as a gift.

Made from a single monolithic limestone, located at the utmost south of Lila, the Sailor-Likeness stood ten times the height and proportionate width of the man it depicted. Due to the ancient, weathered medium from which it was sculpted, the colour of the statue was a pigment not far removed from Lu's true complexion, thus enlivening the already well-captured face of the likeness into the realms of bizarre accuracy.

Though Lu had not worn his beautiful shellsuit after his first night on Lila, Tlephilisse decided to include this attire in her work, as it seemed representative of Lu, and relevant to the scene she had recreated. With its face posed forever skyward, in a posture that imitated the Walker's first encounter with the Web of Scattered Majesties, the Sailor-likeness had been accurately fashioned so that a frozen arm extended always towards the Empryc constellation, whenever it was visible. It had taken the emerald guardian six days to create form, detail, and texture that, elsewhere on Kraj, would have taken a mortal some sixty days or more. The Sprite's efficient artistry had little to do with her otherworldly gifts, however, as she had scarcely used her power throughout the whole process. Her intimidating prowess was instead a talent forged in the crucible of sheer time, for the sprite had developed her skill over a period that would span five mortal lifetimes. Engraved at the pedestal-base of the towering sculpture, in the curious symbols known only to the Sailor and Sprite, was its scenic title, 'A Night of Superlunary Gazing'.

The Sailor-Likeness was not the only gift that Tlephilisse had intended for her sleeping companion, however. Lu had recently become proficient in both the speech and song-speech of Lila and could now understand the many verses that were shared between the trees by the passerines of Empryc. This had inspired the River Sprite to compose a grand lyric of her own, telling of how she had first encountered the Walker and of their first shared days of friendship, and of their lifetime of companionship yet to come. Being as efficient as she was, the Sprite had been whistling and arranging ideas and motifs to herself from day one of her six-day construction period and had structured the entirety of her libretto by the time her sculpture was complete, along with a through-composed melody to which it would be sung.

The day had now come for the Sprite to share her coloratura with the ever-listening Lila, so that it may be recreated in fragmented movements by the songbirds of the isle, and later heard by Lu. She journeyed swiftly to a particularly boisterous grove that lay just outside of the clearing in which she (and Lu, at present) would rest. Nesting here, among a huddled group of large crimson trees, was the majority of Lila's songbird population, who were soon to become Tlephilisse's audience for the afternoon.

After a single, deep inhalation, the emerald songstress began her performance. The first movement of her reflective composition started with a short moment of regiment which erupted into a cascade of exciting phrases, descending from increasingly daring pitches, before rising to a new summit from which to fall again.

Even without the subtle lyrical content that was bound to each note, comprehensible only to Tlephilisse and Lu, the storyline of each movement could be found in the variety of melody and rhythm Tlephilisse had chosen. She could not create her own harmony or accompaniment, with a voice only capable of singing monophonic passages, and yet an echo had begun to surround the celestial soloist. The passerines were responding with what they had learned, creating rounds of short delay, interlacing their lines with Tlephilisse's.

The late Empryc sunset had drizzled all but the last of its reds before Tlephilisse's part finally came to an end. After the sombre murmur of her closing phrase, the green immortal flinched as if breaking from a trance. Then, the River Sprite listened with relief to the breathless echo that resonated from the trees surrounding her. Her carefully considered parts had interwoven just as she had hoped, and now the tropic air was alive with a shimmering polyphony, unlike any that had sounded before. For a while longer, Tlephilisse basked proudly in the slowly fading encore of her composition, before eventually heading inward to her circle-stream sanctum.

Lu had not moved since she had last checked on him, nor had he wet himself or somehow died in his defenceless hypnosis. He had already been dormant for much longer than any of his previous hypnoses.

Furthermore, there was no indication that he would be stirring at any time soon. Though Tlephilisse was concerned for her dreaming companion, she ultimately remembered that there was no limit to the remaining time they could spend together here. After all, they were both of them immortal, to whom six days of stasis were nothing but a short moment. With one last glance at the grey creature that lay between the darklilies, Tlephilisse ascended into a balanced levitation and fell likewise into slumber.

Chapter Six

NIGHT OF THE RED MOON

Something sharp was tugging viciously at the tip of Lu's fingers, and his mind suddenly re-engaged in order to process the sensation. The tugging ceased, and then with a sudden jerk, the Sailor experienced a weightlessness that lasted for only a moment. Lu dared not open his eyes quite yet, for there was an aspect of such weightlessness that reminded him of the reoccurring dream that he feared, where he was held aloft by foul things, and cast into the mouth of a thing fouler still. The texture of grass then returned beneath him, however, and with an exhausted shudder, the Walker forced his eyelids open. And then he shut them again, to rub them in disbelief, for what he saw before him could not be anything but a mirage, from another dream. Sure enough, there stood the splendid Lavender Fox, observing Lu at a distance that seemed warped due to the nature of its size. There was a dim light falling from the sky that illuminated the Fox too poorly to confirm its lavender colour, but there was no mistaking the beast, for it was massive – at least four times the length of any fox Lu had seen before.

The second thing that became apparent to the Reikan was the location in which he now lay. He was in the middle of the ruinous settlement, splayed out in a way that would not be comfortable to sleep in. There were petals stuck to his bare arms, and his clothes had been adjusted. Judging by the evidence he had been moved, from the circle-stream no doubt – he had been taken to the Sprite's sanctum, probably due to an oversleep, but the fox had retrieved him and returned him to the settlement. But why? Why had the Lavender Fox interfered with Tlephilisse's decision? And was Tlephilisse aware of what had occurred, or had she been asleep during Lu's mysterious extraction? For how long had he been asleep? Lu aimed his puzzled expression directly towards his silent vulpine company, half expecting some form of response. The burning silver eyes of the giant momentarily seemed to accept the Walker's confusion and redirected its gaze directly towards the sky. Lu hesitated, as he received a sickly and perilous surge of premonition, before reluctantly tracing the fox's silver eyes towards a veiled and bloodshot moon, by which all his questions were answered.

Lu swallowed back his fear. The night of the red moon had come, and he was not prepared in the slightest. He had not even seen Umbra since hiding it, and he had somehow almost forgotten the ritual by which it must be used.

There was no time to waste, however, and the Walker stood up and gave his new lavender accomplice an uneasy smile. Through forces unseen, the fox had known to assist the sleeping Walker. It was certainly a necessary assistance, and Lu owed it that much. He hoped to learn more about the beast once the job was done.

It didn't take long for the Walker to unbury and equip his effects, which surprised him again with their weightlessness. Soon, he was dressed head to toe in the mesmerising sea-tones of his shellsuit, and the glassblade Umbra was again at his waist. The sabre was not of this world, and it gave off a sighing aura as it was reunited with the hands of the sailor-warrior. Lu frowned at the thing, and imaginarily took himself through the correct sequence of his commands.

'With your fighting hand, sink the blade into the stream; with your free hand, you must cling to the Kraj, or you will be claimed by the shadow forever. Once you are in position, you need not move; Umbra will finish the ritual itself. You will know when it is complete. Then your hands may be cut. Then your hands are ready.'

Enter the circle. Wet the blade, cling to the land. Wait for Umbra to process, and then learn its powers by self-mutilation (Lu shuddered at this thought). Then, from behind the sleeping Sprite, wring Tlephilisse's neck. Do not let her see the blade.

Lu felt confident enough with his instructions and glanced at the red shadow moon; he did not have long. The immense Lavender Fox approached the luridly armoured Reikan, and crouched its rear, inviting the sailor to travel upon its back. Borrowing a frantic trust from his sense of urgency, Lu climbed on the fox without a second thought, and as soon as he secured his grip, the beast began to scurry, becoming seamlessly airborne before the Walker had a chance to hold his breath.

And the pair swam above tree and rock in the cradle of a warm Empryc sea breeze, and Lu had never been so exhilarated. This was the thrill of unknown adventure that he forever dreamed of. Beyond the entrapment of islands and the entrapment of gravity, the Sailor Walker was momentarily free to ride the nocturne wind, and he could already taste the reward of freedom and exploration that would come unto him once his task was done. For a moment, Lu thought he caught a glimpse of a gigantic, human figure in the direction of the south beach, but before he could fully turn his head to investigate, the snake-like fox violently banked into a leftward descent, curving snout-first towards Tlephilisse's Lila sanctum.

They landed with a ghostly silence, and though the sound of wind had rippled and whistled dynamically throughout their flight, the air here seemed undisturbed and at rest; the light patter of Lu's rain was the only audible sign of their arrival, and it was far too quiet to stir the Sprite. Lu then realised his own relief in that they had landed with such grace, for he feared waking the Sprite above all else. She was gentle and deceptively naïve by nature, but Lu knew that these attributes did not represent the true threat of an enraged Tlephilisse's power.

The Lavender Fox had vanished without warning, and Lu now stood alone behind the sleeping celestial. Forever conscious of his limited time, the Reikan impulsively bounced across the shimmering flow of the ringed river that surrounded Tlephilisse and her garden of teething darklilies. There was a prolonged moment when the grey man was floating, not yet landed on the other side; the rain from his cloud companion had paused mid-flow in the air, and Lu temporarily feared that he would not quite make the pass, and therefore splash into the stream below – he should have jumped more carefully.

A breeze caused the nearby trees to flutter, and time had clearly not frozen altogether, yet the Sailor and his cloud were held motionless and aloft above the curious water fence, like flies entangled in the web of a spider. Lu's mind began to slip into thoughts of darkness and remorse; if he was caught in the defensive fetter of an alerted Tlephilisse, then his fly-like ensnarement could end with his fly-like demise. Lu was quivering.

Gravity then escorted the fearful sailor in accordance with his previously instigated trajectory, and the unprepared Reikan landed rather awkwardly on the edge of the sacred garden, his cloud moving in unison. He felt as though the circle stream had studied him, and recognised the Reikan's presence as benign, therefore granting him passage into its centre. Evidently, it was paramount to his entry that he had earned the River Sprite's trust, thus Lu's preparation had been a success. Still shaken by his momentary paralysis, the Reikan smiled nervously, with a stirring of self-assured relief. He could still do this.

Gripping the enchanted hilt of Umbra in his left hand, which Lu considered to be his fighting hand, the sailor-warrior delicately slid the crystalline blade from its unassuming scabbard and raised it towards its lunar patron. For a moment, the Sabre appeared to slither in the half-light of the eclipse, but Lu had seen enough. Kneeling low, the Walker seized a firm right-hand hold upon a well-sunken stone among the sanctum rockery, and then stealthily plunged his streamlined witch-blade into the bed of the stream.

All fell deadly silent, at least to the ears of the Reikan. An immobilising surge of pain shot up the Walker's left arm, and he had to restrain himself from screaming in agony. By no choice of his own, Lu's grey-fingered grip tightened drastically upon the hilt of Umbra, until suddenly the hand did not belong to Lu anymore, and no longer sent any sensations at all to its previous master. The moon's redness now tainted all that lay beneath it, and Lu noticed that even the once-violet darklilies had succumbed to the fast-encroaching plague of scarlet.

Moments after the creeping scarlet had taken Lila and all her inhabitants, a coarse and musty breeze began to spiral from above the clearing, centring in around the submerged sabre. Lu could barely stomach the growing stench, for its scent was of foreign putridity, making it almost intolerable even to his deficient Reikan senses. The force of the miasmic gust, however, was a force felt only by Lu. The surrounding trees and other plant-life, though now stained by lunar red, were calm and altogether unresponsive to the ghostly wind. From behind, Tlephilisse appeared to remain dormant. After glancing towards the Sprite, to check on the status of his sleeping target, Lu's eyes became once again drawn to the circle stream in which his estranged left hand plunged the radiant shaft of Umbra. The water appeared to react to the possessed blade, changing colour from burning yellow to a non-descript brown that almost vanished among the night-kissed scarlet of the corrupted Lila clearing. In that moment, the unusual behaviour of the rippling stream was reminiscent of the way that the Bhia pond would each time indicate the bubbling arrival of its Mistress, thought Lu. Thoughts concerning the Bhia Sorceress would ordinarily inspire the Walker with endless questions, but such was not the case tonight. Tonight, he would serve his Mistress without question. Tomorrow, he would lend himself to her judgement, and receive his reward.

The alien-scented wind then died away completely, and the veil of scarlet had lifted substantially, leaving only a trace of its former pigment upon the sacred garden. The Walker bit his bottom lip in agony, determined to remain silent, for the feeling had returned to his left hand, and yet still it did not obey him. Instead, the hand began to carve this way and that, as if it were repeatedly tracing a single shape upon the riverbed. Lu's possessed appendage became increasingly frantic, as it sliced silently through the mystic waters. The Walker closed his eyes, gripping desperately to the stone on his right. He had begun to feel a heavy suggestion of gravity, pulling in towards the water.

The shape, which Lu now believed to be a star with six unequal points, had begun to sing from beneath its liquid shroud, with a voice that was both mortal and human. In a broken form of Reian, the androgynous, disembodied voice sang a single lyric, drastically altering its melody, rhythm and register with each repetition.

> 'Umbra is running through the water.
> To learn of its shadows, to unlearn its shadows.'

And then, in the blink of an eye, the entire of Kraj itself had turned inside out, through the outline that Umbra had scratched beneath the stream, and Lu found himself dangling from his unresponsive fighting hand, and his rock-bound right hand, for which he now understood the need. Through the portal of the glassblade, all matter had been abstracted into a shifting and formless blend of blood red or lime green, which reminded Lu somewhat of the Red Entity, and the portal from whence it had arrived. There was no recognisable trace of Lila, or of the River Sprite. It was a two-tone world of wheels and of waters, and nothing else. Lu was not afraid, however, and clung confidently to the stone in his right hand; this world was probably the origin of his borrowed sabre, and this climactic stage of the ritual seemed to indicate that all was going to plan. He was grimacing regardless, for the stench of the red-green dimension was unnaturally sour. The Walker's cloud, which usually hung above him, was beneath him, and it was raining upwards, undiscouraged by the reversal of its positioning.

A flash from above caught Lu's attention, where the once-clear shaft of Umbra now appeared to be channelling a stream of sanguine fluid, which slowly lightened in shade to a burnt orange, all the while coagulating, expanding, and filling the blade as if it were replacing the material and texture of the shaft altogether. Lu noticed that the capricious melodies of the singing portal were now being repeated more frequently in the lower registers, as the erubescent re-colouring of Umbra continued. During this process, the sabre had begun to emit an unseeable, pulsating energy, which continued to throb, out into the dark world until eventually the blade was fully transformed.

Then, the singing star fell quiet, and Lu felt his body rushing back up towards the narrow portal, passing through it as if he, his cloud, and all of Kraj were a single flowing body of soft liquid. The world had been spat back out through the window of Umbra and had been carefully returned to its natural order. Lu was back in the exact position that he had been in prior to his temporary visit to the red-green shadow world.

All of the grey sailor's limbs were his own to command once again, Tlephilisse was asleep, and the island was uneventfully quiet. Lu cracked a half-smile, feeling a certain accomplishment on behalf of his borrowed sabre.

Umbra appeared to have completed its task, which meant that there were only two things left to do. With another nervous glance towards the resting guardian, Lu cautiously slid the witch-blade from the water and examined its shaft, which had returned to its regular shimmering, aqueous transparency. The curious force that had entered the blade was not visible outside of the red-green realm. Lu was sure he did not dream it, however, for he believed it to be a visual representation of Umbra's true function. The blade had absorbed the essence of its target's immortality, thus learning how to undo said immortality. With a deep breath, Lu lifted the tip of the blade towards his right palm and slashed clean into the flesh. He winced involuntarily, expecting blood and pain, but there was none of either.

An influx of buzzing, pleasurable warmth, unlike anything Lu had ever felt, now coursed through his fingertips, his arm, and the right side of his torso. It was strength, of the most unfamiliar kind, flowing through his skin and muscles, finding a particularly focussed residence in his slashed hand and its connected fingers. After Lu administered the same dry incision into his left hand, the surge began again; when it was over, the sailor-warrior felt a balanced and symmetrical power within him, which he quickly became fond of. Though it had been acquired for the sole purpose of a terrible act of betrayal, the aura he had absorbed felt both benign and calming. It was almost as if his newfound strength had a separate consciousness from the Walker, as if it were aware of Lu's objective, and now comforted him as the final act drew near.

With a gentle sigh, Lu sheathed Umbra in its viridian scabbard. For now, the glassblade's work was done.

Then, Lu smiled. It seemed ironic to the ageless grey-skinned man that, although the nameless Mistress had given him a beautiful, enchanted weapon in relation to his task, he would not be wielding Umbra as a weapon for the sacrifice, but instead as a conduit. The only weapon he needed now, it seemed, was his hands. He had no way of knowing what to do with his hands, however, other than to choke the Celestial where she hovered. Though he wished that he had not slept through the remainder of his audience with Tlephilisse, he was somewhat glad to be ending the ordeal before he became any more attached to the Sprite. She had to die, now.

And then, in a surge of deathly inspiration (and a desire to finally escape the Lila), the Reikan took two large, soft steps towards his victim, and reached out his hands towards her fragile, floating frame.

The Sprite slowly awakened in response to the nearing patter of Lu's dripping cloud, and her body began to turn to see what was behind her. But she had stirred a moment too late. By the time she had turned halfway to her left, Lu's deranged stranglehold found its target. He squeezed as hard as he could muster, though he was not immensely strong. Yet, the Sprite already seemed to have surrendered to the power of his wicked grasp. She was physically limp, and her left-facing position ensured that her white eyes could only see a peripheral glimpse of her familiar assailant; she could not see the sword in its sheath, but she could see Lu and was evidently rendered weak by the shock of this betrayal. As the weightless, petal-bound and emerald frame of the immortal became cold and slowly lifeless in his hands, some thirty days of well-suppressed guilt and adoration came bubbling to the surface of the grey man's face, and he sobbed over her while continuing to squeeze her narrow throat. The rain of Lu's cloud continued to pour, washing away the tears that fell over the dying celestial.

As Lu's tear-filled eyes met with Tlephilisse's own pair of empty, white orbs, the Walker cried out in the language of the Lila-mortals, Tlephilisse's deceased and only offspring.

'River Sprite, forgive these hands!' he pleaded repeatedly, releasing the evidently broken neck of the Sprite from his cruel, murderous hands.

And then, through the pair of openings in the centre of her delicate face, Tlephilisse sang her final song into the Lila air, which was still coloured by the fading embers of the red moon. Despite all he had learned of the immortal's whistle-speech, Lu could not understand what Tlephilisse was singing. It was high and beautiful, and sombre, but after only a short while, her voice crackled breathlessly and trailed off faintly, exposing the still-captivated silence of the entire population of Lila, who had listened to every moment of the death song of Tlephilisse, the fourth and final River Sprite.

Her broken petal-body slowly melted into a translucent green puddle of water, with a disarmingly sweet aroma, which then began to trickle almost consciously towards the edge of the flowerbed, before spilling off into the river that surrounded it. Soon, all but the last few drops of clear green liquid had vanished into the stream, and no trace of the River Sprite's body remained. As the last droplet fell, Lu broke his entrancement, and glanced into the circle stream. Its water was now an unnaturally deep, berry blue, dotted with bubbling flecks of purple that were deeper still. By the work of Umbra, a sickness had fallen upon it.

Tlephilisse was dead, and her final wordless lament had been learned by a few of the echo-birds that had been roused by Lu's desperate cries, so that her perish song now sounded through the trees surrounding the scene of the sacrifice. Lu cried, and screamed, until his bright orange eyes ran dry, and his throat was torn so that no more sound could pass through. And then he felt nothing, for he had released his congested sentiment, and had found peace again with his unique spectrum of emotion. He was as morally deficient as before – but had let his interest and respect for the River Sprite temporarily convince him otherwise. It was important to refresh his conscience now that the sacrifice was complete, so that he could enjoy the fruits of his reward. Lu suddenly flinched, in realisation of the lack of rain falling upon him. 'My reward...' whispered the sailor-warrior.

The grey-skinned, green-haired immortal slowly turned his head towards the immediate sky. His cloud! Though it had ceased its rain, the cloud remained above his head. And it was growing! Growing in size, and in darkness, the obedient mist that had followed the Walker for so long was now moving in a path of its own, towards the open space in the dawning sky. Had the Bhia mistress, whom he had expected some sort of celebratory appearance from, deceived him? Was there a way off the Lila Isle? How long must he wait before his fate became known? Lu was speechless, as he witnessed the once miniature wisp become a great sky giant, that seemed to cover the entire Lila island. There was a moment of absolute quiet and, if of nothing else, Lu was certain of what would follow.

But nothing did follow. The titan cloud was still and shed not one drop of rain. Menacingly, it cast nought but a shadow over the tropic isle, as if standing in simple defiance of the rising dry season sun. In its sheath, against the Walker's covered thigh, Umbra began to murmur and fidget. Hoping this stirring to be the contact he had expected from the Goddess of the Bhia, Lu gripped the hilt of the blade eagerly, only for his hand to be met with the same paralysing agony as before. Again, his hand was not his own, but this time the possession spread all the way up to his shoulder. Of its own volition, Lu's left arm rapidly hoisted the witch-blade directly up, pointing towards the mighty cloud. With a crackling, heavy groan, a spray of tri-coloured gaseous matter cascaded from the tip of the sabre. Finely concentrated fumes of sky blue, fire orange, and pinkish purple intertwined as they raced towards the heart of the all-encompassing cloud.

Since escaping the sabre's edge, the climbing trigon vapour had created a lingering pathway that reached ever higher, until finally it touched the cloud. From the moment this connection became established, the cloud began to send something back, along the same pathway. Lu could feel the most unusual energy returning to him as it rippled through his arm and into his head. Then, his arm fell to his side, and his blade to the floor. Everything that he had lost to the Bhia amnesia became re-established all at once. He collapsed to his knees, overwhelmed by a bombardment of memories, emotions, and sensations. For every sentiment that now flowered anew, Lu could feel the dust shift and scatter within his ancient brain, as his youth was slowly restored.

Was this the return of his soul? He couldn't be sure – the soul was a vague concept at best, while the energy that came rushing through his body was alarmingly vivid, and by no means vague at all.

Among other forgotten details, Lu now recalled the names and faces of his long-dead loved ones, a myriad of Reian songs and fables he had once adored, and even his own full name. It was Lusini-Sa. It would be 'Lusini-Su' or even 'Lusini-Lusini' now, for he had become more ancient than any of the elders from his time.

There were so many memories that the Reikan longed to examine, but he was unable to focus on any one of them. He felt as though he was overflowing with new information, and that his brain might soon expand beyond the limitation of his skull, causing it to shatter from the inside out. For as long as Lu could recall, so many aspects of his behaviour had felt like an imitation of something that he couldn't quite remember – he had become far more familiar with his forced, artificial empathies, and could no longer recognise the real emotions that they were based upon. All that Lu could ascertain from the oncoming alien emotion was their sheer magnitude.

He was now tightly curled up into a ball under the pinkish haze of a sulking sky and had recoiled entirely into the deepest chambers of his mind. One particularly bitter emotion was beginning to trample above the rest. A rising tumultuous darkness had stirred within him, building exponentially, with no escape. Despite his best efforts, the Walker could do nothing but surrender to its ruthless, towering dominance. The shadow was everywhere; when Lu's eyes were open, it was the shadow of the great cloud; when his eyes were shut, it represented a wicked and relentless guilt, corresponding to an obvious breach of a now glaring moral imperative.

The guilt had evolved and mutated through many oppressive stages of torment within the Walker, before finally latching onto Lu's self-condemnation, and focusing its wrath on his foremost insecurity. He had become a traitor and a murderer, and for what? For all his evil deeds, he had been rewarded with nothing but an even bigger cloud above his head, which would presumably soon erupt into an inexhaustible storm; he would be followed by rain forevermore.

In the false nocturne cast by the cloud's shadow veil, Lu was finally confronted by the prophesied waves of guilt from his black dream. As he became further engulfed by his remorse, the Reikan began to piece together the actuality of the moments that would follow. His memories had unfurled before him, and yet the second abstract movement of the black dream had become increasingly mystifying.

'It *was* I, on the beach! I, who burst into flames, at the touch of a ghastly hand! Of course it was...' he murmured. 'But why?'

As Lu retraced his steps in newfound recollection, he became a young man of Rei once more. Sure enough, it was the Mistress that approached him in the smoke. That much was always clearly suggested.

'Set me free...' She had called; a mere wish in the wind. 'Set me free...'

He had reached out to touch the hand of the wisp apparition, only to feel his spirit leaving his body; feel it drifting off in the early morning breeze.

After that, however, his knowledge came to a dead end. It seemed that whatever had happened to him, body, *and* soul, had been erased from time itself – the work of the Mistress, Lu assumed. Either it was her doing, or that the following events were simply so harrowing that Lu had himself chosen to clear the ordeal from his mind.

He desperately longed for the answer, but his mind was too defeated, exhausted by the total overload of having both his memory and morality returned to him in such a flurry. As he lay in the pink-grey darkness, hoping for his pain to end, the Walker involuntarily began to snuff out the most unbearable of his sorrows, as Tlephilisse once would have plucked weeds from her garden.

Memories and emotions that had so soon returned were already being suppressed, for they were too sensitive and sore for Lu to risk exposing. For a moment, a glimmer of true self had challenged the dark emptiness within the Walker, but that moment was nearly over. It was as if Lu's spirit had been waiting in his cloud all along. Umbra had drawn it out, and returned it to him, only for his reinstated emotional, young mind to fall prey to the most terrible, yet most deserving regret a Lyoya Reikan could have ever known.

Since his quest had begun, the wayward sailor had been searching for the memories and emotions he had lost, of his younger yet visually identical self. Now, with eyes tightly shut, he collapsed into the deepest seclusion of his mind, and he witnessed the death of that lost persona, suffocated by he who had sought it for so long. He could not entirely banish his capability for emotion, or the memories that had remerged, but he had now rewritten his morality; suppressing his sorrows and his fears as much as he possibly could, Lusini-Su had become an emotionally deficient Reikan once more. Guilt would never again be so severe as to bother him, but his anger for the Mistress had only intensified, for he had now sacrificed far more to her than he had originally bargained.

There was a new birdsong in the Lila breeze. It was a song of sorrow, for it was the last utterance of Tlephilisse.

Lu could not translate it, and yet every melody punctured his conscience and filled it with sickness and dread. Between the intermittent phrases of melancholy chorus from the Sprite's perish song, Lu picked up on a few other new melodies that he did not recognise at all but could recognise their language. No doubt he would eventually give in and seek out this other new addition to the Lila song-eternal, in order to translate it before he left Lila for good.

After a moment longer, Lu surrendered to his curiosity and followed the call of the more lyrical fragments from the second mystery sprite-song. In accordance with the apparent origin of this enticing new song, the Walker found himself on the verge of the southern Lila beach, where finally the lyric had become audible. He stepped out onto the white, southern sands of Lila, where he stood awestruck before a breathtaking, monolithic statue. It was an astounding monument to behold, depicting Lu, dressed in his swathe of shell and gemstone, reaching up towards the sky, pointing indicatively to where the Web of Scattered Majesties would be in the night sky. It was a portrayal of their first night together, and it was at least ten times his height. At the foot of the doppelgänger was its title, carved in the unique symbolism known only to Lu and Tlephilisse. 'A Night of Superlunary Gazing', it read.

Lu's hands were clenched into fists, as the mysterious, accompanying tune he had followed began to sift again into his ears, from a dozen nearby beaks. As the autobiographical meaning of Tlephilisse's elusive new madrigal became consistent and understandably clear, it began to serve as a musical counterpart to the Sprite's sculpture. Like the statue, the song was an ode to Lu, and it celebrated the novel friendship he had briefly shared with Tlephilisse.

It told the tale of their encounters from the perspective of the River Sprite. It was eloquent, and it was beautiful. It was, according to the song itself, a gift of gratitude from herself to the Walker, for his patience and companionship. They were gifts both founded on a misplaced trust; for all eternity, they would now act as permanent symbols of Lu's treachery, and Lu was forsaken upon the Lila with them. But still, Lu did not suffer at the hands of guilt or regret, for he had successfully ridden himself of such masochisms. He was, however, boiling with rage and retribution, concerning the Mistress and her devilry. What she had cost him far outweighed the value of his unfulfilled reward. She had lied to him, and he had become her 'Krajian Scythe' under false pretences. She would pay for what she'd done.

Lu turned his head towards the sky and stood to his full height. 'VICIOUS MISTRESS! TAKE THIS CURSE AWAY!' He screamed, through the wretched rasp of his failing voice. There was no sound or sign of answer - not even a coincidental murmur from the slow, silently churning storm above. Before, when she had ignored his pleas, Lu had resorted to foolishness to command her attention, where in that instance he had threatened to attack the Sprite without any further instruction from the Sorceress, forcing her to respond and intervene. These schemes were useless now, it seemed, for the Walker had already fulfilled the Sorceress's request. She likely had no further need for the Reikan, and no longer observed him at all. Unfortunately, Lu had nothing else to do but curse her for her crimes. With a final, sharp inhalation, he tried once more to summon the abstract celestial from her unknown abode.

'You gave me your word and your SWORD!' He raised Umbra slowly, towards the quaking sky. 'I KEPT YOUR VOW... AND YET STILL THE CLOUD REMAINS!

And then the monstrous mist above finally exploded in cloudburst. Tainted light of every hue, tint, and shade fell upon the Lila Isle, as the risen sun finally found passage through the thinning cloud that had blocked its way, now dispersing in precipitation. Down to the land came these sun-kissed cascades, to spitefully remind the dry Walker of a drenching curse he had only recently seen the end of.

Chapter Seven

CLOUDBURST, AND THAT WHICH FOLLOWED

It rained and rained, for what felt like a life-age. Though Lu had lived in a deluge for eras uncountable, he had never felt a torrent such as this. The falling water with which he was familiar had been so gentle and consistent upon his flesh, so mild in temperature. This immense rain, on the other hand, was both violent and unfocused. It was cold and it was harsh, and every drop that thumped down on the Walker's skin came without mercy or even intention. It was as wild and ruthless as the fauna and flora of the Bhia. Wilder still, thought Lu. This rain was as wicked as the Empryc Sea. Eventually, the Reikan found it so unpleasant and irritating that he retreated into his hut in the empty village, to take shelter and become dry again. There was no way of knowing when or even *if* this cloudburst would end, and yet huddled in his shelter, Lu patiently waited to find out, observing the effect that the rain caused upon different surfaces. Before him, the once hard and parched soils of the Lila had softened into a moist and mouldable sludge, whereas every patch of white sand that he borrowed from the beach in order to practise his writing, and was ordinarily dry and soft to touch, had become increasingly firm and dark with each passing moment, bloated by the rainfall it had absorbed.

By mid-evening, the Walker began to notice the gradual relaxation of the downpour, and a creeping sweetness on the breeze had lured him out of his nest. A divine fragrance had slowly risen from the ground that, thanks to his re-established memory, Lusini-Su was able to recognise as petrichor. Long ago, in the sea-town of Rei, it had been the unmistakable scent of dry season's end. Those simpler days were gone, taking the meaning of the aroma away with them, and yet Lu was filled with a comforting nostalgia, nonetheless.

As the setting sun offered the last of its rays through the mist of the waning rainfall, the Reikan found himself dwelling upon an uncommonly positive thought. Maybe one day, if Lu remained immortal, a modern mariner of sorts would make their way through the Empryc Spine to 'discover' Lila and rescue him. Then, he would finally be free to explore the beyond. These clumsy, quixotic dreams and foolish desires were the very vices that had estranged the Reikan in the first place, however, perhaps for now, isolated upon the paradisiacal island of Lila, and away from all else, his troubles were truly over.

Later that night, the weakening rainstorm eventually died altogether. The sinister island-sized cloud, and its shadow of malignance, was gone. A brilliant, pale moon was once again floating in the Empryc sky, and Lu found it difficult to accept that only a single night had passed since its discoloured, bloodshot twin had been hanging there instead.

After a short but leisurely excursion to his preferred umello grove, Lu returned to his cabin where he spent the rest of his evening calmly creating and consuming different blends of juice, before relaxing into a light, dreamless sleep.

Lu was awoken by a ghastly, sharp howl, which seemed to come from just outside of the settlement, towards the nearest beach. The high-pitched shriek was both disturbing and unfamiliar, and Lu decided that it would be wise to equip both his full shellsuit armour and Umbra before leaving his cabin and further investigating the origin of the howl. Before the sailor-warrior had made it to the southern edge of the village clearing, the undergrowth exploded into a blur of purple and blue, and the great Lavender Fox came flying past the Reikan, before rolling into a graceless heap in front of the grey man's hut.

The long, flowing beast was unharmed, but greatly distressed. In the tight clench of its maw was a writhing, limbless creature with scales of various translucent blues, and a crown of three ivory horns upon its snarling, snouted, eyeless head – one upon its snout, and a pair atop of its wretched skull. The wriggling demon slowly began to shrink within the fox's mouth, briefly melting into a thin, aquamarine fog before dissipating into the air completely.

The Lavender Fox grunted in what appeared to be disgust, before rushing towards Lu and impatiently lowering its back. Lu climbed onto his vulpine familiar without delay. A new sorcery was at work, and would no doubt bring him ever closer to the 'greater destiny' that he allegedly shared with the Mistress of the Bhia, whatever that might be.

The Lavender Fox took flight southward, rising quickly above the tallest canopies of Lila. Lu felt an involuntary shiver ripple down his spine, as the cool, early morning air slid through his dusk-green hair and across his scalp. He adored flying upon the Lavender Fox, for the fox determined the course, and Lu could simply indulge in the scenery of the trip. Even the oncoming sight of the great Sailor-Likeness couldn't dampen his mood, for he had already come to terms with mourning Tlephilisse's death, through his appreciation for her art, which he thought was unrivalled. Then, the sand, sea, and what lay beyond, all came hurtling into view, and Lusini-Su felt his blood curdling inside of his ancient veins, and his desire for adventure drastically lessen.

Faint, early flirtations of light from the slightly dawning sun illuminated some of the nearest of Empryc's coast-bound waves, and what now rode upon them. In pairs, and occasional threes, came slow waves of horned serpents to the southern beach, akin to the one the Lavender Fox had apparently defeated. There were no more than ten heading towards the Island, and only a further two that had already made it to the land. Land, for that matter, was apparently of no significance to the sightless wyrms; as the Lavender Fox banked down towards the Sailor-Likeness, and landed upon the summit of its reaching arm, Lu's orange eyes adjusted to the half-light and saw that the wingless monsters were airborne above the land, and had been flying, and not swimming, their way to the shore all along.

Lu dismounted from the Lavender Fox, who then immediately dived into the fray below, biting and gnawing at the serpents that had arrived on the Lila beach. Drawing Umbra from its viridian scabbard, Lu readied himself for battle. For someone who now considered himself an 'assassin', and had been entitled the 'Krajian Scythe' by the Sorceress herself (though Lu hated that title, and found it somewhat embarrassing and theatrical), the Reikan had almost no real combat experience, other than playful stick fights with other children in his youth, the muscle training he had more recently undergone in the Bhia, and the largely unarmed faceoff he shared with the Red Entity. For some reason, however, he was completely unafraid to do battle with the oncoming slither. He did not fear death, if he was even capable of dying, and he certainly relished the anticipation of greeting his mysterious adversary (with visible excitement), but that was not the source of his current bravery. Umbra, despite being infused with the most malignant energies Lu had ever witnessed, gave off an aura of pure power that filled Lu with immeasurable courage. With Umbra in his hand, Lu called and taunted the coiling wyrms, which all turned their blind, tri-horned heads in his direction, allowing the Lavender Fox a moment to finish off the one that it had near destroyed.

For a moment, as a few of the foul creatures began to slowly drift upwards towards him, Lu was reminded of the final scene of his dream, in which he stood atop a great tower, and spectated the aftermath of a great battle, only to be stolen from his pillar by a pair of winged monsters. Lu paused mid-thought, for the first of the blue serpents had made its way to the top of his statue, and aimed its snarling, almost canid fangs in the direction of his unprotected throat. The sailor-warrior sliced at the thing calmly from the left, using the flick of his wrist to curve and strengthen the direction of his blow.

It was a direct hit, for the ghostly serpents all moved with a considerable slowness that was both unsettling and yet ethereal, floating in the breeze like a weed among waves. Umbra sliced clean through the blue-scaled beast as if it were made of air, and the lazy, snarling snout fell drastically short of Lu's neck before vaporising into the same aquamarine mist as the rest, which became lost in a gust of rising wind.

Returning to his initial thoughts, Lu now dismissed the similarities between this situation and his nightmares. The conflict below was not at all comparable, and he was nowhere near as high up as his dream implied. Though the past and prophecy contained in the dream had been correct so far, Lu remained adamant that the bat and the bird would not be appearing on this particular morning.

Again, the Walker was forced to snap out of his tireless daydreaming, as another set of horns approached him to his right. Without thinking twice, Lusini-Su impulsively responded to a sudden urge to thrust his crystalline sabre in the direction of the approaching serpent. As if he had willed it into reality, a blinding, tri-coloured surge of some unknown element exploded from the full curve of the blade and channelled into a monstrous beam of intertwining trigon light that totally engulfed the nearing serpent before it had even had a chance to attack. Lu screamed aloud in both surprise and concentration, as he attempted to steady the blade in both of his hands. The blast sustained for a moment longer before both it and the serpent fell away into the blue-green mist of the ever-building wind. And then the rain began again, and without needing any explanation, Lu could sense that Umbra was spent, and would not be able to perform that sorcery again during this battle.

'Ah! What convenient devilry was *that*?' Lu gasped rhetorically to himself, with a subtle humour in his tone. He gave Umbra a fond glance, before averting his gaze to the white sands below.

Down on the beach, the Lavender Fox had made its way through at least twice as many of the serpent spirits that he had, though there was no physical evidence of their demise. Nothing remained, other than faint residue of the blue mist that scattered in the gale of a growing storm, apparently brought on by Umbra's outburst. As the rain fell on Lu, he looked again at the witch-blade in his left hand. 'It seems you've stirred up quite the storm, my unusual friend.' And then he smiled bitterly and shook his head in self-mockery, for he did not want to make a habit of talking to an object, least of all the blade of his cruel mistress; least of all the blade that enabled the murder of Tlephilisse, his friend.

As far as friends were concerned, however, Lusini-Su had not appreciated the Sprite nearly enough, so he would do well to avoid making the same mistake with the Lavender Fox, who now appeared to struggle as a group of four serpents closed in around it.

Relying solely on a self-induced moment of artificial bravery, the sailor-warrior leapt from the raised arm of his towering likeness and slid down onto its titan shoulder. Then, the rain caused Lu to slip uncontrollably off the shoulder and down the statue's chest, where the tumbling grey man released Umbra from his grip in order to reach for a scrambling hold of the stone, to save him from plummeting to his death. Despite letting go of the blade, Lu was surprised to see that Umbra had somehow found its way back into the scabbard at his side. Unfortunately, he was still only halfway down the statue, standing upon a prominent ridge in the stone imitation of his shellsuit. His heroic leap had been a failure, and despite its best efforts to hold them off, the Lavender Fox would soon be at the mercy of the tri-horned wyrms around it.

Then, Lu had another idea. 'I'm up here! Try for me if you dare, you sluggish, slavering eels!' He bellowed, hoping to catch a few of the creatures' attention. They were still too preoccupied with tiring out the Lavender

Fox and did not notice Lu's taunt. 'Try for me!' He cried, again. He looked at the hilt of his sheathed glassblade. If Umbra had found its way back into its scabbard when he had dropped it, then there was a possibility that if thrown like a spear, it would likewise return to him afterwards. He prepared to throw the sword, getting himself into a sturdy position upon the ridge in the statue. Aiming to hit one serpent in particular that approached the Lavender Fox, Lu launched the blade from his left hand and watched as it soared through the air, and sunk into the white sand, missing its target completely.

The thump of the Umbra's landing startled a few of the serpents, however, and the Lavender Fox was able to escape the entanglement, tear off one of the creature's heads, and then sink its teeth into the menacing, ghostlike body of another. Despite feeling relieved that the Fox had overcome its earlier predicament, Lu now had a situation of his own to deal with. Two of the demons had been alerted to Lu's position and were slowly making their way through the air to kill him.

To make matters worse, Umbra had not returned to its scabbard, and Lu was without a weapon. The Walker glanced at the sand where his sword had been half-swallowed. Contrary to Lu's expectations, the sword had landed and sunken into the ground pommel-first; only the sharp, crystalline curve of the blade could be seen above the sands, and even that was difficult to see, due to its transparency. He was readying himself to jump, near enough to his weapon so he could seize it quickly upon landing, but at a safe enough distance to avoid impaling himself on it. One of the rising blue wyrms was now halfway between Lu and the ground; the Walker saw his opportunity and jumped.

By briefly planting his sandalled feet upon the hornless scales of the wyrm's blue spine, Lu managed to break his fall enough to compose a more stable and controlled landing, albeit a little too far from his sunken blade to grasp it. The creature shrieked and convulsed in mid-air, before recovering from the temporary weight of the Walker. Then, it turned its head and redirected its peculiar drift towards the ground, where Lu was waiting.

The other serpent, which was not yet as high as its similar, was already turning mid-flight to face the Reikan, and was, therefore, a far more immediate threat. Lu had no time to retrieve Umbra from the sand and instead jumped to grapple the pearl-white horns of the incoming wyrm, in an attempt to pull the beast down against the protruding edge of the glassblade in the sand. This was an ill-conceived decision, however. The wyrm was far stronger than it looked, making it impossible to wrestle against, but furthermore, the first mere touch of its horns sent a rippling shockwave of lightning energy down the Walker's spine, forcing him to let go after only a moment.

Now Lu feared death. For all their sluggishness, the serpents were clearly very dangerous, and from his brief encounter with pain, he now had a glimpse of what further pain could amount to. Despite the physical invincibility of his shellsuit, his bare hand-flesh and face were still unprotected against the serpents and their sorceries. In the event of his skin being punctured by those horns, Lu would not wager on his survival.

In clear recognition of Lu's plight, the Lavender Fox (who, by now had finished dispatching its own assailants) sailed towards Lu's opponent and sunk its teeth into the wyrm's especially lithe rear-end. The wyrm flinched, giving Lu just enough time to get close to

Umbra, and dig for the hilt of the crystalline sabre, thus reclaiming it from the sand. By luck alone, the other descending serpent had now aligned itself with its fox-wrestling sibling, and in a single leap and an airborne flail, Lu drove the witch-blade through the skulls of both wyrms, uniting their snarling, wretched heads into a skewered amorphous singularity, which then fell away into a blue nebula.

Already the storm had started to die away, and the light of sunrise fell upon the south-beach dunes. Lu turned to his vulpine accomplice, to offer a faint smile of victory. This gesture was not reciprocated, however, for the Lavender Fox's attention was already focused elsewhere. Lu echoed the seaward gaze of the Fox, to see what had distracted it. The windborne journey of the aquamarine mist, it seemed, had begun to converge as it approached the Empryc Spine. It was returning, all of it, to the source from which the serpents had spawned. There was something out there, among the spines, which Lu could not see.

'What is it? What can you see?' Lu asked the Lavender Fox. The Fox, silent as always, simply dipped its body and allowed Lu to clamber onto its back, before taking flight to investigate the source. It was finally happening, Lu thought to himself; he was finally leaving the Lila Island. As they rose into the air, Lu took one last glance at the Sailor-Likeness, and nodded at it, as if bidding farewell an old friend. In the wind, the song-eternal of the River Sprites could be heard one last time, and Lu shuddered as he heard fragments of both Tlephilisse's gift-song (that spoke of him as a beloved friend), and her unintelligible perish-song. Both would haunt him for as long as he lived, but the latter of the two brought him weakness in a way words could not; it resonated like a curse through the myriad beaks of the passerine. He hoped to never hear it again.

As the pair escalated weightlessly above the sea, Lu returned his orange eyes to the disturbance ahead. The wyrm-dust haze they had followed from the beach led to a distant, enormous curling cyclone of mist and seawater, larger than the Lila itself. Stirring in the centre of the cyclone was a looming shadow, which seemed to come alive as Lu and the Lavender Fox approached it with caution. The shadow twisted, stretched, and elongated until its height matched the altitude of the Fox's flight. Lu shouted above the sound of the throbbing spiral, instructing the Fox to fly higher, but his voice appeared not to sound at all, for it was lost amongst a thunderous crashing of water.

The possessed water was falling away from the shape inside of it, revealing the silhouette to be something that Lu knew only from legend. 'DRAGON!' He screamed with bewildered disbelief, only for the sound to again vanish in the din of the cascade. The Lavender Fox had stopped advancing and now hung almost limp in the air, as if waiting for the monster to make the first move.

The impassable serpentine figure was still some distance ahead of them but seemed deceptively near due to its sheer size, its height equivalent to at least forty of the tallest Bhia conifers above sea level. Three pearl-white horns upon its head and snout, and a whiskered mouth full of dog-like teeth were among the many features that it shared with the small serpents from the beach; it was apparent now that those minions sent to scout the Lila were the tendril manifestations of a much deadlier foe and were each representative of nothing but a mere shimmer of their master's true power.

Unlike its scouts, the dragon had two pairs of dark but variegated eyes. The smaller pair was stacked close above the dominant pair, each so dark and hooded that they appeared to be directionless. The dragon was exquisitely wrapped in silver scales that reflected light so aggressively that they almost outshone the sun itself. From what was visible above the water, it had at least two pairs of limbs positioned lower down on its writhing, coiling rings, but it was clear that a great deal of the beast's body was still below the sea. There was no way of knowing how massive it truly was.

Everything seemed to have come to a standstill. The Lavender Fox hung silently, and the sea around the beast had calmed. Time, and its respective motions, had temporarily halted in bleak reverence of the silver-green dragon. Then, the Lavender Fox continued forwards with an alarming disregard for their proximity to the great serpent. With a mortal fear creeping within him, Lu yelled a distressed scream to the capricious fox. 'No! Stop! What are you doing!' But it was no use - the Lavender Fox ignored Lu, and in a short while they were in the immediate presence of the beast. The dragon's eyes widened, indicating that it had noticed the Walker and his mount, despite the beast being so large that the flying fox and its rider were little more than a grain of sand in comparison.

Lu nervously reached for his side, in an attempt to unsheathe Umbra. The witch-blade refused to leave its scabbard, however, and sent a stinging shock into the Reikan's hand. Eventually, Lu gave up and resigned himself to the mercy of the monster, who had begun to open its chasmal maw, exposing row upon row of gleaming teeth. For the second time this morning, Lu felt reminded of the third stage of his black dream, but before he could dwell upon the resemblance, the dragon began to speak through a grin of fangs that were individually larger than Lu himself.

'You, the killer of Sprites!'

The heavy, intelligent voice of the dragon rumbled through the air, and the echo of each word distorted into thunder as it travelled into the distance. Speckled cloud-remnants of the brief storm from earlier that morning were now fleeing the Empryc sky, driven away by the bellowing speech of the dragon. From behind the clearing mist poured an enhanced, unnatural sunlight that seemed to fall solely upon the body of the serpent.

Clinging to the dragon's spine, the bewitched sunlight gradually blossomed outwards into a divine and immeasurably vast spread of phantom, bird-like wings, which were divided into a formation of four – a larger pair of upper wings, and a smaller, mirrored pair that fell beneath, stretching downwards into the waves. The dragon spoke again, in unmistakable Reian dialect, which Lu assumed was translated by sorcery; the twisted shapes made by the Wyrm's slavering mouth were not at all matched by the voice that followed.

'I am Morl-Majgyn, the apprentice God! I am servant to One of Six; I, sent by the Watchers themselves, have come to execute you for your crime!'

And by the utterance of those last, damning words, Lusini-Su became panicked with mortal dread. Slithering weightlessly between sea and sky, the giant closed its jaw and awaited Lu's response, staring blankly with its four eyes of colour-shifting shadow. Lu reached again for his traitorous sabre, but again the weapon refused to aid him. He grimaced as the pommel stung his fingers and recoiled his hand before gesturing instead towards the almighty dragon that writhed before him. This 'Morl-Majgyn' was both beautiful and wretched, and altogether unsurpassable in combat by any method Lu could think of. It seemed that flattery was his only option.

'What allegiance could you share with a minor celestial creature, such as that Sprite? Furthermore, what allegiance could you, a great celestial creature yourself, have with the unseen Watchers of old?' he cried, cautious not to stumble on his improvised glib.

'My contrition is my business,' he continued. 'I care not for the pardon of Gods unknown. If I must seek forgiveness from a deity, then I would prefer it to come from a corporeal one, such as you yourself! Grant me passage, Morl-Majgyn! Grant me passage, and exonerate me, and I shall forever be in your service!'

But the apprentice God expressed no interest in such beggared worship. With a flick of his reptilian right arm, Morl-Majgyn snatched a crescent blade composed entirely of seawater from the Empryc waves, before proceeding to swing it in a slow, yet unstoppably powerful motion that was aimed at the Walker and his mount. The Lavender Fox, however, did not seem keen to meet the crash of the sabre, and instead turned its head and violently tore Lu from its back and cast him into the course of the gushing blade, before darting out of the way, and eventually out of sight, abandoning the premise completely. As Lu tumbled into the hammering blow of the liquid scythe, he couldn't help but feel both mystified and betrayed by the unstable nature of the Lavender Fox, which had now surely cost him his life. He closed his eyes, as the blade fell upon him.

For a moment, Lu assumed that the bite of the dragon's slash had swiftly, yet inconsequentially, washed over him.

Though his eyes were shut, the sudden coolness of the water hardly seemed to linger after the initial impact. It was as if he had simply been hit by a great, sun-kissed wave. Then, however, Lu opened his eyes to behold a scenario that was far more curious. He had been captured amidst the crescent and was afloat inside of its aqueous (and altogether sorcerous) composition.

'The clearness of the Drownhook never fails to delight me,' sighed Majgyn, 'for I am fond of drowning, of its uses, of its stages, its slowness...'

Lu understood this to be the nature of his death sentence, and smiled morbidly as he quickly realised a flaw in the dragon's choice of weapon, and wondered when, and if, he should address it.

Meanwhile, Morl-Majgyn murmured about the Walker's abandonment.

'Had it not cast you into harm's way, it would seem that your unusual friend could have spared you this fate. It was uncommonly fast, that creature... and I could sense a familiar power within it. I would be pleased to encounter it again one day. Mm?'

The muttering giant returned his four-eyed focus to his submerged prisoner. 'Why are you not losing breath, miscreant? Speak!'

Slowly, Lu opened his lips, unbothered by the water that entered his mouth. 'It seems you are unfamiliar with the Reikans of old, Majgyn! We were seafarers, love-children of land and ocean; the best of us could dive breathlessly for days. I hope you are in no rush, apprentice God – drowning me will be no short affair.'

The dragon produced a lively, yet unsettlingly hollow laugh, and was clearly unbothered by Lu's smug composure.

'I am indeed aware of the Reikans of old, not only of their aquatic tendencies, but also of their misguided arrogance. I was not aware that such a folk still existed. However, since you have demonstrated that very same arrogance, small man, I have no choice but to believe that there is no use in drowning you. A pity, really.'

Despite his brief masquerade of confidence, Lu was under no illusion regarding his own mortality. Since the death of Tlephilisse, things that were lost had been stirred within him; among a flood of memory and sentiment, his mortality had been returned. And yet, as disconcerted as he was by the prospect of death, there was some peace to be found in its belated justice. He had, after all, betrayed the River Sprite. It only seemed appropriate that the Lavender Fox had delivered him to such a similar, and befitting doom.

Then, Lu felt a change among the waters of the crescent. He began to panic, for something was incredibly wrong. Slowly, but certainly, the temperature of the liquid was rising.

He was being boiled alive. 'This is how you die now, heretic!' snarled the Wyrm of silver-green. Lu screamed and tried to swim out of the blade, but there was no way out – its enchanted currents curled endlessly inwards towards the centre, thus forming a chamber that was utterly and frustratingly inescapable to all who suffered it. But the soaring heat of the prison had immobilised Lu long before he could exhaust himself from his frantic and feeble swim.

And simultaneously, the once-cerulean scythe of Empryc water became a flickering curve of lightning, and the shivering body of Lusini-Su, last of the old Reikans, was vaporised among the fires of gleaming white.

– END OF PART TWO –

PART THREE

In which a dream is deciphered, and a trust rekindled; dawns are discovered, and enmities established; two accounts are chronicled, whereby individual beginnings meet a convergent end

Chapter One

INHERITOR OF THE ISLE

And for one unique, momentary interlude in all of Lilan history, its inhabitants were exclusively both meek and mortal. Undisturbed by the draconic, seaward terror that had risen from the waves less than a day earlier, the wildlife of the tropical isle continued to scurry, swim, and soar with no care for their destinies. Tlephilisse, the Guardian Sprite of Lila, had been sacrificed by Lusini-Su, who was executed thereafter for his crime. The immense, writhing shadow of the apprentice God Morl-Majgyn was lifted, as he who cast it vanished from the Empryc blue, and it seemed that Lila's divine participation in the unknown, mystical conflicts of Kraj had come to an end.

Destiny lingered wilfully upon the isle, however, for in one final breath, Tlephilisse had successfully inflicted her role onto her attacker. The reason why she had ordained Lusini-Su with her role would not come to light. Alongside the Sprite, her intentions died unspoken and were left open to any direction of interpretation. All that was certain was that, in the centre of the circle stream where Tlephilisse had once lived, there lay a Reikan of the old world, lost within a dream so vivid that while in hypnosis, he did not assume himself to be dead, and could not recall dying.

No matter how reminiscent it was of Lu's previous recurring black dreams, this slumber was instead something of a parent to those prophetic night whispers. In the embrace of a bewildering oblivion, the grey man witnessed his darkest suspicions become animate. Here, he witnessed the vows of his allegiance dissipate into the same fog by which the Mistress came to him on that morning, long ago.

By his understanding, she was a Storm Sprite that lingered over Empryc. She was one of the thirty-five guardians, who had played God in the realms of men, governed only by the Watchers themselves. Though his interpretation did not feel entirely correct, Lu was utterly enthralled by betrayal and felt no need to linger on the specifics of her role. In the abstract, emerald haze of the unravelling past, it seemed that the Goddess had used Lu as a vessel in which to abandon her duty.

She had stolen his physicality and, in exchange, had saddled him in the role that was her own, temporarily hanging him among the clouds while she gathered the strength to disguise her transgressions more effectively. According to the dream, he had struggled incorporeally above the Empryc for at least a year, unwillingly casting spells of intermittent calmness and shower, and of merciless storm over Rei - a town still mourning his disappearance.

That year-long imprisonment came to a sudden end, when the enchantress returned to a similar Empryc shore, with her power somewhat restored, and a handful of followers that she had accumulated on her travels. Led by their Mistress, five of the hooded acolytes marched into the shallows, uniformly robed in lilacs and blues, where they raised their hands to the sky, muttering frantically all the while. In the near horizon, beyond the deathly rocks of Empryc, the shadow cast by the isle of Lila became an island of its own, sunken deep into the rising rock that had borne it just slightly above sea level. Thus, the Bhia was created, where Lusini-Su was released from his disembodied prison of clouds, and where he continued to be imprisoned, now physically, in an inescapable pit of ever-blue conifer. This was a camouflage of the Mistress's invention, for she still needed him to remain both alive and enrolled in order to fill the vacancy she had created in her escape.

Time then galloped exponentially onwards in the dream, gradually approaching a pace so absurd that Lu could hardly bear to observe it. The continuation of time at this relentless speed was a most harrowing denotation of the true longevity of his reclusion in the Bhia. Turning restlessly in the thick of slumber, he watched hordes of overgrowth and decay become one with his ageless past self in a dream-speed sequence until shortly he had been unrecognisably engulfed by it.

The dream then leapt drastically on, merging the likes of the Mistress, and the Lavender Fox, which Lu assumed to imply her control over the beast. Either Lu's vulpine companion obeyed the Mistress, or it was the Mistress herself in another form. Either way, she was responsible for its actions.

Finally, the dream presented Lu with two final offerings of equally perplexing ambiguity. The Walker could not tell if what he saw was a vision of the past, the now, or of the future, but could nonetheless recognise the collective attire of the legion that now stood before him. Hooded and enrobed in emerald, lilac, azure, or a combination of the three, stood a great number of the

Mistress's acolytes upon a midnight beach of sand and stone, by the anxious tide of a shore that was utterly foreign to the Reikan.

Though each person was transfixed on a unique portion of the beyond, all were singing in unison; the words of their peculiar verse echoed into the moonlit night until their resonance was pulverised by the crashing of waves.

'Here begins the age of men, for the gods will fade in fear of wind and tide. Here begins the age of men...' they called, with no indication of fatigue or climax. It seemed to the Reikan that this would continue forever.

Lu felt a twinge in his awakening brain, as the second of the final abstract moments of his dream was presented to him. All became dark, and the Walker could feel his body stirring elsewhere, in a more corporeal plane. Before his eyes could open, and his trembling lips could pull his first waking breath, a disembodied voice filled the chasm of the dreamless dark. For a moment, the voice was none other than the final melancholy whistling of Tlephilisse, the River Sprite. Slowly, the sound became a mess of rhythmic displacement and instead represented the collective passerine throat of the Lila chorus, creating a somewhat identical melody, but in the higher register of the songbirds.

The morose din evolved twice more, first into a curious tongue similar to that of the Lila mortals, yet in a more primitive dialect Lu could not understand. Then, finally, the repeating phrase arrived, with a stammering clunk, at the language of old Reian, and Lu understood them as clear as day.

'On Lila you shall remain, for you have carved a place in the balance, and you must steward it.'

And Lu awoke, and he gasped, and his lungs were filled with a familiar air, and his back lay upon a familiar land.

He was gracelessly spread, face up, across the teething darklilies in the centre of the Lila circle-stream. Supplied by an unexpectedly generous burst of energy, the Walker shot up onto his bare feet and immediately wondered what had become of his sandals and garments. He was naked, with his grey skin exposed to the rays of an early afternoon Empryc sun.

Two things then occurred to Lusini-Su simultaneously. He remembered that he had died, in the boiling blade of a great dragon warlord, Morl-Majgyn, the 'apprentice god'. His second realisation was of a far less morbid nature; his sandals and shellsuit were beginning to materialise around his flesh, as comfortably as they had been fitted prior to his demise. There was no sign of Umbra, however.

How had he been restored to life, and his clothes along with him? He pondered his black dream for a moment longer and came to no conclusion, though his contempt for his Mistress had doubled.

He had been little more than her decoy from the start, since even before his true memory could recall. Now it was clear why he had been cast into the Bhia forest, and why a cloud had followed him all the while. He had been an unwilling substitute for the Storm Sprite, and a cloud remnant of said role had continued to pester him even in his human form. It was also now apparent that the Mistress had fled from the eye of the Watchers, which further explained why she desired to remain unseen by Tlephilisse and required an assassin to dispatch the River Sprite who, Lu assumed, contained a power that the Mistress sought. Foolishly, he had absorbed that power and fed it back into the sky, and thus back to the Mistress, as she had planned.

Lu furiously considered how the vulpine servant of the Mistress had allowed Lu to fall into the drowning knife of Morl-Majgyn, after aiding him for so long prior to his demise. Had he needed to die, to fulfil the Sorceress's plan? Had the Mistress planned for his resurrection, or was it instead the work of the Watchers, or Tlephilisse for that matter, in order to grant the Island of Lila a new guardian. That was, at least, what the final voice of his dream had suggested.

With a shake of his head, Lu removed his shellsuit, for he was boiling beneath the afternoon sun. He had again spent too long inside of his thoughts and now needed to focus on the physical truths before him. He was, again, trapped upon the Lila Isle.

Lusini-Su screamed wordlessly aloud with frustration and a few birds in the nearby trees scattered from their shaded nests. He had been given a second chance and might even be immortal. He would escape the Lila, no matter the cost.

After his anger had subsided, the Walked trudged on, in the heat, carrying the separated fragments of his shellsuit behind him, in a sailor's net that had washed up, and had been salvaged by Lu, not five moons earlier. First, he arrived at his old storeroom, and retrieved a container of one of his buacoctin mixtures, which he wolfed down in seconds. Then came the slightly more arduous walk, to the southern beach, where he had first encountered the airborne, slithering wyrms sent by Majgyn.

The breeze was calm, and the air was warm, and there was no sign of those serpents, nor was there a single trace of the gigantic dragon in the seaward horizon. Lu turned back around, to face the great stone Sailor-Likeness that also inhabited the southern beach. His eyes widened with anger, and immediately Lu reached for his weapon, only to remember that he no longer carried his bedevilled glassblade. Stood atop the utmost promontory of the likeness was the Lavender Fox.

'Mistress!' Lu snarled, his voice crackling from the damage of his earlier scream. 'What is this foolery? Why would you have me die? And why, still, do I live?'

But the Lavender Fox seemed uninterested in Lu's heartfelt fury, and instead gently lapped at its front paw. Lu prepared to shout again until a creeping chuckle echoed behind him. The Reikan wheeled round in the white sand, and as expected, there stood the Mistress of the Bhia. She was almost human, if not a little too tall, with pale blue skin that was surrounded by an unusual rain-like mist.

'My dear Lu, you have much to learn of the ways of Kraj. Of course, I would have you die, for now the eye of the Watchers has been deceived most believably. I must admit, however, that I had not expected Morl-Majgyn to be their immediate choice for the task, nor had I predicted that Tlephilisse would gift you her role. I had intended to resurrect you myself, once my strength was restored. That has worked out nicely in our favour, truth be told, for the power I had saved for that task can now be allocated to other things.' Her voice shimmered with candid beauty, without a shred of animosity or dishonesty. Lu furrowed his brow and continued to digest the words of the Goddess with contempt.

'Nothing has changed, Lusini-Su, our bargain is intact. I had to omit a few of the details, otherwise, you would have never agreed.' She smiled at him, before directing her smile at the Lavender Fox, who also appeared to be listening intently to the Sorceress's inviting, velvet tone.

Lu attempted to regain some of his earlier fire.

'How can I trust you? Through the images of a fell dream, I have seen how you used me in the past! *What* are you?'

'I cannot afford to tell you, should you ever align yourself with my enemies. It is for your own good that, for now, you are none the wiser. You saw, perhaps, that I had spent a short while in the role of Storm Sprite, among the Thirty-Five. Trust that this was all you needed to know, for the safety of us both, and the destiny that we share. It was not the Watchers who cast you into the black dream, Lusini-Su. That was my doing. I had hoped to save you some time through that explanation, though we have ended up discussing it regardless.'

'What would you have me do next?'

'There is much to be done. The Watcher-creators are not necessarily our enemy, for the moment. Besides, it matters not; even if enemies they were, they are too strong to defeat, too distant to reach. They reside elsewhere and have business elsewhere. And fear not, adventurer, we shall also explore the elsewhere.'

Lu tried to stifle a grin, but his excitement had gotten the better of him.

'I would like that very much, more so than any other reward you could offer me, Mistress of Bhia and beyond. I must concede with my confused furies. It seems, despite my misunderstanding, that you have kept me alive thus far for a reason.'

Lu was still not wholly used to the Mistress's more personable appearance, for she was the closest thing to human company he had experienced in an eternity. Still, she emitted a disarmingly pleasant aura of both unearthly grace but also of comfort and homeliness. She was the only living acquaintance he had, aside from the Lavender Fox, though Lu was less than sure of the Fox's true nature or allegiance.

With a faint upward turn upon her lips, indicating that she found some humour in the thoughts she had seen within the Walker's frantic mind, the Mistress comforted him.

'You are not just an assassin, Lusini-Su. And I am not a warmonger, though it would be easier to pretend that I was. But it seems that Majgyn must be stopped. The Watchers have, for some reason, prepared him to become a ruling God upon this curious world, and as his power grows, he will become a threat to all those who are not mortal or otherwise ordinary, such as you and I.

The Lavender Fox padded delicately across the white sands and stood beside Lu. Even with its rear end seated, the beast stood at least the same height as the Walker. Lu offered the creature a friendly wink, which it seemed to acknowledge. The pair remained silent, as the Mistress continued.

'Know that I have seen into his mind in a way that the Watchers cannot. He will turn even on them, in the end; of this, I am certain.

Morl-Majgyn is neither a dragon nor a man. He is a Nirath sorcerer of the Old World, Mulusthe. When the Watcher-creators abandoned Mulusthe, the most expansive and tiring of their creations, Majgyn was spared for his talents and mystical prowess, along with a few of his shades, for reasons unknown to me. He is the last living Nirath, but he means to restore the ways of

Mulusthe upon Kraj. And believe me, Walker, when I advise that Mulusthe was no desirable habitat for the meek or peaceable.'

As was the usual case with Lu's conversations with the Mistress, the sailor-warrior found himself resigned now to all that she spoke of, no matter how improbable it seemed.

'Mulusthe... Is that where I have seen, through the portal of the blade, and the portal from whence came the Red Entity?'

'Mulusthe is gone, Lusini-Su' replied the Mistress, with a hint of relief in her aqueous voice. 'What you saw is a private realm, a shadow world of red, that myself and a few of the faithful have managed to create from the salvaged remnants of Mulusthe that are found here on Kraj. A realm that we devised for the sole purpose of containing all that cannot be long contained here. Yes, the Xollec Entity now resides there, among many other relics of Mulusthe, thanks to the work of Fym, my second in command. There, they are hidden from all who are aligned with the Watchers. There they sleep, to be called upon when necessary. It is Fym who you must seek, who will aid you in your quest to defeat Majgyn.'

The Lavender Fox yapped agreeably, as if to express its own excitement for this mission. Lu, however, was less than impressed.

'*My* quest? What chance does a creature such as myself have in defeating one such as Majgyn? Apprentice God, he called himself... Yet from a stance as lowly as mine, he was certainly a God, and nothing less. You send me to my death, Mistress of mine!'

To Lu's frustration, the Mistress seemed incapable of responding to all that he expressed with nothing other than laughter. Impatiently, the Reikan watched the Mistress chuckle, awaiting her answer with little faith that she would successfully reassure him in this instance.

'He thinks that you are dead. As do the Watchers. That is why you needed to perish in the way that you did, under the watch of the demon and his masters. They know you only through the eyes of Tlephilisse, and therefore only by the lies that you sold to her. Though I am sure that they were aware of how you inherited her role, they cannot see through your eyes, and therefore have no way of knowing that you have returned to life...'

The Sorceress's eyes widened, and she gestured her hands towards Lu, who was distractedly wrinkling his nose in thought.

'That reminds me, Lusini-Su. I must reallocate the Azdin I would have otherwise spent on making you immortal. Since the River Sprite has already seen to that immortality, I shall endow you with other gifts.'

'Azdin?' Lu had never heard such a word.

'Sorcery. Azdin is the energy from which all sorcery is derived. Some storytellers - and fantasists - would have you believe that magic is simply science yet to be discovered, or learned. This is risible, however, to those who are truly sorcerous. Azdinic sorcery needs not obey the laws of any realm. That is what makes it sorcerous, of course.'

Lu looked away with embarrassment, for those fables had certainly influenced his understanding of magic. The Mistress was mocking him.

'I shall not suffocate you with information at this time, Lusini-Su, though I will give you an example of how this gift may be used. Azdinic magic behaves much like wealth, or valuable possessions. What magic you currently possess can always be spent on what spells you can afford to cast, should you know how. The more Azdin you possess *without* spending it, the faster it regenerates and grows. In turn, as that Azdin is saved and cultivated, it further lends itself to a higher rate of recuperation. Unless one is initiated by an Azdinist such as myself or one of my highest acolytes, mortal humans will not live long enough to accumulate sufficient Azdin to use it, let alone understand how to.

You, on the other hand, have lived countless lifetimes. There are no pre-ordained champions in the world of sorcery, Lu, yet you are now circumstantially blessed with the greatest untapped well of Azdin of any human who has ever lived.'

Lu shook his head and ran his hands through his unkempt, dusk-green curls. 'Then you are dismayed, perhaps, that I did not die when Majgyn boiled me alive? For you had doubtless assumed my strength would return to you. Besides, what could you offer me with your 'reallocated Azdin', if I already possess so much of it? My brain is strong, Mistress, do not take me for a fool.' He clenched his jaw involuntarily, immediately regretting the intensity of his response.

And for once, the Mistress of the Bhia did not laugh at all, but instead approached the Walker, crouching towards him until the tips of their noses fell just shy of being connected.

'The greatest untapped well of Azdin of any *HUMAN* who has ever lived… I do not think you a fool, Walker. However, I am certain of your plain ignorance, though I will not allow it to offend me. The Azdin required to both resurrect and then immortalise *you* -' she lowered her voice, and relaxed the austerity of her tone, 'would have been of a magnitude that no other being will ever achieve, not even Majgyn.'

Swallowing back his obvious fear of the Sorceress, Lu lowered his chin to his bare, grey chest. 'Forgive me' he whispered, 'for I am not well adjusted to the renewal of my emotions.'

'So I can see,' smiled the Mistress, who had returned to her usual suspicious benevolence. 'I can see all that troubles your mind, Lusini-Su.' Quickly, she planted a kiss atop of his lowered head, before stepping twice backwards, to where she had been before.

'There is only one thing, besides resurrection, that comes close to being worth such a high price. That is how I will spend your reward.'

'What is it?' Lu enquired, curious as to what could be as costly as immortality.

'I will enhance the rate of your Azdinic regeneration' replied the Mistress. 'There is only one other human with this blessing, with whom you must soon be introduced.'

'Fym?' recalled the grey man.

'Fym. She is the greatest human sorceress and adventurer. She is immortal, and she has learned all that there is to be learned about Azdinic sorcery. You must meet with her so that she may teach you. You must meet with her, so that you can unlock your ever-growing potential, and then overcome Majgyn together, as equals.'

Lu nodded, with impatience, and walked closer to the sizzling shoreline of the south beach, until his feet were beneath the lulling tide. The Lavender Fox followed quickly behind the Walker, in a somewhat similar fashion to the way that his cloud had once followed him. He stared out, across the sharp expanse of the Empryc crown, and through his nose, he inhaled the brine-dense breeze that was sailing back inland.

'I accept this task. I wish to leave now, Mistress. But I must ask, what of Umbra? And what can you pledge to me, to secure my trust, if not Umbra again?' He turned round to face the wise, blue woman on the beach, awaiting her response.

Sharply, the Mistress raised one arm and pulled the glassblade from the air, as if it had been sheathed in nought but the wind.

'Umbra *shall* belong to you again, Lusini-Su, but you are not ready to wield it, nor can you guarantee its security against any common thief who might desire it for its un-krajian appearance, let alone against those who might recognise it as something more. No, for now, the blade stays with me.'

She paused solemnly for a moment, before placing Umbra back into the breeze, from which her bejewelled hand then returned with something else in its grasp. It was an egg of brilliant blue and gold, of a diameter not dissimilar to that of the buacoctin shells that lay nearby.

'I have guarded her for too long, but soon she will finally prepare to hatch. As proof of our alliance, I entrust her into your care, Lusini-Su.'

The Mistress released the alluring egg from her hand, and it glided smoothly towards the Walker, who accepted it hesitantly from its ethereal drift. He inspected the shell closer, but aside from its surprisingly small weight, Lu found no particular features upon its peculiar surface that might suggest what lay inside.

'She?' Lu asked, hoping for some clarification, as opposed to more of the Mistress's enigmatic nebulosity.

Though she had clearly sensed the desire for clarity in Lu's mind, the Mistress offered a faint smile instead and continued to speak hazily.

'She...will grow ferociously, in size and in intelligence, and must remain hidden from the ever-increasing number of eyes possessed by the Watcher-Creators. The wisest decision, it seems, would be to place her in the arms of another who now escapes those same eyes. Know that, by my own choice, I have placed my full confidence in you; I am bound to this egg; I would never risk its safety by betraying our allegiance.'

And for reasons unknown to Lu, he felt unusually inclined to accept the Mistress's vow to be true, despite having a distinct lack of evidence that the egg was of any value to the Sorceress at all. She then appeared to mutter something or other, and a large dark green, woven pouch rose softly from the sand before Lu's feet, alongside a few folded garments that Lu could not yet recognise. He knelt to pick up the clothes, when suddenly he noticed himself to be completely naked, his grey flesh exposed from head to toe.

'Much like Umbra, I am afraid that your shellsuit and matching undergarment would be far from ordinary in the land that you are soon to explore. I am aware, however, of your growing care for your appearance...' She glanced at the sides, and back, of Lu's hair, which the Reikan had shaved down with shells, with no shortage of meticulous effort, so that only the short, curly locks from the top of his head, grown over the last month, swinging freely against his face. 'And thus have devised some more culturally appropriate clothes for you to dress in, whilst attempting to retain some uniqueness that I believe will satisfy your tastes.'

And momentarily, Lu had changed into his new garments, and found them both befitting of his body, and of his tastes. First, he had donned the pair of knee-length, linen trousers, which were remarkably comfortable for both their looseness around the thigh and for their feather-light weightlessness. They were somehow dyed to a shade of unusually rich, twilight purple, which happened to be one of Lu's favourite colours. Similarly weightless was the lace-up cotton tunic of citrus green he then pulled over his head, and the long, swaddling cloak of cool onyx black, that seemed almost vitreous under sunlight. The latter could be fastened at the neck by a single silver link, that depicted a pair of reptilian claws both clasping a single, blue jewel in the centre. Lu folded the hooded cloak for now, wrapping it around the blue and gold egg, before placing both inside of the large pouch he was also gifted.

'Umbra, and your shellsuit, will be waiting for you in the citadel of Daleia, at the heart of Daleia-Dal. Until then, you must strengthen your mind and spirit by sourcing your own provisions. Tonight, the Lavender Fox will fly you to the place of your birth. There is no need to rush, and you can afford to settle down for a short while.'

Lu frowned. No rush? Had the Mistress not suggested his mission was urgent? He opened his mouth to speak but then remembered that his thoughts were not private, and waited for the Mistress to elaborate on her words.

'It is essential that you find time to rest and strengthen yourself, Lusini-Su. Familiarise yourself with the new age of Koau, and the world you left behind, and seek company among those who are human, for a change.'

She grinned sardonically, before continuing with (and concluding) her advice.

'Without me, you must seek the library of Daleia, and the sages who frequent and defend it. They are expecting you, though they do not know who - or *what* - you are. To enter the citadel, in which the library resides, you must present something of scholarly importance, something that must be written by you. The citadel of Daleia, and in turn the city of Daleia-Dal, was built upon the accumulation, categorisation, and exchange of rare knowledge - its primary trade. This lingering custom of the city is one you must adhere to and respect in order to gain the trust of the sages who dwell in its core. My advice is that you spend a month or so in Rei, or 'Awreia' as it is now known, so that you can put your flawless memory to the test by documenting your tale thus far.

Once you are content with what you have written, leave for Daleia-Dal. Avoid prominence, and keep to yourself while you find your feet, before eventually offering your complete written account to the scholars in exchange for permanent admission into the citadel, as a student.'

'Should I not merely speak of this "Fym", or even yourself, so to be recognised?'

'You must do the opposite, Lusini-Su. That would make for far too easy an infiltration on behalf of our enemies, of which there are many. Anyone could steal that information from you and break in if it were that easy. No, you must not attempt to ease this stage of your mission, for it is essential that such formalities remain in place, so as to eliminate the possibility of an interceptor.'

Lu smiled, recognising his Mistress's desire to conclude their meeting.

'You have told me very little, Mistress of the Storm, defier of Watchers. Tell me, at least, when I can wield this

Azdin, and see the benefit of the enhancements you have granted me? I feel no different, of course. And, on another matter, why can your elegant, lavender servant, the Fox, not join me on my quest? Already, that creature has been quite the companion to me.'

But the human-bound Mistress had begun to evaporate, becoming water, and then pure mist, and then nothing at all. Lu was left standing in the shade of the early evening, beside the Lavender Fox, who would soon escort the Walker to shores he had not seen in an untold era.

'It seems,' Lu murmured, turning to face his vulpine companion 'that we are going to travel tonight.' With his right hand, he stroked the woven texture of his pouch, in which he now carried that peculiar blue and gold egg, which was wrapped in his black cloak.

Seeming to understand the Reikan's words completely, the Lavender Fox brushed against Lu's side, before lowering its back, and allowing Lu to climb upon it. Then, with one heavy flick of its dazzling, tremendous tail, the Lavender Fox climbed into the shadow of the Empryc night, rising quickly, seemingly into the very starlight that now illuminated their route.

Lu glanced backwards as if to make sure he did not dream. Finally, he would be rid of the Lila Isle, at least for now. Finally, he was going to witness what had become of the world that lay beyond.

Chapter Two

PORT AWREIA

Nearly two full days had passed since Lusini-Su, and the Lavender Fox, arrived on the shores of Rei, in the deepest silence of the night. The Lavender Fox had quickly departed, once Lu was safely upon the ground, and Lu had spent the remaining phases of night scouting the beach rocks for a safe place to rest. Then, he had awoken to the smell of cooked food and the distant, colourful sounds of music and bustle. Groggily, he had staggered along the coast until he had reached his destination, Port Awreia.

Rei had come a long way in the age of Koau, since its humble beginnings as a fishing town of mariners and gentle folk. Now, it seemed that the entire continent of Taromet's sea-borne trade arrived upon these very waves, passing through Awreia in a regimented fashion. Still, from the few townsfolk that Lu had encountered during his first full day, the people were just as pleasant, likeable, and well-meaning as ever.

At first, Lu had struggled to adapt to their dialect, and the tinge of their accent, for it had changed immensely since he was a mortal Reikan. Several Awreikans had commented on the speech, and the greyness of this new vagrant, for unlike the people of Rei, the Awreikans were far less varied in appearance and skin tone, mostly sharing a very similar, light grey-brown complexion. All comments were made only in the kindliest manner, however, Lu had already begun to realise that the Awreikans were an accepting, easy-going people and that they had no qualms with the unknown, much as his own people had been, long ago.

Now halfway into his second day of exploring Port Awreia, Lusini-Su found himself finally facing the obvious task before him. He had nothing but the beautiful garments and pouch (and the egg within) that was supplied by his Mistress. With no lodgings, or weapon, or writing equipment to begin the work he needed to start, it was clear that the Walker needed to acquire some local currency in order to truly settle here. He wandered through a food market, glancing here and there as some of the stalls were being dismantled for the evening, whilst new night stalls were being constructed, offering pre-prepared fire-cooked foods for the late-working sailors, fishermen, and traders who desired such things. Lu had never seen or even considered such a thing. It was fantastically creative, and the food smelled utterly intoxicating to a man who had not eaten hot, well-prepared food in uncountable lifetimes. He would purchase some as soon as he could secure an income.

Eventually, in the night, Lu was awoken by a particular rabble that gave him some inspiration.

'Night-sailors, night-merchants! See here that I've found a shard of ruby from the wreckage of The Merralyn!' boasted a short, but strong woman dressed in the heavy insulation of warm, brown leather and stained red cloth. In her hand of warm, grey skin, she clutched a small, iridescent ruby, which immediately attracted the attention of the few night-shifters who were nearby.

'By the blue waves!' exclaimed one of the sailors, a younger man of barely twenty years. 'That'd be worth a fine amount – suppose there are any more, which one might find in the light of tomorrow morning?'

The first sailor threw back her head of thick, bushy black hair and laughed. 'No chance, Tatael, my friend! That wreckage is sunken far beyond the reach of even the best divers. It was by luck alone that this small remnant has washed ashore and into my hands. No matter - I shall be eating well for the week!' She glanced at the jewel in her hand, and smiled, before swaggering off into the night.

And by that alone, an idea sprang into the Walker's mind, as a scheme to obtain work in this busy, trading seaport. He remembered how Morl-Majgyn had initially tried to drown him in the core of an enchanted aqueous hooked dagger, without realising that Lu could remain submerged for a great deal of time. The Awreikans must have a short supply of breath, therefore preventing them from diving deep into the sea. He stood up quickly, wiped the skin he'd shed from his eyelids, and then scurried after the carrier of the ruby.

'Night sailor!' He called, to which the woman responded immediately by pivoting her entire frame in a single step, by the heel of her leather-booted foot.

'Hello?' she said, with a hint of impatience in her tone.

'My apologies, night sailor.' Lu blurted. 'I haven't visited this place in a very long time; I don't know your name.' The Reikan tried to include as many Reian contractions as he could while he spoke, in an attempt to seem more personable.

The sailor acknowledged Lu's peculiar accent, regardless, but seemed intrigued by his mannerisms.

'Demja. Call me Demja. What is it, foreigner?'

Lu tried not to smile at the irony of being called a foreigner in a land that was his home long before it was hers, before giving his name and rambling an elaborate lie in which he claimed that he was an incredibly experienced diver, with unparalleled control of his breathing.

'...And so, if you'll take me in your crew, I'd be pleased to come aboard and work as a scavenger upon your ship. That is – if you are in charge, of course.' Lu smiled, believing he had appeared a convincing diver.

'I am indeed the captain of my boat, but it only sails a handful of fishermen at a time. Here's a good idea – how'd you like to work alone? I'll loan you a small wooden boat, and you can sail out over to the Merralyn wreckage point in the early morning. I'll...err... mark it on a map or something or other.'

Lusini-Su nodded, his orange eyes never breaking contact with those of Demja the Captain. This was it, his opportunity to make a living here in Awreia!

'You know, of course, that I'm taking a slight risk here, young Lu. If you're as much an...uh... sea searcher as you claim to be, then I'd be a fool to guide you to such opulent treasures...and give you a boat to get there. I'll be needing some insurance, you see.'

And then Lusini-Su became a little more collected, and sceptical, and set his hand upon his woven pouch. He was certain of what Demja would ask for and now debated the risk.

'I carry only one thing of importance to me, Captain. You wouldn't rob me, I hope.'

The thick-haired, muscular night sailor chuckled, as Lu pulled the exquisitely beautiful, yet organic-looking egg from his bag.

'That certainly looks the part, diver! I was, however, not going to trouble you for something of true importance. I highly doubt anyone can make the dive, and besides...' The Captain burst into a full-blown raucous laughter, before quickly calming herself. 'Besides, forgive me, I don't suppose I'd be able to sell that egg, regardless of its importance to you! I don't even know what it is!' Lu felt his stomach settle, as Demja continued with her explanation.

'I was going to ask that you lend me your lovely cloak at dawn, which is when I finish working, at the far east end of the harbour. There and then, I'll hand you a map and show you your boat.'

She glanced at the egg once more and shook her head with a chuckle before Lu returned the thing to its pouch.

'We've a deal, then!' Smiled Lu. 'I'll get rested for the morning and meet with you at dawn! Thank you, Captain Demja, for the opportunity to settle into Awreia.'

And then Demja nodded affirmatively, before returning to delivering (and, Lu assumed, collecting) imports to and from the market of the night. Lu returned to where he had huddled himself to sleep and fell back into a light, abstract dream of warm seas and warmer winds.

Later, the dishevelled Reikan got to his feet without hesitation, awoken by the day-bringing angle of sunlight directly upon him. He had chosen his location well, for he seemed to have roused on time.

Eagerly, Lu headed to the agreed meeting point where he waited for quite some time, admiring the many vessels of various design, quality, size, and value that surrounded him. Then, while Lu was observing a quarrel between three ravenous seabirds, Demja arrived unaccompanied, upon the bounce of a languid, but rhythmic strut. With a yawn and a polite grin, the Captain handed Lu a fairly neat, well-drawn map of the Empryc coast, with some annotation as to relative distances along the side of the illustration. As the Walker opened it out fully to examine the detail, Demja jabbed a short, painted-black nail towards the symbol denoting the location of the wreckage. 'Most items that sit beneath this area of waves were uniquely crafted for The Merralyn. Bring your haul to the place that we met last night, and then I'll offer you a job.'

Lusini-Su nodded in acknowledgement, and carefully handed Demja his folded cloak. He was (self-consciously) still unused to such blunt communications; he had been starved of casual social intercourse for as long as he could recall. His only recent acquaintances had been inhuman, telepathic, or otherwise mute. They walked along the harbour together for a while, without speaking, before the Captain finally directed Lu to a medium-sized reed sailboat that floated jauntily between two others. Though its capacity was certainly limited to three sailors at best, it seemed to be sturdy in its own right and of fairly recent construction, as it showed no signs of serious weather erosion. Supporting the single, reed sail was a pair of eucalyptus masts connected to either side of the vessel, with a few adjustable cords that could be used to influence the sail while travelling. Attached loosely to the stern was a reasonably sized steering oar.

She winked impishly, before taking a bite out of some bread that she had been carrying. 'I'll be seeing you later, Diver. Good luck!' She said, her mouth still full of food. By the time Lusini-Su had prepared the boat for his first voyage, Demja was nowhere to be seen.

It took the ageless Sailor a good few hours to manoeuvre the reed boat out of the harbour. To his relief, surprisingly little had changed about sailing since Rei had become Awreia, regardless of the countless eras that had probably passed. It was his skill level, however, that had returned all too slowly. Despite his powerful memory, his limbs had to be retaught. Still, the sun was kinder here than it was on Lila, and the breeze refreshed his limbs whenever they grew tired with exertion. Lu was still not satisfied with his fitness, but it had come a long way since he awakened from the moss. Eventually, he was gliding (with occasional elegance) above the abundant coralline beauty that lay beneath the waves of the coastal Empryc shallows.

It was soon a hot midday, and the Sailor had somewhat reached his destination, according to the map. The water had become deep but had retained all its enrapturing clarity, by which Lu had been able to spot the amorphous shape of the sunken wreckage that he intended to maraud. Lusini-Su was thirsty, and he was becoming hungry, but knowing that he only had to take a few things in order to secure Demja's trust, the Sailor quickly removed all of his clothing and his pouch and placed them safely in the centre of the boat, before clutching his carrier-net and diving straight into the water.

Lu swam down with ease, and the genetic blessing of his sub-aquatic eyesight allowed him to enjoy the spectacle of what he approached, and all that surrounded it. Unknown to all but Lu, the sailor-warrior now shed a few tears of joyous reunion, for he had missed the undersea sights of fauna and flora more than he had missed the entire population of Rei, or Rei itself.

Once he had arrived at the half-lit wreckage of The Merralyn, Lu wasted little time investigating the glamour of the broken vessel. Driven by the irritations of thirst at sea, Lusini-Su quickly located and then snatched a handful of wildly dispersed rubies, jewellery and other gemstones that were situated around, beneath, or on top of the many shards of the broken hull of The Merralyn. Like the much smaller vessel loaned to Lu by Captain Demja, this seemingly enormous craft was built mainly with tightly compressed reeds, which now escaped their bonds, alongside beams and ropes that were fitted together in a feat of engineering that, counter to what Lu had thought earlier, was of an intellect somewhat more advanced than those of Rei. There was so much rope along the seabed, in fact, that Lu could not picture how the ship would have appeared when in use; he simply assumed that most of it had been pulled taut in various directions in order to stiffen the beams or act as some form of joist. The design was intriguing, but much of the wreckage was in utter darkness, with only certain portions that lay visible in the path of the sun's diving light. Nonetheless, now that Lu had found what he required, he was keen to be on his way, and so with a fluid, single movement, he launched himself from the wreck under his feet, and soared unbrokenly through the water, towards its surface.

With far more ease than before, the Walker returned to the east side of the harbour and carefully stole and drained a few market-sized umellos to quench his gasping, dry mouth. Later that night, when Demja had begun to work, Lu approached her with his findings in hand, to which she grinned in disbelief, before rewarding him his first commission.

In no more than twenty days, Lu had progressed rapidly from being a nameless vagrant in Port Awreia to becoming the most whispered name among the sailors of the town. For every valuable item Lu retrieved from The Merralyn, Demja had worked hard to sell them and repay her diver half of her takings, which Lu agreed was fair due to his own lack of know-how or salesmanship. As Lu's work grew ever popular among the people of Awreia, and the riches of the wreckage became eventually thinned to nothing, Demja broadened the horizon of the business by promising to the people of Awreia that, for a price, her 'diver' would retrieve anything valuable that was lost beneath the waves in known locations.

Though Lu's workload had become increasingly strenuous, he enjoyed the daily promise of stimulation, and within his first five commissions had already managed to afford his nightly residence in the cheapest of the three inns of Awreia. Staying in what was little more than a single room in a stranger's house, Lu had first discovered this new, nameless 'inn' from the mouth of Demja. She was a friend of the innkeepers, who were desperate to begin their business. He was, therefore, the first and only lodger of these first-time, zealous innkeepers - a friendly and generous pair of men, who Lu had already become very fond of.

The sailor-warrior had also become rather fond of his routine. At sunrise, he would leave for work, taking with him whatever food the innkeeper Haln (who was the hairier and broader of the pair) had left for him. He would eat this as he travelled through various jobs, before returning for an evening meal (also prepared by Haln) and then retiring to his room, to work on the writing exposition that his Mistress had tasked him with. Haln was a wonderful cook and catered proudly in accordance with Lu's growing distaste for meat. Ever since the Walker had befriended and then slain Tlephilisse, he had become perturbed by his prior disregard for non-human life. The Sprite had valued and cared for all things equally and shepherded the flow of life-energy through all of Lila's creatures. Out of admiration for Tlephilisse, and his growing sympathy for the more peaceful, herbivorous beasts of Kraj, Lu had begun to exclude animals from his diet whenever possible, in hope that it might ease his conscience.

For the most part, he had managed to work unseen, and was therefore known by name and name alone; very few people in Awreia would recognise him by his face. With his chronicle nearly up to date, Lu's anonymity served its preconceived purpose of veiling his preparation to exit Awreia. While largely conflict-averse, the treasure-starved Awreikans would not be pleased to learn of his plan to depart.

One evening, thirty or more days since his arrival, Lu completed a particularly indolent sentence upon a trembling, word-filled page, and sighed deeply, before the immense bulk of masculinity that was Haln the innkeeper stepped politely into the doorway.

'Quite the unusual story you've...err... got there!' yawned Haln gaily, startling Lu who nearly flung his costly but exhausted silver ink stylus into the air. Grinning politely at his jolly landlord, chef, and friend, Lu submitted to the infectious nature of yawning, before responding bluntly. 'It's finally done Haln. Up to date.'

Haln nodded with a facetious display of understanding, before approaching the Reikan for a closer glance at the papers.

'Inspired by your travels, I understand, although no one has been to the Island within the Crown, it is impossible!' he laughed, though Lu understood that it was not in mockery. 'You've got quite the imagination, of course, of course... Forgive me; I couldn't resist reading through a few of the pages when I last cleaned your room! It's good work, interesting work; the dreamery makes up for your lack of experience in storytelling, of course!' He offered Lu a playful wink to punctuate his joke, before handing the Walker a dish of salted vegetables and rice, sparsely dressed by a thick, creamy sauce derived from the flesh of the buacoctin. This was one of Lu's favourite evening meals, and he eagerly accepted the dish from Haln's gigantic hands.

'I'm in your gratitude, Haln. You and your partner have allowed me to comfortably pursue an obscure task during my visit to Awreia, though you have charged me little for my stay. My time here, however, has reached its end for now, though I hope to return to this wonderful sea-gazing inn as soon as I can.'

Haln appeared positive, but for a twinkle in the corner of his eyes, and he coughed and nodded as if to signify his sorrow. Noticing the tears in his innkeeper's eyes, Lu smiled reassuringly, before continuing to speak.

'In return for your hospitality, I've a gift for your business. You see, I've earned more than enough to afford my stay, my travel equipment, and my inks, and have no use for the rest of my fast-acquired wealth. So I leave it to you, to grow this one-guest building into the thriving business that you deserve.'

Lu gestured towards a locked box beneath his table, before handing Haln a recently made key. 'All I ask is that you preserve this room, for when I return!'

Chapter Three

BANDITS OF THE MIRE

Lusini-Su roused instinctively to the first embers of dawn, after spending the rest of his evening condensing his effects into an equipment and rations bag he had purchased recently from a friendly merchant in the day-market. The style of fine basketwork had initially attracted him, and after some consideration, Lu decided it would be appropriate for his journey.

Within the waist-fitted bag, he had carefully packed a hollow-gourd for water, several small parcels of bread and other food prepared by Haln, a fishing knife (though he had not packed it with fishing in mind), and a well-protected, neatly rewritten copy of his logbook, which he intended to present to the scholars of Daleia-Dal. At his side, he carried two things. One was the small pouch gifted to him by the Mistress, which contained the mysterious egg of blue and gold. The other was a simple, bronze short-sword that he had found during his first week of working as a diver. It had suffered no damage from the water and was of a substantial enough density for Lu to find enjoyment in swinging the thing around.

As Lu reached the outskirts of Port-Awreia, a distant, wiry shadow called out from behind. 'Leaving? Are we leaving?'

Resting a precautious hand upon the pommel of his sword, the grey man wheeled back around to face the shadow that addressed him. Young, thick-haired and handsome, was Tatael Ram the sailor. He stood at least a head taller than Lu, though Lu did not see the man to be a threat. Tatael Ram, like Lu, worked for Demja; Lu was aware of more than one story concerning Tatael's cowardice, as such tales were fundamental to Demja's sense of humour.

'Yes, I'm leaving. I've an errand to run beyond the border of Awreia' replied Lu, now approaching Tatael.

Tatael snorted in response. 'And it seems all the money in Awreia wasn't enough for you, dream stealer.'

'Dream stealer?' Lu frowned at the young sailor in confusion.

'That night...when Demja returned with the ruby from The Merralyn, that inspired your brief profession. I have been diving for those jewels since the day they were sunk. Since I was young, I've been an avid diver, inspired by the ancient men of Rei...something of a myth, their abilities; a myth that has driven me to dive ever since.'

Lu took one step back, as Tatael began to raise his voice.

'I know what you are, Reikan. I've read enough to understand! By leaving, you not only put our business in danger, but also our lives! The King of Light will discover you, for they say he is drawn to the unnatural! If he hears word of a true Reikan, I fear Awreia will be razed!'

The Mistress had made no mention of any King of Light, and Lu couldn't help but smile at the unimaginative title, doubtless belonging to either a mortal ruler, or a completely fictional being that Ram had invented. He felt threatened by neither. Waving at the frenzied young sailor, Lu slipped into the woodland beyond the town's border, calling 'I'm leaving, Tatael! Reclaim your dream if you want!'

And as Tatael's colourful curses vanished beneath the ambience of the wild, Lu pulled out the map that would lead him to Daleia-Dal.

For a few days, Lusini-Su found immense joy in the traversal of the woodland, which had slowly become a jungle. Limestone, lichen, and many vascular plants now marked a vague path through what was an otherwise impassable, tiered dungeon of tree, marsh, and shadow. These were almost the adventures Lu had been longing for, though he kept a wary eye for the larger beasts that sometimes prowled in the night - he had not lived twenty or more lifetimes to become a creature's midnight meal.

Regarding meals, Lu had not been so careful with his own. In fact, due to his voracious strength-building diet, he had already eaten nearly everything that he'd packed. More than once, he had unravelled the egg of blue and gold and imagined cooking it. This was only to feed his sense of humour, however, and he swiftly ended his playful ideas whenever he remembered the Mistress's power to intercept his thoughts.

By the third day, Lusini-Su had begun to concede that this adventure was not what he had expected, nor was he the adventurer he had thought of himself. He had spent so much effort building and sculpting his body and strength during his month in Awreia that he had not considered how far his stamina would take him, and therefore had miscalculated how long his rations would last.

That night, he pulled the egg of blue and gold from its pouch, and whispered to it before settling down to sleep between a pair of thin, smooth trees in the thick of the jungle.

'This is not at all like the fantastical stories that I've heard or read, it seems', he muttered to the egg, stroking its peculiar texture with his thumb. 'For those characters seem only reliant on food when it is of importance to their story.' The egg offered no response, as usual.

Lu smiled with a tinge of bitterness and traced the burning veins of gold that danced around the egg of brilliant blue, before setting the egg back down into its pouch and wrapping himself in his cloak of onyx black.

Before sleep had scarcely caressed the Reikan, he had become aware of a distant chatter in the wilderness. Though he knew little of the world, Lu feared the worst – there had been talk of bandits, and mercenaries robbing travellers near Awreia, and Lu carried things he could not afford to lose. Without hesitation, the sailor-warrior shifted his logbook and the pouch containing his egg into a gap behind one of the slim trees, before uprooting a nearby cluster of gigantic, dead leaves and covering the hiding place of his valuables.

There was little time to do anything else, other than clutch at his short-sword in his left hand, snatch for the fishing knife with his right hand, and suffocate his small fire with his feet, as he waited for the rogues to pass.

In total darkness, Lu now focussed wholly on the sounds made by these creeping strangers. There were at least four of them, and they said very little to each other aside from a few peculiar, instructive murmurs that Lu could not quite grasp. A dim, controlled lamplight now glimmered beyond a nearby tangle of marsh-grass, and then they were upon him.

Upon a wave of brown, grey, and silver arrived four violent bandits, and a fifth who kept some distance, and Lu was certain he would soon die. He was outnumbered, lamp-dazzled to near blindness, and entirely unable to distinguish where each bandit limb ended and the next began. Still, he thrashed and coiled among the blades that came towards him, managing to wrestle away the weapons of two of his attackers, though he could not see well enough to trace their retreat.

Before Lu could recover his breath, the open moment allowed a third bandit to swing what appeared to be an axe on a chain, which missed its mark and instead smashed into the mud, rendering a catastrophic implication of what it could do to Lu's flesh. The Walker dared not allow such a casualty, however, and cut off the assailant's arm with his pathetic short-sword, thwarting any attempt to retrieve the sunken flail.

The fourth of the armed bandits was yet to make her move, though Lu could see her shimmer in her lamplight, behind the bulk of the armless man. He could not reach her for now and instead stumbled backwards to dispatch the two he had already disarmed. To Lu's relief, one of the disarmed bandits had not moved; she kneeled where he had disarmed her, in surrender to his blade. He did not kill her, and instead searched frantically for her companion, panicking as he heard what he believed to be the approach of the fourth bandit from behind.

The other man he had disarmed had only just found his weapon, for he had been patting the unlit ground frantically as Lu drew near. Then, as the frenzied rogue brought his blade into view, Lusini-Su ran him through with a blast of pragmatic urgency. As the skewered man struggled helplessly upon the short-sword, Lu dragged his fishing knife through the man's throat with blinding mercy, finishing him off.

He could not dwell on the prospect of killing, for something now grasped at his right shoulder, and then his left. It was the one-armed bulk of a man, and for all the Walker's strength, this giant mercenary could not be shaken off.

The Walker's panic had fled, however, for he now believed to have the upper hand against these witless, ill-prepared rogues. With one foot, he thrust himself backwards from the trunk of one of the slim trees, causing the armless man to fall uncontrollably backwards. As they tumbled and crashed into the darkness, Lu jolted his arms free and then drove his sword into the belly of the brute. The man died gasping with a horrific croak, as Lu pushed his blade deeper, using it as an aid to regain his footing.

Before Lu could reassess his surroundings, and seek the three bandits who still lived, he felt a cold, sharp prick upon his back, followed by a chill that seemed to reach his every limb. He glanced down in shock, to find a black spear protruding through his abdomen. The pain had yet to follow this sign of certain death, and so with one last swipe, the unfeeling sailor-warrior swung himself back around, blade first, until his short-sword met and severed the neck of his murderer. It was the disarmed woman whose life he had previously spared for her surrender.

Now, in a union of lamp-lit lifelessness, the sweet face of her severed head, and the entire body of the Reikan, collapsed quickly to the ground.

In the throes of death, Lu's eyesight began to fail, and pain corrupted his senses. He lay within the centre of a triad of bandit corpses and would soon be joining them in their peace. As his ears and body thumped with the aching sound of his struggling pulsing heart, he could hear two voices chattering, and rummaging through his bag. One, he assumed was the fourth bandit and lamp-carrier, and the other was the fifth shadow that had witnessed the ordeal from afar. He could not see their faces, and it mattered not. To the scuffling sound of robbery and the bandits' complaints regarding his dull possessions that were not worth stealing, Lu's body began to fail. Moments later, he was dead.

Chapter Four

THE VANITIES OF PROGRESS

As quickly as he had died, the grey man was again rousing in an uncomfortably familiar setting, upon a bed of teething darklilies.

'Now I understand. I understand the nature of this curse...'

He was situated in the centre of the circle-stream, at the heart of the Lila Isle. He was without a weapon, or a single piece of clothing, the latter being a more prominent loss; his clothes were a unique gift from the Mistress.

But as Lu stood up, in fast acceptance of his missing effects, he was presented with another, far less conceivable forfeiture. His body had changed; a month's hard-earned musculature, and a month's curling length to his dusk green hair, all now vanished in such a way that Lu believed he had travelled backwards in time. He gasped, with a hint of theatrical irony, as he ran his hands over his half-shaven, shorthaired scalp, and slender frame. He had been proud, and sometimes even transfixed by the physical transformation he had undergone while working in Awreia, so as he gazed into his reflection in the river-ring around him, he could not help but feel a tinge of disappointment that accompanied his otherwise gladness to be alive.

The Walker soon dismissed the madness of his earlier thoughts regarding the possibility of time reversal, for as he glimpsed the mid-morning blaze he was reminded of the dry climate when last he occupied this Empryc isle, which had relaxed considerably since. He was still living in the present, though his resurrection had revived him in a previous body – the body with which he had murdered Tlephilisse.

Her final incomprehensible whistle, which again sounded among the passerine, had ensured his eternal bond to the role he had stolen from her. He was immortal, in an unconventional sense, for he was susceptible to death, but could return to life.

Lu sighed, and walked out of the clearing, in the direction of the Sailor-Likeness. It had already crossed his mind that, despite cheating death for the second time, he had no way of knowing how many chances this role would allow him. He still feared death, for any death could be his last. Even then, he was not fond of the form he had been returned to, and would, at the very least, still avoid death for the sake of protecting his hard-earned fitness. As his bare feet stumbled over rock, grass, lily, and mud, before finally reaching the comfort of white sand, Lusini-Su grew troubled by another matter. How would he cross the treacherous spines of the Empryc Crown? How would he escape the Lila?

The Reikan, gaunt and grey, needed not ponder his escape for long, however. Atop the likeness perched the Lavender Fox, its eyes enthralled by myriad birds that fluttered and flaunted nearby. Lu smiled with relief, as he approached his supernatural acquaintance.

'Even for an immortal, I consider myself lucky - lucky to have such otherworldly friends!'

The fox's ears twitched at the sound of Lu's voice, and in the blink of an eye, the beast has begun to float down from the Sailor-Likeness, in the direction of the Walker. Without a word or grunt, the two prepared for flight, and were soon sailing upon the brine-scented Empryc breeze.

Once they had crossed the teeth of the Empryc Crown, the Lavender Fox became somewhat restless, as if recalling their encounter with the dreaded Morl-Majgyn in these warm waters, two flights prior to this. Without warning, the fox began to glide down towards the surface of the sea until eventually the pair were completely submerged.

Lu tried his best to grip onto the scruff of the fox as they snaked beneath wind and wave, but the fox had no intention of escorting Lu any further. With a single, elegant roll, the fox separated itself from the Walker's grasp and then proceeded to explode from the water and disappear into the sky. Not at all bothered by the depth of his abandonment, Lu quickly swam his way to the surface for a welcome kiss of air. He was a great distance from the land, but the Lavender Fox had done all he had needed it to - he was across the Empryc Crown. It was doubtless a busy creature, loyal to the Mistress, thus Lu felt nothing but gratitude for its continuous aid; he could swim the rest of the way.

Afternoon came, though Lu felt he had been swimming for days without rest. Whenever the waves became too difficult to fight, he dived below, avoiding the brunt of their resistance. Even then, he was often helpless against the will of the water; sometimes he longed to simply surrender to their smothering. He now felt some frustration towards the Lavender Fox after all, for he had greatly misjudged his ability to swim, due to the reincarnate degeneration of his physique. Nonetheless, he was now approaching a well-sailed route, and several boats had slowly entered his peripheral vision.

It was not long before a large fishing vessel drifted close enough for Lu to scream out for aid. A stereotypically scrawny, young Awreikan watchman quickly acknowledged the naked, panting Reikan, and cast out a rope to hoist Lu up onto the deck.

Once aboard, a few of the sailors (including the ancient and near-motionless captain) recognised Lu despite his hazy presence in Awreia, and he was offered basic clothing, two meals, and a safe passage to the shore in return for fair labour during his stay.

As was the way with Reikans and Awreikans alike, these people were generous and caring, all while preserving their tough, sea-spirited wit. By the day's end, Lusini-Su had recovered most of his strength, and had even made friends with a few crew members who had instructed his jobs upon the ship, which was called 'Horral II'.

As night began its cool, blissful descent upon the shores of Awreia, the haggard captain of Horral II made sure to dismiss Lu of his duties and allow him overboard as the ship glided along the coastline. The sailors were mostly now aware of Lu's journey to Daleia-Dal, thus directing the Reikan to the beach closest to the jungles in which (unknown to the sailors) he was slain. With an honest bow, Lusini-Su thanked the captain and his sailors, aiming his fire-eyed stare with particular focus on a couple of friends he had made during the short voyage. Their names were Runil and Darathus, and without once questioning his circumstances, they had made Lu feel both welcome and valuable to their camaraderie. The grey man had not felt such platonic, selfless friendship since before his time in the Bhia. He would miss these sailors dearly and hoped to meet them once when he was permitted to return to Awreia.

For now, however, another matter rumbled impatiently at the core of Lu's skull. The questionable safety of the egg, or what may have hatched from it, was of the utmost concern to the beach-crossing Reikan. If it came to any harm, the Mistress would most certainly wreak a terrible vengeance on him, and he would lose every freedom he had toiled for.

Even if, by chance, the egg was still there, there was also a possibility that some tree-burrowing beast had snatched his book.

With no food or provisions other than the clothes given to him by the sailors of Horral II, Lu scuttled back into the overgrown jungle before him, not once taking his mind off the egg, the logbook, and their safety. Tearing through the vines and branches, and climbing or otherwise circumventing countless natural obstacles, the sailor-warrior was growing somewhat familiar with his surroundings once more. Like fire, he climbed across a tree-fall passage that married two ends of a steep, waterfall valley, which he now recognised as something he had crossed before due to a human-made, withering hut that could scarcely be seen at the bottom, behind the cascades. He had nearly made his way back to the place he was attacked.

By nightfall, Lu had reached the slim, twin trees near which the egg and papers were hidden. His bags were, as expected, nowhere to be seen, and neither were the clothes he had died in. With a shrug, the Reikan trudged towards the hollow in which he had hidden his valuables.

The Walker's ancient heart nearly stopped in his chest, as his eyes scanned the empty hollow where the egg and logbook were stowed.

'Stolen!' the grey man hissed.

Then, Lusini-Su buckled to his bony, exposed knees and allowed himself to sob. He did not know if he had the strength to trace the bandits now, and even if he could reach them, he carried nothing but the tattered clothes he was given aboard Horral II – without weapon, armour, or sustenance, he had no chance of defeating them.

Driven by agony, and the fear of otherwise losing everything to the Mistress, Lu had no option other than to run back in the direction of Awreia, where he believed the bandits would return, to sell the stolen goods.

His naked feet were sore and splitting from the sharp rocks and branches he had been relentlessly scaling. His heart was beginning to struggle from the immense strain of his exertion, but he could waste no time to stop, eat, or sleep, for the longer he waited, the less likely he would be to see the criminals again. By next nightfall, Lu had discovered a fresh trail of prints in the mire that clearly implied the traversal of more than one pair of feet, leading on in the direction of Daleia-Dal.

While there was still some light falling between the vines, from both the setting sun and the rising moon, Lu forced himself on and allowed the trail to lead him up and out of the jungle, through a gradual clearing that led towards an open, rock plain. In the distance, he caught a glimpse of a great spitting fire and a pair of shadows. Careful to remain unseen, the Walker kept his distance while studying the distant figures.

Sure enough, there stood a bandit by the fire. She was roasting some sort of fresh meat above it, while barking short and stifled responses to the second human, who appeared to be huddled and whimpering, against a tree.

Lu's orange eyes were struggling now, as he peered through the distant smoke to make out what lay behind. Of the five who had ambushed him several nights prior, four were bandits and the fifth had sulked in the distance. There had been only one survivor of the four bandits - the torch-holder. It was she, Lu assumed, who was now cooking meat above the blaze, her face obscured by a hood. This suggested that the fifth, distanced member of the group was the shape that appeared to crouch and struggle at the base of the tree.

No matter how Lu aimed his sight, he remained unable to clearly see the face of the crouching bandit, but the shudder of their seated silhouette gave the impression that they were tied up, or otherwise bound to the tree. Lu no longer felt threatened by the rogues. He would attack at dawn.

Lu spent the rest of the night awake, in preparation for his attack. He had not even seen whether the bandits still carried the egg or logbook, or any of his belongings at all, but he could come no closer to their camp until he was ready for battle. During the night, he sourced a few displeasing means of food and refreshment, and slowly built his strength somewhat, while planning the assault, resting his body, and cleansing the cuts, bruises, and other damage upon his feet and arms.

In what seemed like no time at all, the sun had started to climb, and Lusini-Su crawled to the opening from which he had occasionally been observing the pair.

Eventually, the dominant bandit stirred and began to rummage in one of her bags for something. Lu slowly discerned that she was preparing some form of morning meal for herself, which was the precise event he had been waiting for.

Without a sound, the Reikan scurried in a curving fashion so as to approach the bandits from behind. Still, he could not see the person who was asleep against the tree, but he could now see that they were indeed bound by a rope that continued around the trunk of the tree.

Lusini-Su glanced down at his feet, taking care to remain silent as he drew near enough for combat. His plan did not require him to be too close, for he was too weak to wrestle an opponent, least of all a skilled, rogue leader. Instead, his method of attack was akin to that of a coward or child, enhanced by a skill he had developed on the Lila.

The Walker clenched his jaw, snorted in a breath of preparation, and then hurled one of two large, angular rocks he had been carrying. Immediately his target collapsed in pain, for his aim had been true; the projectile had smashed straight into her shadowed face.

Now was Lu's chance. He dashed forwards, snatching a dagger from the weapons piled near the fire. On the impact of Lu's high-speed blunder, the rest of the weapons were scattered, one reaching the feet of the man tied to the tree. The Walker turned his eye to see the man and became instantly limp with shock.

The fallen, hooded rogue was already stirring, however. Momentarily, she was back on her feet. With a grunt, she spat out a thickness of blood that may have contained a tooth. Stunned, Lu was helpless as she approached him, and swiped a sword from the dry mud.

Now she lunged at him, still a little dazed by her concussion. Lu jumped to the side involuntarily, narrowly avoiding the blade. Gracelessly, the Walker stumbled back, as the rogue regained her footing. There was a fair distance between them, enough to launch his second stone, but Lu was transfixed upon the man who now freed himself from his bonds.

It was Tatael Ram, the sailor! Lu realised that the young mariner must have hired the bandits to capture, or even kill him after he'd departed Awreia.

The rogue lunged again at Lu, startling him enough to retaliate. With a whip of his dagger, the Walker managed to parry the rogue's blade just enough to save himself. Then, with the rock in his right hand, he swung at her in an attempt to club her unconscious. He missed, and the dark-faced bandit snarled as she kicked him in the thigh, and then as he buckled, she kicked again into his chest.

Lu was now lying, breathless, on his back, as this ruthless huntress prepared to end his life. Then, her footsteps halted, and she exhaled violently. Craning his neck, while remaining on his back, Lusini-Su attempted to make sense of this delay to his next demise, only to witness the bandit collapse as Tatael withdrew a short-sword from her back.

She was dead.

There was a brief silence, as the eyes of the Walker met those of Tatael Ram. Then, Ram fell to his knees and began to weep.

'Please have mercy, immortal one! Have mercy on this foolish sailor! I have already suffered for my crime, for once you dispatched of her associates, she bound, robbed, and starved me! I have slain her, see! We are allies now.'

And instantly Lu was reminded of something that had not occurred to him for the entire duration of his attack. He had come back from the *dead.* Though he had become accustomed to immortality, his return must have stricken Tatael and the bandit with immense fear. He smiled, realising that he could likely have arrived and demanded his belongings, and they would have submitted out of reverence for his immortality. Lu straightened his back and walked dramatically towards the Awreikan sailor.

'What would you have had them do with me, Tatael?'

Tatael began to shake, and stutter, before eventually mustering the ability to reply. 'The King of Light... The King of Light would have spared Awreia in return for an ageless Reikan of old.'

'The King of Light?' Lu smiled grimly in memory of Ram's previous claims of such a ruler. The 'King of Light' must be real, after all.

'And you would have delivered me to this King of Light, had your bandits not murdered me?' Lu asked, patronisingly.

'Yes... but they were given no choice, as they did not expect such a worthy opponent, I assume.' Young Tatael Ram seemed closer to madness with each quaking word that left his dripping lips.

'But the egg, and the writing - I saw value in that!' continued Ram. 'I begged for the leader to allow me to bring them, with your corpse, to the King of Light. But she tied me up, and punished me, for I had been a fool. She robbed you of your clothes, and threw your body into the swamp...'

'Where are they – my belongings?' Lu had become fond of the power tied to this exchange and wished to hurry Tatael on. Tatael scurried towards the largest of three bundles sat beside the tree he was previously bound to, and began to unravel the clothes Lusini-Su was murdered in. 'Throw them to me, Ram!'

The young sailor tossed the folded garments towards the Walker, followed by a pair of familiar sandals, which Lu placed gently to one side. Immediately afterwards, Lu rushed into Tatael with an unexpected tackle, and the youth was knocked senseless against the tree.

Lu set about retying the sailor to the post of lifewood and removed all useful tools from the surrounding area. No more risks were to be taken during this expedition.

By the time Tatael Ram had awoken, Lu was freshly changed, weapon-equipped, and packed for travel. The twilight purple trousers he had been gifted by the Mistress now boasted stains of both mire and blood, and there was a single narrow slit in his tunic of citrus-green from his impalement, but his wondrous cloak of swirling black seemed as otherworldly and un-krajian as before, fastened by the dragon-clutched blue jewel that never dimmed. To the Reikan's relief, his logbook was still wrapped, and completely unharmed. Safely, he tucked it back into his main bag. The egg, however, had changed somewhat since last Lu held it. Snaking about its brilliant blue surface were its veins of gold, which now seemed greater both in their number and the depth of their indenture. A cold, throbbing energy seeped infrequently through these cracks, in a manner so hypnotic that Lu felt an urgent need to re-cover the thing before he became fully absorbed by its mystery. Tatael began to struggle in his bonds, acknowledging his predicament.

'Lu! What have you done? I saved your life!'

The Reikan glanced up at the bound, squirming Awreikan and smiled cruelly, exposing his neglected teeth. 'You are a snake, Tatael, and I would deliver you to Demja myself if I weren't so busy. I will leave you here with nothing but a few foods. You must earn your freedom.' And then Lu fled, pulling behind him a third bag, belonging to the rogues, containing all their stolen belongings.

After a day of lugging the bandits' effects as far out of into the jungle (and out of Tatael's sight) as he could muster, Lu collapsed from exhaustion. With Tatael far behind him, he had no need to continue this act of dominance. It was time to be rid of anything needlessly heavy that would otherwise hinder his progress.

It took two more nights of traversal, beyond the jungle and swamp, and into rocky, yet flat fields swathed in the warm haze of morning, before the Reikan finally realised that he was without his map. His visual memory, it seemed, was still so retentive that he had covered most of his journey by simply picturing the map's image in his mind.

While this greatly satiated his ego, Lu could not help but think of Tatael Ram. The young, yet jaded sailor doubtless knew of Lu's destination, and would follow on to Daleia-Dal, should he seek the Reikan again.

A few other things were troubling the Walker since his recent conflict with the bandits. Despite his confident display of swordsmanship in the dark and the success of his well-thrown projectile, he was now into the deep thicket of a combat-bound adventure with very little true skill with any weapon. When the belongings of the group were laid before him, he had considered brandishing the axe-flail, or perhaps a pair of daggers, or even the huntress' grand, two-handed sword. But he had stopped himself, for he had no knowledge (or aesthetic interest) in any weapon save for Umbra, or for now, the familiarity of his short sword. Vanity had limited him to the sole attraction of single-handed blades, for he likened himself a little too much to the destiny-bound heroes of his favourite childhood fables. In truth, for one who deemed himself the sailor-warrior, or was unwillingly titled 'Krajian-Scythe' by the Mistress, he was at constant risk of failure; in fair engagement, he would not defeat the most basic of swordsmen.

Lu was a day or less from the (apparently bustling) city of wealth and life, and the citadel of scholars within it, and the thought of company was now most of what still spurred the tired steps of his aching, sandalled feet. The friendships he had enjoyed so far in his life had never been plentiful, and yet in his current absence of company, Lu missed Tlephilisse, and Haln, and Demja dearly. He sometimes even wept, mourning the River Sprite. He longed for the unbridled, adventurous radiance of the Lavender Fox. The cool, weightless shape of Umbra still lingered on his thigh, where it had rested for so brief a time. He even missed the deviance of the Sorceress (though he dared not explore that emotion). In the silence of nightfall, he even craved the homely patter of his cloud.

Chapter Five

DALEIA-DAL

During his descent, after clambering over tall, red sandstone and silver rocks, both topped with lively grasses and shrubs, Lu could finally discern the shimmering, distant mass that was Daleia-Dal, amid the damp haze of sunrise. Bringing his hands to his thin, grey face, the Walker wiped away some sweat, and dry skin, before massaging his trembling fingers through his recovering mane of dark, green hair. He was nervous but eager to immerse himself in a new city, full of new people.

By the time that Lusini-Su had reached the outer rim of the frenetic city, he was already infatuated by it. There were traders, stalls, houses, and inns for as far as his eyes could gaze. Merry children, and animals, played happily in the open spaces, while merrier adults laughed and discussed as they worked or walked.

He entered one of many beautiful metal archways about the border of Daleia-Dal, which was followed by a path of varicoloured stone, leading him gently through the first layer of this societal paradise. Colour after colour seemed to leap out at Lu, sometimes from bouquets of dazzling flowers grouped and sold by passing merchants, and sometimes from fabrics worn by the people wandering by. Even the subtler shades that dovetailed in the brickwork of the buildings were rich with intentional artistry. Narrow, clear streams and ponds decorated many of these buildings, occasionally interweaving and creating webs that networked delicately throughout the city. Lu was unsure of how these waters remained clear, or in motion, for he saw no river on the outside of the town, but he refused to question such beauties, for they seemed wholly appropriate in a place of such fast-paced elegance.

Once he was a little further into the streets of Daleia-Dal, Lu began to feel greatly at ease. Not a single Daleian had been phased by his dishevelled, traveller's appearance, or his complexion. They were, themselves, a grand mixture of skin-tones and bone-structures – some of which Lu had not ever seen before. It seemed that, whilst the patchwork town of Rei had slowly coalesced into the more uniform peoples of Awreia, the opposite had occurred for Daleia as it transformed into Daleia-Dal. From what Lu had learned, both from his childhood and then from his month in Awreia, the city of Daleia-Dal began as an inland offshoot of Rei, formed by a handful of scholarly Reikans.

It seemed that during however many life-ages Lu had spent in the Bhia, the tiered, greenstone citadel of Daleia had amassed a serious amount of interest and trade for its renowned libraries. Humans from all over the continent of Taromet, and elsewhere in Kraj had come offering knowledge, and fiction, in return for a place in Daleia's community, until eventually, its tall but humble citadel could not contain another resident, thus the expanded city of Daleia-Dal came to be. Now, Daleia-Dal was a vibrant menagerie of hybridised culture, with the most revered and guarded library, full of elite intellectuals, at its silver-green core. It was this very core that, by the Mistress's insistence, Lu intended to penetrate.

Eventually, the sailor-warrior felt confident enough to approach a few of the merchants and sell some of the mercenary loot he had held onto for this purpose. By nightfall, he had raised more than enough money in the ever-changing currency of the land to afford himself to stay for a week or so in one of the cheaper inns of the city. He intended to save the rest of his earnings for a slight indulgence in the fashions of the land.

For now, however, he had settled into his room with a few writing implements he had purchased, in order to add the events of the last week or so to his ever-expanding narrative. Afterwards, he would go to sleep, to recover his strength.

By the time he had finished writing, however, Lusini-Su had become interested in the murmur of the tavern below his room and decided to venture downstairs in order to socialise with the local drinkers.

Many of the women, men, and wonderfully androgynous intermediates were simply so intoxicated that Lu, ever sober, found it impossible to maintain a dialogue with them. They were a happy and harmless lot, so Lu left them to their laughter and instead approached a more intelligible group of drinkers on the far left of the homely room.

Though styled in the most triumphant and beautiful jewels and clothes, many of these Daleians seemed a little more unsettled than those he had seen earlier in the day. There was a word, or rather a name, on their lips, that Lu had hoped not to hear again, and yet it lingered in conversation for longer than Lu could believe.

'He comes from the far east continent, some say...' muttered a round-faced drinker, who was both old and attractive in their gown of pink and red. 'Though no one knows who he serves.'

Lu shuffled closer on a stool of worn leather and elm, until eventually, he had (albeit awkwardly) joined this group of conspiracists and sceptics.

'My brother lived in Jundra-Dal, not ten day's ride from here...' stressed another of the Daleians, a slim man no older than Tatael, with a luxuriously dark complexion, and long, silver hair. 'But from the rumours I have heard... the seething fire...'

The person in pink and red leaned in and comforted their now-sobbing friend with a delicate, but secure embrace.

'Recently, the King of Light has been less of a rumour and more of an actuality, it seems. Let's remember that our beloved home is of great importance in these lands. This sorcerer is not a conqueror, so I understand. He is a gardener, and this continent is his garden. We will do well not to resist him when, or if, he finally reaches Daleia-Dal...or he will see to us like weeds.'

Eventually, Lu had heard enough of this 'King of Light' and left the tavern without consuming a single drink. From what he had gathered, this sorcerer was no recent visitor to the continent of Taromet but had usually been little more than a scapegoat for certain catastrophes, high-profile murders, and the occasional rumoured town-fire that, more often than not, was nothing more than an illusion to those who witnessed it.

Recently, however, there had been a change to these occurrences. Neighbouring kingdoms and cities of Taromet had sometimes 'vanished' overnight, whether it be to fire, or pure darkness. The King of Light was no longer acting behind a veil of mirages, or rumours.

He was a real, and somewhat encroaching storm, which seemed to be working its way towards the west of Taromet.

As Lusini-Su lay disturbed in bed he found himself dwelling on something that the Mistress had said to him when first he returned from the dead.

'When the Watcher-creators abandoned Mulusthe, the most expansive and tiring of their creations, Majgyn was spared for his talents and prowess, along with a few of his shades, for reasons unknown to me.'

Was the King of Light one of Morl-Majgyn's followers, from the 'old world'? Illusion or not, the King of Light's blaze-summoning sorcery described by the Daleians certainly sounded at least as impressive as any power boasted by the Mistress herself, though Lu knew little of such matters, and could not help but feel distressed by the Mistress's failure to mention such a nearby threat.

The next morning, Lu had near-forgotten about the King of Light, for he was to head into the streets in search of some of the exquisite jewellery worn by the Daleians, which he had coveted since his arrival.

After an incredibly filling breakfast, catered with remarkable ease to his diet, Lu left the inn with the purse full of coins that he had saved for his quest for beauty. While he could have exchanged this wealth for a better short-sword, or some form of defensive clothing or equipment, Lu was both fond of his worn, Awreian blade and considerate of the Mistress's promise to reunite him with Umbra once he had been inducted into the inner citadel. He also felt no urge to redress himself, for the clothes she had gifted him (which he had recovered from the bandits) were incredibly unique and lightweight, to a degree that Lu considered irreplaceable. Again, he was reminded that he would be reunited with his shellsuit in the citadel also.

In what felt like no time at all, Lu had spent half a day (and most of his money) in the markets of Daleia-Dal. He had now twice pierced the lobes of both of his ears, with a pair of additional piercings in the curve atop the left ear. All his punctures were filled with thin metal hoops of gleaming pink-silver, save for the front puncture in both lobes, which he had stylishly reserved for a pair of unique, dangling half-moons that had reminded him of Majgyn's blade. These, too, were crafted from fine pink-silver metal, though the crescents themselves were a richer, sapphire blue, and had individually cost him more than the combined price of the other four hoops.

Upon the middle finger of his right hand, now, was a sleek ring of the same pink-silver metal, engraved with unique (the merchant assured) feather-like detail. Finally, the Reikan had haggled, quite poorly, for a delicately linked, thin necklace to complete his set of silver-pink accessories, thus relinquishing the rest of his loot-traded money. He only had enough left now for essential foods in the market, but was pleased nonetheless; for once, his vanity was somewhat appeased.

It was mid-afternoon by the time the freshly decorated Reikan approached the greenstone gates of the inner Citadel. Standing in casual conversation aside the opening was a pair of tall, well-built Daleian men, dressed in robes that Lu assumed to be the uniform of the scholars who dwelled within. They were unarmed, though their size and obnoxious beauty were enough alone to disarm any who dared pass the gates. Lu approached the scholar-guards, while rummaging for the revised copy of his logbook. While glancing in his bag, he noticed that the egg of blue and gold was again restless – since he had arrived in Daleia-Dal, it had become dormant and less radiant. Now, it had stirred again, and fidgeted in its swathes. Lusini-Su reached in and ran his thumb gently over the shell, whispering an urgent yet motherly hush before covering it again.

'Afternoon, gentlemen!' Lu smiled, in an honest attempt to seem friendly. 'Lu is my name. Am I addressing the guards of this citadel?'

The younger of the two beautiful, green-robed watchmen instantly receded, allowing the slightly older and presumably more experienced man to respond. A pale man of almost greyish-white, who appeared to be about thirty years of age, he had not one hair upon his scalp, cheek or brow. There was a single tattoo on his chest, half covered by his robe, outlining a peculiar bird reminiscent of the giant that had once haunted Lu's dreams.

'Yes, for lack of a better title' he smiled. 'What do you seek?'

He had mistaken the Walker for some sort of visiting traveller, due to Lu's prehistoric accent and complexion.

'I don't seek at all. Rather, I offer my writings in exchange for admission into this citadel. A friend advised me to present my work to you, for its value would likely not be recognised elsewhere.' The Reikan handed his precious, neatly bound papers to the green guard, who had begun to chuckle.

'That is an optimistic sentiment, young Lu! Your friend should have taken more care to tell you; there have been no newly admitted scholars in Daleia for a hundred years!'

The younger guard stifled a brief, voiceless chuckle from behind his partner, while Lu shuffled with worry.

'You will read this, guard?' Lu urged. The guard flicked through the papers in his hand, before handing them to his companion.

'We will read it. Return late evening, to collect your work. We will have found reason to refuse you by then.' They both laughed mockingly now, and Lu found himself retreating with a weight in his heart with which he was unfamiliar.

The afternoon passed so slowly that Lu had begun to wonder if he was suffering from some anxiety-induced madness. His grey, sandalled feet tapped uncontrollably on the floor of the tavern, as he called for yet another mug of a nameless, fire-heated brew. Whatever he drank was the same stuff that ruined those who were now falling about the place, and yet he was, for the most part, unaffected. If anything, he was jealous of his belligerent, flirtatious neighbours, for they seemed to have drowned their worries and cares. It was an inconvenience that this had not worked for him, as he wrestled with a bizarre fear of rejection. He was, after all, fairly proud of his writings. He had no real skill with blades or strength, nor had he the wisdom of his elders. The words he had written were not elegant, rhythmic verses of poetry, but his ability to recall, command, and present his immense memory was truly unique.

Though recently he had doubted himself for his inadequacy when wielding a blade, Lu truly valued his ever-refining skill of bringing his story to life with words. He was proud of it, and had half-convinced himself that there was no better man for the job, in order to relax his nerves.

Evening came, and the Walker was already at the door of the Tavern, bidding farewell to the few casual friends he had made over that afternoon. Before long, he had made his way back to the centre of the city, where the two scholar-guards appeared to be retiring for the night, as two others waited to take over their watch. The older of the original guards was clutching Lu's work and grinned as he saw the Reikan approaching.

'Ah, he returns!' the watchman laughed. 'You have my apologies in regard to your success, Lu. This...' he handed the logbook back to the Walker. '...This is simply a fiction derived from madness. And not a particularly compelling fiction, at that.'

Lu immediately felt his heart sink as he received his papers from the elegant, robed Daleian.

'Then you don't understand it, it seems...' Lu muttered, feeling an intense urge to defend his work. 'These events are true! There is great value in the things I have learned, value that can only be entrusted to the library of your scholars!'

Both of the day-guards now stood in silence, as if waiting for Lu to bring his aggression to a suitable cadence.

'That is what I have come to believe.' Lu concluded once he recognised that social cue.

'I will grant you this, young Awreikan...' began the younger of the guards, as Lu winced at being referred to as an Awreikan.

'Your knowledge of old Rei is remarkably clear and seemingly true. You speak of things that predate our best resources if I am not mistaken.'

Lu rallied and made sure to appear attentive as the soft-spoken youth continued.

'The shadow isle you speak of, 'Bhia', has always been in our hidden charts, so it is impressive – or worrying, rather – that you are aware of it. However, you speak of your younger days in Rei as if it were a time before the Bhia existed. We have no record of this, though I feel inclined to believe you, if only for the way you speak of old Rei itself.'

Slowly, Lu felt his hope return to him. 'I was born in old Rei.' he interrupted, hoping to allure the watchman further into belief.

'So it would seem.' The older, hairless man interjected solemnly. Both Lu and the younger scholar fell silent, allowing the man to continue.

'I apologise, Lusini-Su, for mocking your work. In truth, it is unusual - to the extent that I do not recognise it as a document suitable for our library, and therefore for admission. Truth be told, we had never seen such a work of unbridled, directionless confusion. You both have given me reason to believe that there is value in this text, the very kind of value that we've not seen often enough to recognise. We are the lowliest of scholars, us watchmen of day and night, taught only to deny entrance to those who do not already belong. Perhaps it is time to break the trance, however, and pass your work to our superiors – it may mean more to them than it does to me.'

By now, both Lusini-Su and the younger, more effeminate day-guard were awestruck by the confidence of the older scholar's words. Lu was ensnared by a restored sense of pride, hope, and curiosity, meanwhile, the young guard was clearly enthralled by the prospect of a new admission – an event that he likely believed would not occur in his lifetime.

Lu eventually opened his mouth to respond, but the guard began to speak again. 'I'll present your writings, with the aid of my brother here, to the others who dwell in the citadel. It's likely that they'll want to test your knowledge of old Rei, for a start. If you can manage questions whose answers are known only to those of the great library, then your claims and stories will be accepted as truths.'

The watchman looked Lusini-Su up and down, before nodding goodnight, and gesturing for his brother to leave with him for the night.

'We will reconvene tomorrow evening, Lu!' he shouted, as the pair disappeared behind the silver-green walls of Citadel Daleia.

And so another evening, night, and then day went by, which Lu had spent resting, exercising, and grooming himself. It would take nearly a month to return to the body or hair length he had developed in Awreia, but he would try his best to satiate his desire for visible wellness sooner if possible. Among the rippling and bountiful human activity of Daleia-Dal, Lu found himself strangely un-tempted by the flirtations of people, of wines, and of greed. There were so many overwhelming treasures in one place that the Walker felt no need to immerse or indulge in any one direction – it was enough to simply bask in the company of such things without falling to their vices. As the evening approached, the Reikan made sure to update his writings, and mentally rehearse his memory and knowledge of old Rei in preparation for whatever the scholars might ask him.

Chapter Six

VOANMJUR

'Good evening, Lusini-Su! You are an alarmingly prompt... err...man!'

The hairless, handsome watchman with the bird on his chest had struggled momentarily to place Lu's age, likely due to Lu's written claims of absurd longevity, or the ambiguous essence of life-experience that sometimes haunted the Walker's eyes.

Lu smiled in place of a spoken response, not wanting to delay the news any longer - had the scholars accepted his work?

Sensing the Reikan's impatience, the Watchman laughed and nodded his head affirmatively. 'The Sages of Daleia would like to meet you, after all! Follow my brother, Mimun, into the Citadel – they will see you within the hour.'

The younger, more delicate watchman then emerged from the silver-green stones, with a grin upon his face. 'This way, Lusini-Su! See you later Salun!' The youngster seemed particularly excited at the prospect of Lu's induction – Lu wondered if the Citadel was perhaps somewhat starved of foreign company, and thus in need of a new face.

As Mimun, the younger robed watchman, escorted Lusini-Su into the great, tiered stone citadel of Daleia, the Walker found himself remarkably unbothered by the ancient, exquisite architecture through which they were traversing. Mysterious inscriptions decorated boulder-walls, but all were faded, unreadable and obscured by winding tendrils of parasitic, thin white plants that clung to the stone. The citadel was circular at the base and narrowed little by little on each level, but as Lu entered its inner chambers and greenstone-stairways, he could no longer recall the outline of the citadel's exterior or the bustling joy of the city that surrounded it. There were endless rooms, doors, and pathways that led outside, onto raised gardens of plants that were sometimes mundane, sometimes magnificent, but always unfamiliar.

They had barely halfway scaled the floors of the tall, but compact Citadel when Mimun came to a steady stop outside the entrance of a chamber that seemed no different to the others they had passed.

'I cannot escort you any further, friend Lu. I hope for you to have a successful meeting, though it's a fairly selfish hope; I would much like a new friendship. Goodbye for now!'

And then Lu was alone. Confidently, he entered the room of sages.

The sailor-warrior took a seat at a noticeably new wooden table, to which his seat was attached. After a moment of inspection, he realised that the table, and its connected chairs, were all in fact part of a large living plant that seemed to emerge from the room below them. There was no rough outer layer crumbling away from the peculiar tree, for the table had the appearance of a wood that had been sanded, and treated with oils, and yet a few living flowers of pale yellow, white, and pink blossomed at the ends of certain seat-branches, as if to remind its seated occupants that it was still alive.

Once the Walker had successfully torn his attention from the table, he realised that he was not alone, and was yet to introduce himself.

'Good evening, great scholars of Daleia! My name is Lusini-Su, and I am tremendously grateful for your audience.'

Excluding Lu, there were five individuals seated at the table, and all but one of them were robed and hooded in a cloth that was familiar to the Reikan. Of emerald, lilac, yellow, and azure - these were the robes of the chanting acolytes in his resurrection dream. The fifth was a middle-aged, impatient-looking man in garments of military or possibly even royal importance.

Without a response to Lu's introduction, the formally dressed man prompted the face-hidden four to speak. 'Let us be done with this, ask him your questions. I have other things to oversee.'

A woman in emerald bowed her head lightly. 'Very well.'

She placed Lu's logbook on the table. 'This was an interesting, if not concerning read, young Awreikan. We inhabit the only library in the known world that possesses these histories. Such records are the key to this citadel's wealth and are kept well-guarded for the purpose of power, and refinement until our knowledge is complete enough to catalogue and distribute certain histories in exchange for wealth. It is our trade, here in Daleia-Dal.'

Lu opened his mouth to respond, but the emerald sage raised her hand and continued to speak.

'Our records of old Rei are not yet complete, and yet here in your fanciful narratives of swords and sorcery, you discussed the sea town's youngest moments as if you had witnessed them first-hand. You are either a thief or a dreamer with a coincidental imagination. The other explanation, in which you claim to be an ancient Reikan, is an impossibility that I refuse to believe.'

Lu frowned, as a stinging headache accompanied the stern words of the emerald sage. If he answered her questions correctly, she would think him a thief, but if he failed to respond, he would be dismissed as a liar.

Nonetheless, the Walker surrendered his honest knowledge to the group of sages, answering every question about the era of his youth to the best of his memory, and even occasionally correcting the sages' own understanding of old Rei. The militant, royally dressed man did not speak another word, but his impatience had begun to seep into the minds of those who surrounded him, infecting the tempo of the discussion.

It was becoming difficult for Lusini-Su to respond at this pace without mentioning his mission or Mistress, let alone the name of the woman he was here to meet. He had, at first, wondered if Fym was the emerald sage who interrogated him, but he soon banished these thoughts; the emerald sage had clearly become irritated by the Walker - he doubted that the Mistress would select such an impatient person to be her closest, and greatest apprentice.

It was the very moment that Lu began to carefully explain why he wished to join the scholars of the citadel when the sage in azure stood upright and said, 'Enough. We've heard enough of your half-learned history, spy, and we have no need to endure this conversation for a moment longer. Salun! Escort this man to the oil-pit and discover the names of his masters. Lord Beol and I have other matters to discuss before he leaves, and I will not allow this thief to steal another hour of our time.'

Oil-pit? Lu was faced with a realisation that prompted a union of acute stress and fear. For the whole time that they had been gathered, the lilac sage (who had done nothing but whisper into the ear of the yellow sage) had been the very man who originally granted him the opportunity of this meeting. Was Mimun, with whom Lu had fallen quickly into friendship, aware of his brother's place among the sages? Was it truly the same brother who, without any reluctance, would now escort Lu to a place of (by Lu's understanding) torture? Regardless of his sprite-given ability to return to life, Lusini-Su was certain that he would still feel every moment of pain from whatever torture could be derived from this 'oil-pit'. He stiffened up in surrender to his terror.

Salun unveiled his perfect, hairless face from beneath the lilac hood, and grappled Lu's malnourished torso, before flinging the Reikan over one of his great shoulders. Lu could not muster a struggle, as the giant man carried him out of the door, and towards the stairway. Soon, they were ascending, but Salun's grip on the Reikan had lessened, until eventually, the sage let go of Lu all together, allowing him onto his feet.

Lu glared up at Salun, his orange eyes demanding an explanation.

'Lord Beol must be gone by now' whispered Salun. 'There is no need for any more dishonesty.'

Lu's body continued to automatically trudge up the stairs of the citadel, but his mind was hard at work. What could that mean? Lord Beol certainly seemed outlandish in the company of the sages.

'The fenland ruler thinks that he has deceived us. But we were prepared for this form of treachery. He was not always so austere, was Lord Beol, but he comes to us now as a puppet, gathering intelligence to save his land from the King of Light. By condemning you to execution in his presence, we have yet again escaped the suspicions of the King of Light's men. We even decidedly referred to you as a spy, in order to subtly alert Beol to the punishment that becomes of spies here in Daleia.'

Lu felt a great relief. 'You don't think I'm a spy?'

'Oh my dear Lusini-Su, we believe everything you've said. In fact, we know it to be true. We needed to hear it from your lips so to ensure that you weren't an interceptor, like our friend Beol. Once you spoke freely of Rei, we knew you to be the Lusini-Su that we were told to expect.'

Lu stopped walking, for he had reached the top of the stairs. 'You were expecting me?'

Salun grinned and gestured towards a blood-red door unlike any that Lu had seen so far in the citadel.

The hairless sage waited for the Walker to proceed, before following on into the room that lay beyond the sanguine entrance. The entire chamber appeared to be a near-endless hall, contained by walls of black marble, patterned with curious flecks and vein-like strands of sapphire blue. There was nothing in this elongated midnight – no windows, or furniture, or plants, or even people. The light that filled it came exclusively from the throbbing blue on the walls, and yet the room seemed illuminated and without shadow. Once Lusini-Su had entered, however, he was immobilised by wonder, and Salun continued ahead.

'In order to trust you, and expose to you our best-kept secrets, we must be thorough in our initiation. Come, there is much to do.'

Lu frowned involuntarily at the sage's keenness to continue on into this endless corridor.

'Come to where? There is nothing, Salun!'

Still, the Walker plodded on. His stomach was now unsettled, though it could not have been hunger that stirred there, for he had eaten not long before his arrival. Then, after a while longer of scuffling through the blue-black illusion, his destination became rapidly apparent.

'I would like to introduce you, friend Reikan, to Voanmjur!'

Enough bile had risen in the Walker's throat to necessitate a frantic gulp in order to prevent vomiting. Lu's stomach, and brain were now afflicted by dreadful nausea, though he now understood why.

Ahead, the destination 'Voanmjur', as Salun had called it, was not behaving like that of an ordinary horizon. Instead, what Lusini-Su saw ahead was a bird's eye view of the most lurid and fluorescent landscape that he had ever witnessed. It was as if, in his step-by-step approach, he was descending upon this adjacently eschewed land that awaited him.

'Sal...Salun! What will be the manner of our arrival? Do we approach a nearness whereby a new gravity will take effect, pulling us face-first into the ground? Or is this Voanmjur truly the plane of awkward obliqueness that it appears to be? I can't–'

Salun was gone. Lu turned his head to search for his missing companion, but the endless halls of marble that stretched behind him were seemingly vacant for as far as his orange eyes could see. He had no choice but to progress further towards the sideways land of Voanmjur that neared on the horizon.

Much to the Walker's relief, there was no moment of dramatic gravitational realignment as he arrived at the wall of bewitched ground before him. Instead, during his last moments of traversal, his steps appeared to slowly curve through the air, as if he walked up a hill. Soon, his walking posture had rotated by the full magnitude of the horizontal displacement that had separated his path from his destination, and his feet eventually greeted the land as if they had never left it. Lusini-Su was standing upright, in the brightly coloured, yet hazy wilderness of 'Voanmjur', which was populated solely by alien plants of bizarre luminescence.

The Walker had hardly regained his balance in this dream-like landscape when he noticed the presence of a familiar company. Not five steps ahead, yet barely visible through the swathes of the dusk-like haze, stood the Lavender Fox. Lu smiled, and almost bowed at his companion, before attempting to approach the beast as if to stroke its soft, weightless mane.

The Fox yipped, before recoiling drastically. Startled, the Walker reciprocated the retreat in the opposite direction, keeping both eyes fixed on the unusual behaviour of the fox.

His eyes were struggling to focus, however, for he was seeing duplicates, shadows, and reflections of the Lavender Fox, and could no longer ascertain which was the original.

Then, the illusion was both shattered and actualised, and Lu realised that he did not hallucinate – these familiar creatures were now all separate entities. In all directions, and at different speeds, the countless fox-replications each dispersed into the clouded, unseeable mystique of this plane, known only to the Walker as 'Voanmjur'.

Lusini-Su did not require Salun, his missing guide, to explain the task at hand. The puzzle was blatant – he must identify the true Lavender Fox, though he was unsure of how. This mattered very little to Lu, however, for first he needed to become comfortable with the nature of his current location and felt a strong urge to test the agility of his omnipresent target. With a blinding scurry, Lu darted into the way of a huddle of foxes, and all burst into nothing but a cool mist upon the impact of his attempted grapple.

And such was the case for every shadow and shimmer of the Lavender Fox that Lu tried to touch in Voanmjur. Running between glittering pools of perfect translucence, and ferns of rich red, brown, and glowing green, the Walker had near exhausted himself within half of an hour since he had arrived. Furthermore, the Fox now seemed to torment him with an occasional yip or bark, though these otherwise friendly vocalisations were only seen as a taunt due to Lu's ever-self-consciousness inability to solve the mystery he had been presented with. He had no liking for this task at all.

'The foxes move beyond any speed my body can grant me...' Lu panted to himself. 'This is a puzzle, not a race... this is a puzzle.'

He glanced again towards a pair of foxes that murmured and groomed impatiently to his right. Both foxes set a light shadow on the ground, and both foxes appeared to possess enough weight to flatten the plants beneath them. The sailor-warrior allowed his eyes to linger, before darting them elsewhere in search for another theory.

'This is a puzzle...'

Lu turned his head back to approach the foxes he had been analysing. There was a new idea his head, though it was a little too predictable for him to have much faith in it.

Surrounding the foxes was a series of pools, which seemed to freckle the entire realm of Voanmjur. Did the ethereal sister-foxes each have a reflection in these pools? Was that the answer to the riddle?

Lusini-Su knew that he could only approach the pools to certain proximities before incurring the inevitable scattering of the currently placid Lavender Foxes.

Slowly, he edged towards the pair with his eyes fixed exclusively on whatever shape was being cast into the shallow water ahead.

There was something, Lu observed, flickering in those pools. As he drew nearer, his heart began to sink for he had clearly wasted time pursuing yet another false theory – there was clearly a reflection of a fox in every pool before him.

The Walker prepared to dash out again at the two foxes ahead, for he had become near enough to at least make use of his approach; there was no point in thinking about reflections any longer.

As he readied himself for the launch, the reflected fox in the pools began to move. Startled, Lu halted his body and recommenced his gaze into the rippling shallows. The fox in the water was not a reflection of either fox sitting on the other side. Lu focussed his ember-toned eyes with disbelief, as the reflection of the Lavender Fox appeared to walk from puddle to puddle, as if each were merely a window in a wall.

Without hesitation, Lu recklessly plunged his hand into the closest puddle (that the fox had not yet reached), only to be rewarded with the most excruciating agony as his grey flesh smashed into a particularly sharp rock below the surface. He yelped in pain and the two foxes in front of him, the fox in the water-window, and a few others that had accumulated nearby all scattered into the mist, and Lu was left alone.

'Curses!' Lu rose to his feet and kicked the rock that had injured him. The dense palm on the side of the thumb of his left hand had been punctured and wounded deeply by the sharpest point of the debris. His blood-covered fingers had become numb, as every sensation between wrist and fingertip had been overridden by throbbing agony. It would heal, but for now, his hand was of no use. 'Dezon!' he hissed, which was a new favourite curse word that he had learned from the drunks of Daleia-Dal. He assumed it was derived from the Reian equivalent, 'Dez'.

For another half an hour, the Walker plodded through the warped and bewitched mystique of Voanmjur, contemplating the way by which he might reach the true Lavender Fox that lay behind the pools. His stomach had become incredibly unsettled again, though this time he knew that it truly was hunger, and not some side effect of the magic that had brought him here. The feelings of hunger and thirst were a welcome distraction from the pulsing pain in his left hand, which had only become more severe as Lu exerted himself in traversing the pool-scape.

For all his discomfort, however, Lu had a suspicion that the hardest part of the puzzle was over, for his observation of the pool-confined fox was a matter of nothing but luck; he could have wandered for days before noticing any inconsistencies in the reflections of the duplicates.

It must be, he considered, that the key to seeking the true Lavender Fox was simply to locate any of its mirages and wait for their reflections to develop behaviour of their own. This time, he would reach correctly.

Soon enough, the Reikan reached a particularly colourful patch of plant-life, where known and unknown flora had become overgrown and interwoven, resembling serpents of red and gold, entangled in polygamous courtship. Here was a gathering of three shimmers of the Lavender Fox, accompanied by sufficient pools and puddles for the possible appearance of a reflected fourth fox.

The Walker waited for a moment, while he decided from which direction to approach. So far, the foxes seemed to flee when Lu was about four strides away. While there were many pools around them, he required an angle whereby the place of his four-stride separation between him and the foxes was nearby to the larger and more optimal waters, so to get a clearer glimpse of his target.

Once Lusini-Su had decided on a waiting spot, he made his way towards the huddle with such attention to his silent steps that it reminded him of the night that he assassinated Tlephilisse. He shuddered, and lost concentration, but nothing changed. He was in place, and the foxes remained grouped.

And Lu watched the pool-reflection of the huddled foxes converge, as predicted, into a single beast which then began to travel from puddle to puddle until the sentient reflection drew near to the pool beside him. Lu hesitated. He had planned to wait until the Lavender Fox approached him, before reaching into the pool that the fox was situated in, to grasp it. But now, with the mirror creature close beside him, through a veil of rippling, shallow water, Lu felt no need to reach out to the creature and instead followed a new instinct to simply sit and wait for this submerged, otherworldly Fox to come to him.

His instinct was right. The reflection of Lavender Fox glanced up, directly into the Walker's orange eyes, and then leapt diagonally, propelled by its tail, until the beast exploded from the shallow water, restored to its original shape, size, and mass. It landed with a thud, and grunted abruptly, which appeared to banish the illusory foxes in an instant. This was undoubtedly the true Lavender Fox.

The Lavender Fox approached Lu and nuzzled his shoulder with its great soft head. Upon completing what he believed to be his task, Lu's senses returned to him immediately and he clutched his left hand with agony. Quickly, he ran and dipped it into a pool, and cleansed it of the mud and dried blood that had already gathered in his wound. The water stung, but his injury needed cleaning, for he dared not risk an infection on his fighting hand. A dominant, sharp, and somewhat familiar voice began to chuckle from above.

'Cut it off and spare yourself the pain.'

The Walker hurled a glance into the skyward chasm that encapsulated the realm of Voanmjur. There, in the not too distant reaches, sideways as was the nature of Lu's descent into the realm, stood a proud rogue.

It was she who led the bandits of the mire, and who was slain by Tatael Ram in an act of cowardly repentance. The Reikan shuddered – was immortality far less rare than he believed it to be? And despite her previously apparent skill in combat, it seemed farfetched to Lu that this rogue had single-handedly penetrated the guarded walls of the citadel.

'How did you find me, rogue-leader of Awreia? Who do you serve?'

'Cut off your fighting hand.' She retorted, interrupting the Walker's question. Lu's eyes fluttered between his throbbing wound and the rogue above him.

'Who are you?'

'Cut off your fighting hand!' the Bandit urged. She was gripping something in her hand, but she was too distant, and too veiled by fog, for Lu to get a clear view. Then, a choked scream descended upon the land of Voanmjur, disturbing both the Lavender Fox and the pools surrounding it.

'NO! DON'T-' but the voice of Salun choked and spluttered into submission, for it was his throat in the hand of the Rogue.

The Lavender Fox had split itself into its many shimmering illusions, and all were rife with erratic fear. The Walker had hoped to mount the beast, ride to freedom, and possibly even attack the deathless rogue on his ascent. Instead, he was trapped in the alien landscape of Voanmjur with nothing to do other than converse with the unusual woman above him.

'Would the King of Light truly want for you to deliver a handless Reikan to him?' scoffed Lusini-Su at his captor. 'Let us be done with this. You are too skilled an opponent for me to defeat in battle, Rogue, especially with this bleeding hand of mine. Take me to your King of Light, and collect your bounty... I'll allow no more of this torment, I have no time for it.'

And for the first time since Lu's arrival in Voanmjur, he could feel the egg of blue and gold shifting with disturbance in its pouch. He had almost forgotten about the weightless thing and had only set the pouch aside occasionally, when he had dashed for the mirages of the Lavender Fox. Was the egg hatching? Lu desperately hoped that it would not hatch at this moment, for he had no time to investigate its behaviour.

The deathless rogue was yet to respond to Lu's comments regarding the King of Light, but as Lu glanced back up away from his pouch, he could see his horizontal adversary performing some sort of gesture through the mist.

A dagger, half the length of Lu's forearm, began to sizzle noisily into existence upon the ground beneath the Walker, in one of the eerie pools. Steam was rising off the blade as its apparent heat combatted the water it was submerged in. Lu shook his head in frustration. What form of torture was this?

And predictably, the rogue spoke once more. 'Cut off your wounded fighting hand, and I will allow Salun – and his brother – to live.'

'Mimun...' muttered the Walker in dismay. His mind now conjured up scenes of the young and kind watchman, and how they had silently agreed to be friends, once Lu had been initiated.

With a sigh, Lusini-Su dropped to his knees and fished the dagger from the pool. It was an ugly blade, with exaggerated crossguards at both ends of its handle. There was a small, pearl insignia on the handle, and a warped collection of runes upon the blade, which looked more like random scarring than an intentional inscription.

'The dagger will find its way through bone in a single stroke...' the bandit smiled.

Around him, the many copies of the Lavender Fox were yelping and screeching with agitation, but despite their clear distress, not one of the foxes dared challenge this bandit or her demands. Not one of the foxes seemed inclined to intervene, as Lu rose to his feet, dagger in hand.

It seemed peculiar, thought Lu, that despite once fighting a small legion of wyrms side by side with the beast, the Lavender Fox had no visible interest in protecting him on this occasion.

As Lu prepared himself to bring the blade to his weeping flesh, a slight glimmer of optimism rippled in a nearby pool. The sole, converged reflection of the Lavender Fox was calm, if not encouraging, as it stared up at Lusini-Su. As before, the truth was to be found here in the puddles of Voanmjur - not in the antics of the multitude of false foxes that perilously writhed nearby. Comforted by the possibilities that this suggested, Lu hacked at his injured left hand, instantly severing it from his arm.

The Reikan screamed in total excruciation. Though the rune-knife had somehow lopped off his hand without a problem, he had half expected this to be a painless illusion. The pool-dwelling Lavender Fox had instilled Lu with enough confidence to go through with this act of madness, as if it was part of the riddle. Instead, the Walker had collapsed onto the ground as blood streamed from his wrist. Lu's eyes were squeezed tightly shut, but as the deluge of agony travelled up his arm, he found himself concentrating on the sound of approaching footsteps. The rogue had descended into Voanmjur, and he would be too helpless to resist her.

Then, the sailor-warrior felt the softness of lips pressing against his forehead, planting a prolonged and soothing kiss. He flinched in fear and pain, before a serene calm flooded his body, and his pain was relieved. The source of his alleviation was the kiss, and soon he was numb to all but the feeling of the lips as they finally broke contact with his skin. Eventually, Lu opened his eyes, only to be confronted with a sight unlike any he had ever witnessed before.

The deathless bandit's hood was finally down, and Lu was now staring in beguilement at the face that lay beneath it. Gazing back was a pair of wide, hibiscus-red eyes, framed by flesh of midnight blue that was streaked with other blues, of both lighter and darker shades. Her head was round and her cheekbones were prominent, and her hair appeared at first to be shaven, until Lu noticed the meticulously short layer of tight, bone-white curls that clung shallowly to their roots.

The dark-blue rogue's lips were stained red with blood, for her mouth was pressed against her right hand, which was also covered in blood. Lu glanced at his missing hand. It was his blood, now dripping from her peculiar grin.

'I commend you, Lusini-Su, for passing this test. We see now that you are not an imposter-double, summoned by the King of Light, nor are you acting under some bewitched agency that is not your own...' She smiled pensively, as if to reminisce events where those alternatives had already occurred.

Lu recoiled in horror, as the rogue swallowed whatever blood remained in her throat, before standing up and offering him her hand. Unlike her bleak, dark attire from their previous encounters, she was now robed in a flowing garment of yellow and blue patches, woven together unlike anything Lu had ever seen. Eventually, the Walker accepted the rogue's bloody hand that, to his surprise, pulled him to his feet as if he weighed nothing at all. Their previous fight had not even hinted at such strength.

'I apologise for the part I played in your previous demise, Lu! Once I had heard word of Tatael's desire to have you brought to the King of Light, I made sure to involve myself. That way, I could be sure that the document and egg you carried would remain safe and undelivered to their masters, regardless of the success of Tatael's scheme. From what I understood at the time, the real Lusini-Su would return to life, whereas an imposter would be expendable, so I did not hesitate to let you die. I am grateful you have returned, of course.'

Any realisations (and therefore questions) that had sprung to Lu's mind were immediately answered quite effectively by her words. This was not a rogue or an assassin that stood before him. In a wash of emotions, the Reikan managed only one word of frail utterance.

'Fym...' He whimpered, now recognising the power of the individual that stood before him, whose mouth was red with his blood.

She smiled slightly. 'Fym Sallow. I am the one that you seek.'

The Lavender Fox, who had silently re-emerged from the rippling illusions of the pools, approached the Walker quietly from behind. Then, with a lurch, it grasped Lu firmly by the leg and raced up towards the sky, before flinging the Reikan diagonally into the whirling blue corridor that had led him to Voanmjur. The pouch containing the egg and all of Lu's writing remained upon the ground, beside the feet of the mysterious 'Fym', and the sight of the Witch-Rogue reaching for his belongings was the last thing Lu saw before he was no longer within Voanmjur, the self-contained realm of pools and plants.

Lu shot to his feet and investigated a buzzing sensation that murmured upon the stump of his missing left hand. The wound was glowing a gentle pear green, and some feeling had returned to his arm, but still, he was handless. Was this damage permanent? Would the elusive Fym grant it back soon? Lu smiled wryly. If nothing else, he would be able to kill himself and restore his body to a previous time in order to regain his missing hand. Out of curiosity, he tried to move his missing fingers, only to be surprised at how easy it was to do so. In fact, when he closed his eyes tight shut and continued to focus on those movements, his fingers did not feel like they were gone at all.

The Walker's trance was broken by the sound of an abrupt, forced cough. Lu turned to his right, to see Salun standing tall beside him.

'You are still under the glamour of the most powerful human Azdinist in history. Do not mourn your hand - it will return after your initiation...'

Chapter Seven

DEN OF DAWNS

Lu shivered uncontrollably as a momentary breath of wind ambushed his legs and torso. His eyes darted downwards, to survey the air that bothered him, only to find that he was now dressed in tattered garments that would commonly be attributed to homelessness.

'Surpass this illusion and find us in the Dawn' Salun commanded. 'Then and there, your initiation will be complete.' And then he was swallowed by a splash of violent pink until nothing remained in the place he had stood.

Confused, but not at all shocked by the nature of Salun's exit, Lu then found himself drawn towards a glassless window at the end of the veined-blue corridor. By the time he had seemingly approached the window, he stood again in the citadel of Daleia, and there was no sign of the endless blue-black marble hall that had led him both to and from Voanmjur. The Walker was distracted, however, by what he could see outside of the opening in the wall of the greenstone citadel.

It was the city of Daleia-Dal, or instead, the city of Daleia-Dal had it been painted with the murk and gloom of a thousand nights. The streets were empty, and the buildings were derelict. The miserable, shadow tentacles of an unknown sickness seeped between every crack, gap, and orifice in the abandoned city. There was no sound, save for a ghostly hiss rising from the ground. Lu steepened his gaze down towards the land directly below his window and then stumbled back in fear.

The walls of the Citadel were teeming with faceless, shapeless ghouls. Eerily, they floated up to greet the Reikan at the window of the tower, at a speed that was slow enough to seem menacing, but consistent enough for the Walker to hurriedly pull away and seek an escape.

He stumbled down the stairs of stone, noticing that the citadel itself had also become a decrepit husk of its former self, offering no living plants or art, other than a few crumbling statues here and there. Eventually, Lu reached the entrance of the citadel, where speedily he managed to slip beneath the rising phantoms that now hovered nearby the highest rooms of the haggard building. With the nocturne ruins of Daleia-Dal ahead of him, Lu pondered every possible answer to Salun's riddle.

'Surpass this illusion, and find us in the Dawn', the watchman had said. No matter how the sorcery worked, its 'illusion' was apparent enough, thought the Reikan. After pacing a little further into the darkness, Lu smiled. A fool would perhaps consider a more literal solution to the words of the handsome watchman, and simply wait the night until dawn. Unfortunately, Lu's ears had detected a peculiar emphasis on the way Salun recited the word 'Dawn', leaving the Walker with no choice but to pursue an alternative meaning. With a sigh, the tired Reikan continued into the shadows of the city, in search for the Dawn.

With a thud, and then a crack, Lu ransacked yet another building in the hollow city. He was starving, and near broken by thirst. Had it been hours? Or days? He was not sure. He had spent a great deal of time avoiding the drifting ghouls, or 'sleep-bringers', as he had begun to call them. Whenever the mysterious shapes drew near, Lu found his body near-overwhelmed by drowsiness, so he avoided them in fear of what may occur during the slumber that they wielded. There was a cyclical nature to the darkness upon Daleia-Dal, as if night rolled into night, with no dawn or day to break the blackness. The Walker had long since given up his hunt for Salun or the enigmatic 'Fym'. Now, he was simply trying to alleviate his boredom and suffering by examining the goods that each abandoned house had to offer. There was no food, or life to be seen. The perimeter of the city was barely conspicuous beneath the midnight shroud, so Lu dared not venture towards or outside its walls, in the fear that those amorphous, intermittently patrolling demons would also be lurking elsewhere in the unseeable beyond.

Lu's eyes began to roll in his head, as his body slowly succumbed to the weakness of hunger and thirst. He had been avoiding sleep to the best of his ability, in order to remain alert enough to escape the shadowed fiends that searched for him. Now, however, he had no choice. In the empty room he had only just broken into, the Walker collapsed. As his eyes flickered open and closed, he caught glimpses of sleep-bringers that had followed him in. As his consciousness faded, and the darkness surrounded him, the Reikan wondered why he was in the ruins to begin with.

~

'Can someone bring his drink forward! He's beginning to rouse.'

'He didn't fare too badly, at least compared to the rest of our initiations!'

'Step back, give him some space. He's twitching.'

Lusini-Su was awake, though his eyes were still shut. He could hear voices nearby. Some were familiar, but most he had never heard before. He clenched his torso as he attempted to lift his body, but he was incredibly weak, and his body felt abnormally stiff. Eventually, and with a great deal of discomfort, he managed to open his eyes slowly.

Sunlight, of the haziest oranges and pinks, kissed everything it touched so passionately that Lu's eyes struggled to make out a single shape or face for some time after waking.

While his eyesight was still adjusting to the cascades of dawn, something that felt like a glass chalice pressed against his shaking lips.

'Drink, now, Lusini-Su. You need this more than you know.' Spoke the voice of Fym Sallow, the sometimes rogue and sometimes sorcerer.

Lu opened his mouth, and allowed the cool, familiarly sweet contents of the chalice to fill his throat, before pulling away to try and swallow it. Strangely, his body appeared to have forgotten how to do so. To his embarrassment, he spent a few moments having to relearn how to drink - all the while his was vision returning, illuminating the many faces that were watching this awkward process.

As he sipped at the glass chalice, his eyes scanned his immediate surroundings. Directly in front of him was the handsome, striking face of the Azdinist, Fym Sallow, who watched Lu with patient, red eyes as he slowly looked around. Beside her was the Lavender Fox, who also seemed cheerfully content in watching the Reikan return to his senses, occasionally nuzzling Fym fondly.

Salun, and his joyful brother Mimun, were also close by, but they were the last faces that Lu recognised. He was completely surrounded by strangers, all dressed in the robes he had seen both in his dreams and in his initial meeting. When he had finished looking around him, he took another shallow sip and glanced down at his flesh, which caused him to spit out his drink in shock.

Swathed loosely in the tattered clothes that he had been wearing in the ruins of Daleia-Dal, his body was little more than skin and bone – far worse than the physique he returned to whenever he was reborn on the Lila. How long had he slept? His body had clearly been washed and seen to, however, his frame was more fragile than ever before.

Fym noticed his expression of alarm. 'Drink, Lusini-Su' she advised.

So he gulped down the remainder of the familiar-tasting liquid, and sure enough, his strength and appearance had seamlessly returned to normal by the time he was finished.

Wiping the spill from his face, Lu looked up at the Azdinist with a face that begged for endless answers.

Fym smiled a little. 'After rereading your accounts, I thought I'd try to appeal to your preferences by mimicking the flavours of your favourite concoctions of buacoctin and umello.'

Lu nodded, now understanding the familiarity of the flavour. 'What had happened to me? My body? Why did

I tread that anguished, shadow land?' He rubbed his eyes with his grey hands. 'What were those...creatures?'

A stifled chuckle from the crowd reminded Lu that this conversation was being spectated.

'Welcome to the Den of Dawns, Lusini-Su.'

Lu's eyes reached up again for the colour that fell from above, feasting on the beauty of the orange and the pink. 'What does that mean? This is not Daleia-Dal...'

'Indeed. First, you needed to experience the most basic sensations of a cuthrealm. That is why your trust in the Lavender Fox was tested in Voanmjur.'

Lu nodded, to show that he was listening. He had, in fact, temporarily forgotten about Voanmjur - those events seemed like a life-age ago.

'You were then sent to the cuthrealm of night - of *every* night. The cuthrealm of night suffers harshly at the hands of time, and so do all who dwell within it. Those who have already lived the endless dark cannot fully return so, in the form of shades, I and a few others came to bring you sleep, so that you would experience less pain in the process.'

'Pain?'

'The Den of Dawns is a cuthrealm forged from an endless array of sunrises, each stolen from the ends of separate nights. To visit a place of endless dawns, one must have first lived through endless nights. As Azdinists, it is our greatest protection, against Majgyn and his followers. Only a chosen few may enter.'

The Lavender Fox appeared to purr proudly at this notion, as if to remind Lu that it was one of the chosen few.

'Endless nights!' Lu wasn't sure whether to smile or to be concerned by the claims of the Azdinist. 'How long have I been asleep?'

Again, the crowd blurted out a short laugh at the Walker's outburst. Fym, who was also smiling, put a long hand on Lu's shoulder.

'Your body is eight days starved. As I have said before...time is a frantic thing in the cuthrealm of night. While those eight days passed normally for your body and for Daleia-Dal, an impossible length of time had passed in the place that you lay.'

'And what of this place – how did time pass here?' Lu probed, without fully believing (or understanding) the words of this midnight human sorceress.

'The same amount as Kraj, eight.'

Lu sighed and nodded his head wearily at the Azdinist. 'I see. I gather that these lengths of time are intentional? So that the process of initiation is swift in the cuthrealm of night, and so that time here in the Den of Dawns allows for easier intercourse with the time of the outside world?'

Fym nodded. 'You are correct. Spend a year in the Den of Dawns, and a year shall pass in the outside world. I've been able, when necessary, to sever a piece of the Den of Dawns and create a smaller cuthrealm in which you can spend weeks, only to return on the same day you departed. It costs a great deal of my power but has proved exceptionally useful when I've needed to practise skills or learn histories with a limited amount of time.'

'And your body wouldn't age a day?'

'Precisely' Fym smiled.

There was a silence while Lu mulled over the sheer absurdity of Fym's claims before a member of the crowd began to make her way over to the pair. She was carrying a few indistinct bags on her shoulders and pulled something larger on a wooden cart behind her, and Lu began to smile uncontrollably when he recognised some of the shapes of her burden.

The hooded woman handed the items into the strong, open arms of the high Azdinist, Fym Sallow, who then one by one returned them to their rightful carrier.

'I believe it has been months since you have dressed in your warsuit, Lusini-Su.'

And surely enough, sat in the carriage behind Fym was every piece of Lu's beloved shellsuit, gifted to him by the Mistress. As he approached the carriage and delicately caressed the alien craftsmanship of the intertwined shells, he wondered if he would be seeing the Mistress again soon.

Once the Walker had finished inspecting the immaculacy of his shellsuit, he returned his gaze to Fym, who handed him back the items he had left in Voanmjur.

'It has been a delight to guard this egg - if even only briefly, and read your papers, but now I must return these things to you. It is essential that you are the one to care for this egg; it will only hatch in the presence of an ancient such as yourself. Even I am not old enough to fulfil such a role.'

Fym's words instilled a slight importance in the sailor-warrior that he had not felt in a while. He was chosen by his Mistress for many reasons, his age being a considerable factor. Momentarily, he was reminded of the unspent 'azdin' that had been building within him, which was now multiplying faster than ever, thanks to the gift of the Bhia Goddess.

Lu readied his lips to ask Fym Sallow about her dealings with the Mistress, but before he could speak, the Azdinist lifted a familiar scabbard before the Walker, and he forgot all that he was going to say.

'It is again time for this blade to return to its destiny-bound owner. For hundreds of years, I, alongside countless acolytes, spent great effort on seeking the many palun shards of the old world that were scattered here on Kraj. This blade, named by that which completes it, has been under construction since I first learned my role.'

After handing Lu the scabbard, Fym looked fondly into the Reikan's face.

'I look at you, and I know you, Lusini-Su. I look at you and I see myself - all the suppressed fear and confusion, and the desire to be left alone. To be-'

'Ah but then you are placing a little *too much* of yourself into me, Fym!' Lu blurted impulsively. 'I am afraid sometimes, yes, and I do often suffer from confusion – the events that link us are unusual, of course! But I share no desire to be left unbothered by the wonders of fate. I am excited to be part of this adventure. I was trapped for far too long without a purpose or a name.'

Fym smiled. 'For now. You are older than me, Lusini-Su, but I began my journey when I was only young, whereas yours has only just started to unfold. It sometimes seems as though our roles should have been swapped. I would have chosen your lifetime of solitude, and you would have adored my centuries of adventure. Some of them, at least.'

Lu nodded, in faint agreement. He wasn't really sure of the nature of Fym's adventures, but he felt inclined to agree that he would have preferred them to the monotonous rot of the Bhia. And then he pulled Umbra from its sheath, and his love for the glassblade returned immediately to his heart.

'I have not known this object for long, Fym. But I thank you for creating it, for it completes me in a way that no weapon ever could – I am no great swordsman, and yet with Umbra in my left hand, I feel as though I am the greatest.'

'I know the feeling that you describe. Meet Lustre!'

Fym raised a hand to the sky, and from clean air, she unsheathed a blade unlike any Lu had ever seen. Light, rivalling the sun itself, poured endlessly from every inch of the immense weapon, to the point where Lu could barely make out the shape of the blade itself. It was impossible to tell where the steel ended, and its radiance continued. Unlike Umbra, Lustre appeared to be a less curved, much straighter and more direct sword. Lu almost felt a sting of jealousy. Lustre emitted a similar otherworldly aura to Umbra.

'You will learn of Lustre's importance soon, and even wield it yourself. Tonight, however, we have another matter to discuss.'

'Majgyn? Or the King of Light.' Lu placed the sheathed glassblade to one side and ran his fingers through the thick of his dusk green locks. His hair felt soft and healthy – it must have been washed while he was unconscious. He smiled, for it seemed comical that a swordsman as poor as him could be so privileged as to encounter and use such exquisite blades.

Fym almost mirrored the Walker, as she massaged her short-shaven, white-haired scalp with long, tattooed fingers. 'Both.'

Now that introductions and formalities were dropped, she appeared to undergo a slight change of character. There were buried shadows in her eyes that were beginning to rise to the surface, though Lu could not make sense of their meaning. For now, he was happy to accept the sanctuary offered by the beautiful Azdinist, in the equally beautiful Den of Dawns.

Like the cuthrealm of night, the cuthrealm of dawn was not dissimilar to Daleia-Dal, save for a lack of normal merchants, walls surrounding the city, or the citadel in its centre. The glow of sunrise tinted everything with rippling pink and orange, but all the buildings and statues and monuments appeared to be made of the same greenstone as Daleia itself.

For some reason, as he passed by the buildings, Lu followed a strange desire to stroke his hands across the nearest walls of each one, as if to make sure that they were all truly real. The walls were cool and pleasantly textured, and for a while the Reikan found himself in a state of euphoria, whereby everything he witnessed in the Den of Dawns was, by default, the most interesting and excellent thing he had ever seen, smelled, heard, or touched. Some of the crowd, including both Salun and his younger brother Mimun, had followed behind the Reikan, the Lavender Fox, and their sorcerous guide.

Before Lu had a chance to ponder their destination, the group arrived at a courtyard of ornately designed statues, similar to those in the citadel of Daleia. At the end of the courtyard was a large square building, laced with pillars and statues. The combined smell of fire and seasoned food billowed from every window, entrance, and exit of the building; it was a banquet hall.

'Tonight, you feast in the Den of Dawns, as a welcoming to your new home. Then we will speak of many things, including how we came to be acquainted, and the tasks at hand. A conversation with someone else who has first-hand experience of the Mistress will be quite cathartic to you, I'm sure.'

After inhaling another deep whiff of the food he was soon to eat, Lu smiled at the Azdinist with a humorous, mock madness in his eyes. 'More than you could ever know!'

Fym laughed at Lu's response and then pushed forward through the tall, wooden doors at the front of the hall.

Chapter Eight

AWREIA GOES AWRY

Jokes of every kind were being hurled across great turquoise tables, thinly decorated by patterns of swirling gold and silver that were etched throughout the wood. Lu was sat somewhat centrally in the great hall, between Mimun, who was to his left, and Fym Sallow on his right. Salun was sat to the left of his brother, Mimun, and the Lavender Fox had retired for the evening, so Lu was making an effort to learn the names of some of the other acolytes that were celebrating his arrival.

From a door at the back of the hall, a great number of people dressed in beautiful all-black uniforms then emerged, carrying boards of food, and drink. Others were carrying plates and cutlery, placing assigned dishes and platters on the tables in front of whoever required them. Lu had, of course, specifically requested a meal that included as few animal ingredients as possible. Fym, and her staff, surprised him by respecting this wish without mocking him at all and promised to prepare him something special.

In no time at all, Lu was dipping chunks of warm, freshly cooked bread into a delicious combination of oils. The bread was dark, and firm on the outside, but once broken revealed its soft and fluffy composition, in which myriad slices of juicy varicoloured olives were interspersed.

Halfway through consuming the bread, the Reikan had finished off his small dishes of oil. With hesitation, he moved on to the deep bowl of dark purple soup that had accompanied the arrival of the bread; he had been waiting for it to cool down. The soup was both filling and sweet, masterfully prepared by the cooks of the Den of Dawns. Once Lu had dunked and eaten his last piece of bread, he wasted no time in seizing the soup bowl and slurping down the rest like a ravenous dog. His dining etiquette didn't stand out too extraordinarily, however, as the food was clearly so fantastic that it had nearly everyone else behaving in a similar manner.

Not long after Lu had swallowed the last drop of his soup, another course arrived. After seeing what had been set before him, the Walker shot a glance to his right. Before he could speak, Fym laughed.

'Don't worry yourself, Lusini-Su! We hadn't forgotten about your dietary needs. Though that may look like pig meat upon your plate, I can assure you that it isn't. Give it a try and let me know what you think!'

Lu sliced his way through what appeared to be a cut of pork,and glanced around to make sure he wasn't on the receiving end of some unfriendly joke. Next to him, Mimun had already sunk his teeth gum-deep into a mouthful of some fish or other, and no one seemed to be watching Lu, other than Fym. Lu quickly bit down on the food on his fork. It was pork, of some sort, and it was distressingly enjoyable to the tongue. After swallowing it with a look of discomfort, he frowned at the Azdinist.

'Why do you tease me with this delicious meat, Sallow?'

Fym's eyes seemed to sparkle a little, as if she saw a compliment in his words.

'There are two things that separate the food on your plate tonight from any other meal here, or anywhere else.'

Lu frowned again and was about to voice his complaints before the blue-skinned Daleian continued.

'Not only is that the first and only meal I have ever prepared for someone else,' she continued 'but it is also, I believe, the only meal ever prepared using sorcery.'

'The taste and texture... Is it an illusion?' Lu was intrigued.

'A minor illusion, yes, but I did still have to prepare it and season it once I had crafted the basis of the meat substitute!'

Lu smiled and continued to eat the food that Fym had made for him. Like Lu's talented friend Haln the innkeeper, Fym had truly slaved over cooking something special for the Reikan. Lu was honoured and now looked forward to getting to know her even more.

The acolytes and their guest soon devoured every luscious morsel of food that had been set upon those turquoise tables. Goblets, tankards, and other glasses brimming with ale, beer, and wine then replaced the plates and cutlery. The room was bustling and roaring with laughter and song, and everyone was drinking except for Fym and Lu.

Lu turned to the Azdinist. 'Why am I here, Fym? I say this with absolute gratitude for your hospitality, of course!'

Fym sipped at her glass of pale green pear juice and whispered:

'We share one destiny, Lusini-Su. The Apprentice God, Morl-Majgyn, seeks to impress his silent, ever-watching masters. He will be granted total dominion over this world and could risk tipping the balance of all that is pure on this earth. We must be the ones to slay him, in the end.'

'But what about our silent, ever-watching Mistress? Where is she, and what is she? What agency compels her; I fear that we do not know the side we serve.'

Fym stared deep into Lu's old, orange eyes. 'Unfortunately, though she has been my teacher from the start, I still only know a little more about her than you do, Lusini-Su. It is for our safety, as I understand, that we know as little about her as possible.'

After some consideration, Lu beckoned one of the servers to pour him some wine. After a sip of dark red, he had sufficient encouragement to speak openly about his experience with the Mistress.

'I must apologise, Fym. I know you have served the Sorceress for much longer than I have. My fears are the fleeting worries of a lonely Walker, with little else to ponder. Besides, I do feel inclined to trust her, especially since she placed that egg in my care. I can't read her; I can't explain her actions - or her tone. And yet, when she passed the egg of blue and gold into my hands, I sensed the purest of sentiments, as though she was a mother forfeiting a child.'

Fym nodded and took a swig from her replenished glass that now smelled of apples. 'You possess more sorcery than you know.' She elaborated no further on the subject of the egg.

As the evening endured, Lu found himself drunkenly learning about the beginnings of Fym's own allegiance with the Mistress. Fym was born to Daleia-Dal but left at a young age due to the townsfolk's persistent infatuation with her unusual complexion. Driven out by discomfort, she had travelled very briefly, seeking the answers to her uniqueness, only to become wholly fascinated by the Krajian histories and sciences she had discovered in the process. Eventually, according to Fym, she found herself living deep in the forest that separated Awreia and Daleia-Dal where, isolated, she continued her studies into the unknown. It was here that the Mistress of the Bhia eventually approached Fym and invited her to the Den of Dawns.

The Azdinist left much unspoken, as she summarised the nature of her allegiance with the Mistress, but Lu was becoming a little too intoxicated to mind. He was particularly intrigued by the fact that it was the Mistress, and not Fym, who initially created the Den of Dawns. The Lavender Fox, the egg, and Fym's mastery of Azdinic sorcery were among the things left largely unmentioned. She was, instead, intent on simply explaining the nature of her quest – gathering shadows from peculiar realms, until at last she had enough to forge Umbra, a sword that now sat safely in Lu's chamber.

'As you know, Majgyn is a ruthless apprentice of the Watchers, intent on proving his competence as an orderly God. He is the most powerful being on all of Kraj, and though he hides behind his forces and his shades, he could destroy the Den of Dawns in an instant if he knew how to find it.'

Lu finished off a third glass of wine and reached for some more bread that had recently been sent to their table.

'You are a great Azdinist, Fym. If you've not enough strength to defeat Morl-Majgyn, then of what use am I?'

'None, at the moment' said Fym, candidly. 'Even at the utmost zenith of my Azdin, I would pose nothing more than an irritation to the Apprentice God. It is you who will tip the balance, Lusini-Su. Now that your Azdin is growing at an unnatural pace, combined with the amount you have already stockpiled in your longevity, you are primed to be the strongest human Azdinist alive. I was the Mistress's only student, and now you are to be mine.'

'And what of the King of Light? Do you fear his approach?'

Lu drunkenly pressed for more information regarding this servant of Majgyn's, but Fym was in no mood to entertain it.

'We have time, here in the Den of Dawns. Plenty of it. Tomorrow, I shall recount my past to you in its entirety. Your writing is invaluable to our library, and I would choose none other than you to document my history alongside yours. It would also be an opportune time for you to learn more about me, soberly,' she glanced at the grinning, drunk Reikan '-if we are to become teacher and student.'

Lu nodded with growing admiration for Fym. By her teaching, he was to become the 'strongest human Azdinist alive'. Regardless of the wine's involvement in tonight's conversation, the promise of magic was enough to excite the Reikan more than ever before.

'Shall we say midday, tomorrow?' he asked the witch of deep blue.

'No. I will simply wake you when you have had sufficient sleep' she replied. 'Besides, you will struggle to locate mid-morning here.'

Lu glanced at the windows in the banquet hall. He had forgotten that he now resided in a place of endless dawn.

'Are you leaving this festivity early, then?' said Lu. The Azdinist's company had been refreshing. She was the only person he had met who fully understood the bizarre role that was thrust upon him. It was maybe the reason that Lu found Fym attractive, in some way or another, though he was still unsure of what action his feelings entailed.

'Yes, I must retire for today. I have spent much of my energy retrieving you from the cuthrealm of night, and creating the elixir that restored your strength.'

'And the false pork?' Lu smiled, not wholly sure of whether his comment was a relevant contribution or just a humorous remark.

'No, the pork required no effort at all! Worry not, Lusini-Su; there will be no shortage of similar meals, provided you stay to train with me.'

And together they laughed, as Fym Sallow stood up and prepared to leave the table. After offering a wave to a few of her servers, she pulled her yellow cloak around her sturdy frame and vanished into nothing. There was a brief moment of applause, and then the drink-driven celebrations resumed.

Lu was amazed at the spectacle of Fym's exit, but his mind was somewhat preoccupied by his attraction to her, and his inexperience with such emotions. He called for his wine to be refilled, and then shifted his gaze, ready to converse with Mimun who was already drunkenly laughing with a loud, blonde-haired woman that Lu didn't recognise. Harnessing a brand-new confidence bestowed by the Daleian wine, the Walker glided around the table of blue and green, and perched beside the two acolytes. If tomorrow onwards were to be days filled with toil and heroism, tonight he could afford to enjoy the novelties of inebriation for a little while longer.

~

What sounded like the slow, heavy purring of a gigantic cat was now stirring Lu back into consciousness. His eyes were still shut, as he tried to discern the source of the sound. Something was on top of his torso, weighing him down enough to dissuade him from sitting up. Was the Lavender Fox sitting purring upon his chest? He couldn't be sure.

Slowly, his eyelids seemed to peel open in spite of exhaustion, and he was staring up at the ceiling of a chamber that was not his own. He lifted his head, and immediately set it back after spotting the origin of the purring, as well as the amused face of Fym Sallow who stood on the other side of the room.

'Fym, is there an Azdinic incantation that alleviates shame?' he croaked.

Fym clapped her hands together and chuckled, before walking out of the room. 'Meet me in the courtyard as soon as you are ready.'

Lu was lying in a bed, naked, half-under the sleeping body of the golden-haired acolyte from the night before, though he couldn't recall her name. The rest of her body was sprawled across the dormant shape of Mimun, who was curled up in an uncomfortable position to Lu's right.

Lu put his hands up to his own scalp. There must have been some amount of drink left in the Walker's body, because though he tried to remember details from the night before, all that came to him was a throbbing ache in his brain. His memory was not so excellent after all.

Slowly and delicately, he managed to roll the girl off his body, and more onto Mimun. The handsome younger brother of Salun responded slightly to her weight and began to wake up, causing Lu to panic and stand up off the bed. There were bruises on his body, and his muscles were sore, but he didn't dare wait for Mimun to explain. He dashed out of the room as silently as his bare feet would allow, as they slapped on the cold marble floor. He was now in the middle of an unfamiliar corridor, with no clothes on. His room was not in this building, and he would have to go outside, and brave whatever commotion was brewing outside in the courtyard in nothing but his skin

As Lu stumbled groggily into the gardens of the Den of Dawns, his vision was near-stolen by the light of the eternal sunrise. The crowd that was gathered there immediately noticed his arrival; whispers (in which his name frequented) began to ripple through the huddle of robes. Lu began to worry if Mimun and his friend were not the only people who witnessed last night's apparent antics.

'Does Lu know? It must matter dearly to him' he heard one of the acolytes mutter. Though he was aware that another, more ordinary person would feel inclined to cover their naked body in such social circumstances, Lu experienced no such shame, for he was intrigued by the topic of the crowd's murmur. He stomped in the direction of Fym Sallow, who was in discussion with Salun towards the back of the huddle.

'Fym, I would walk to my chamber to fetch my clothes, but I must ask what news has stirred such a gathering?' he asked, with forced confidence.

'I have only just learned it for myself, after leaving Mimun's chamber when I woke you up.' Fym replied. Her tone was overly controlled, as if she was stifling her own stress. 'If I am honest, I wouldn't have disturbed you had I already known.'

'What is it?' Lu's voice had begun to adopt a stress of its own.

'From what I've heard, I think that... It appears that Awreia is under siege.' Fym paused, as if disturbed by a detail she had omitted.

Without hesitation, Lu began to walk in the direction of his chamber.

'I must go to Awreia, Fym. I have to try; I am in debt to its people.'

The Azdinist tried to say something in response, but Lu was already at the entrance to the nexus leading to his room.

In no time at all, Lu was dressed in his shellsuit, and equipped with a short-sword similar to the one he had travelled with on his journey to Daleia-Dal. As much as he had missed the touch of Umbra, and longed to wield it once again, the sailor-warrior could not allow Umbra to fall into the wrong hands if he died at Awreia. Once he was a more skilled swordsman, and had learned sufficient Azdinic sorcery from Sallow, he would feel more confident to equip the glassblade on his travels.

Before leaving his room, Lu checked on the egg of blue and gold, to ensure that it did not verge on hatching. By the demand of his habit, he stroked his fingers along the egg's veined indentations, and then re-covered the alien thing with a sheet of cloth.

Outside, Lu was met with the concerned face of Fym Sallow who, though she appeared to have calmed herself since he'd last seen her, now seemed unsure if she should let the Walker leave.

'The events that are taking place in Awreia are beyond your control, Lu. I would urge you to let the acolytes survey the situation, while you stay with me and begin work on the document.'

Lu felt disappointed by the Azdinist, and awkwardly slid past her domineering frame.

'I'm sorry Fym, I am immensely grateful for your welcome into this beautiful realm of dawn, but I have a duty to protect my friends in Port Awreia. I cannot be permanently killed, and I will not risk bringing Umbra. I fail to see a reason why I can't involve myself in the protection of my home!'

Fym Sallow's tired, red eyes softened, and she raised a hand slightly, as if inviting someone new to their conversation.

'Very well, Lusini-Su. But whatever pain or sorrow is to be discovered in Awreia is a sorrow you must bear alone I warn you, and will have no sympathy for how this may affect you.'

And from above, the Lavender Fox descended, landing directly beside the sailor-warrior. 'I am yet to receive any information as to the condition of Awreia, or what manner of siege she has fallen to. Be careful, for you do not know what awaits you.'

'And the Mistress? Will she come to our aid?' Lu frowned. He had not anticipated such a long absence from the enchantress of the Bhia, considering that it was she who sent him on this path towards the unknown.

Fym Sallow massaged her sculpted jaw with the fingers of her right hand and then offered the Reikan a final, sardonic smile.

'She has played her part, for now. She will likely be engaged elsewhere until you have succeeded in a solid mastery of Azdinic sorcery, after completing the rigorous training I have planned for you. Never try to anticipate her, and never try to command her. She will arrive only when she needs to.'

The Azdinist began to walk away, before turning to speak once more.

'The Lavender Fox can travel seamlessly between the Den of Dawns and the true world. Farewell.'

Lu gave a frustrated nod and then climbed upon the Lavender Fox. It was time to protect Awreia. The pair sailed skyward, like two tangled feathers caught in an upward draught. The pink and orange hues of the sunrise cuthrealm disappeared gradually beneath them, until Lu could see nothing but colour that seemed to slowly shift into a cloudless sky blue. Without noticeable transition, they were now flying fast above Daleia-Dal, over the plains marked by shimmering greenstone and crumbling red sandstone, and then over the dense tropical forest, which seemed to have no bottom to its tangled depths.

In no time at all, the Lavender Fox was gliding above Port Awreia.

'Hold back for a moment, my friend.' Lu stroked the head of the fox, hoping to pause above Awreia before their descent, to consider a method of entry. From their height, the Port seemed almost calm and unbothered; it was just a clump of rooftops and gardens, lined by its Empryc harbour.

Then, Lu urged for their arrival and the Lavender Fox dipped slowly towards Awreia. As they approached from on high, the ugliness of the sea-town's siege became morbidly apparent before Lu's eyes.

Some buildings were ablaze, while others were simply in ruin. The streets were decorated with the torn-up bodies of countless Awreikans, and there was no living person or beast to be seen. After landing, the Reikan bid the Lavender Fox farewell, as he walked solemnly among the ruins. There was no army, or fiend patrolling the town, and yet Lu did not feel alone. A formless, overbearing presence seemed to linger in the wreckage of his home; it was as if Lu's senses refused to detect something that stood nearby. Lusini-Su drew his short-sword from his belt and made his way to the inn of his most beloved friends.

Sometimes, the Reikan stopped mid-stride to glance around. Shadows, that were not his own, seemed to slide and shift behind him. But even the twisting, silent shadows that appeared to pursue him were not enough to distract the Walker from the condition of his destination.

There was hardly anything left of Haln and Pernim's Inn by the time Lu had arrived. Fire had all but stolen the entire building, leaving nothing but rubble, and a menacing tower of black smoke hanging high above where the Inn once stood. Lu glanced for a moment longer at the titan of smoke. For some reason, it reminded the Walker of the cloud that once drifted above his head, though it shared none of its features save for the fact that both clouds cast a melancholic shadow upon their subjects.

Lu waded into the wreckage of the Inn, stopping still in his tracks once he reached the middle. For a moment, he felt nothing; there was no sorrow, no sentimental grief.

It was only once Lu's eyes had adjusted to the murk of the grey, black, and brown that he began to see certain things that evoked an emotional response. Firstly, the building seemed larger than before. Among the ashes, the Walker found charred materials that suggested that the Inn had been renovated, supposedly with the funds he had left for Haln and his partner. The short-lived dream that his two close friends had worked so hard to achieve now lay in ashes and rubble.

Then, from the other side of the wreck, Lu's burning orange eyes became fixed upon a shape at the far end of the ruin. He ran towards it, as tenseness arose in his chest and throat. It couldn't be. It was.

Fire-bathed, and dressed in soot, the scarred bodies of Haln and Pernim lay curled together in a black and bloodied mess. Lu screamed with anguish and knelt beside them. 'This is my fault!' he wept, buckling over Haln, a friend he had loved so dearly. 'Haln... I should never have left you.'

The face of Haln was motionless, stripped of life and most of its skin. Haln's body, however, began to twitch. As if animated by some emotional delusion, Lu watched as the body of Pernim struggled beneath the arms of the gigantic man. Pernim did not speak, and his eye sockets were blackened and burned out, but he lived. Horrified, Lu felt as though the innkeeper was silently addressing him. Lu's eyes were stinging with tears, for they were not used to crying.

'If I were a great sorcerer...if I were Sallow -or the Mistress- I could have healed you Pernim. I'm so sorry that I brought this upon our town.'

Lu unsheathed his short-sword and, with eyes full of the same adoration and respect he always had for the innkeepers, he drove it through Pernim's withered chest and into his heart. 'I loved both of you' he wept.

Now he was filled with fear and sorrow, both masked behind his rage.

'KING OF LIGHT! SHOW YOURSELF!'

The torn voice of the sailor warrior echoed through the ruins of Awreia, seeking out the arsonist in question.

Immediately, Lu heard a chuckling from behind him. He spun around in the ashes of the Inn, to be met by the fierce eyes of a familiar face.

'Tatael...'

Not five strides from what was once the entrance of the Inn stood the Awreikan youth Tatael Ram, dressed in a silver-white mail that rippled and flowed like velvet, and a pair of blood-red trousers. 'Good afternoon, Lu.'

'You are... you're the King of Light?' Lu's voice cracked, as he waded through the remnants of the Inn, carefully approaching his betrayer.

Tatael grinned. 'Idiot. For someone of your years, I would have thought you to be more intelligent.' He paced back and forth, with an awful swagger. 'The moment I freed myself from the place that you abandoned me, I made my way to the fenlands. I had heard word of a disturbance in Lord Beol's province and thought to investigate it for myself.'

Though tears were obscuring what he saw in reality, Lu now saw a clear image of Beol from his memory, sat outlandishly in the company of the sages of Daleia. 'So Beol *was* a spy!'

'Indeed. His realm is under the watch of Light, and in order to protect it from this-' Ram gestured at the ruins of Awreia '-he acts solely in the interest of his new master.'

Though his heart throbbed from the loss of his Awreikan friends, Lu sighed with considerable relief. The elders of Daleia had suspected Beol correctly and had kept all information regarding the Den of Dawns a secret from their guest.

'By the time I reached Beol, he had visited Daleia-Dal or, more specifically, the citadel of Daleia. This proved useful, for I came with the interest of seeking the King of Light, of *joining* the King of Light. When I mentioned the existence of you, an ageless Reikan, Lord Beol became overly quick to trust me and brought me to his master. He remembered you from Daleia, did Beol.'

Lu was weak with rage. 'What venomous corruption led you to this, Tatael? Razing Awreia, the sanctuary of your family... and friends! You told me, before I left, that you wished to spare Awreia of the King of Light's wrath, that I should surrender myself to him in order to save our home!'

Ram chuckled. Once again, Lu felt the invisible presence of the creeping shadows about him. Something hot was seizing his arms. He struggled, but whatever grappled him was too strong.

'And yet once I kneeled before the King of Light, I realised the nature of my most honest desires. The King has granted me power. With a small force to command, I laid waste to this dreadful port, full of vacuous people, so as to find the one that threatens the King of Light. I'm here to steal your secrets, Lu. I'll do whatever is required to get them from you.'

The invisible, searing presence that restrained the Walker now dragged him forward, behind Tatael Ram who walked proudly without uttering another word. Lu did not struggle for long, for he was helpless to the grip of whatever phantoms surrounded him. Soon, they had reached the harbour.

When at last Tatael came to a halt, Lu adjusted his eyes to the familiar stretch of the harbour before him. Something that resembled neither a boat nor beast floated in the water nearby, and Lu quickly discerned Tatael's reason for stopping.

'I'm sure you recognise this area of the coast - our destination' smiled the Awreikan. A wild morbidity flickered in the boy's eyes. Lu nodded, eyeing the shape that floated in the water. Bobbing between the boats tethered on either side, it was a sort of cage or basket, not of wicker, but instead fashioned from something else. The cage was fastened to a crude rope lever system that appeared to loop through a metal hook on the harbour side, and then back into the water.

Tatael made a slight gesture with his hand, and it appeared that the invisible arms of light that were gripping Lu then ceased their hold, and began to tug at the pulley system, bringing the cage up from the water to where Lu was nervously standing. Lu's mind was becoming clouded, overrun with sorrow and disbelief. He was near dissociated from all that was happening around him.

'I have a gift for you, Reikan, that was prepared by my master. Come, take it from me.' Tatael beckoned the Walker towards him, as he pulled something from the pocket of his ash-stained orange breeches.

Lu approached Ram slowly, feeling for his short-sword before remembering that it had been confiscated.

Lu spat on the ground in front of the Awreikan.

'I resent you, Tatael. I resent you for what you have done. I warn you of this: despite your best, I can never truly die. I will hound you tirelessly. Torture me -for years if you must- but here in the blazing ruin of Awreia, the greatest damage has already been inflicted. A day will come when I am free again, through death or otherwise. And then I shall return for you. And you will fear me, and you will run. But you will die, Tatael Ram. You will die.'

Tatael applauded and mocked Lu for his words. He pretended to quiver and back away in fear, before lurching forward in an attempt to snatch some of Lu's Daleian jewellery from his ears, but Lu wrestled him away.

'What is your gift, you wretched eel! If there is none, I would rather you kill me than touch my face again.'

Tatael laughed and opened his palm to reveal a single seed. 'A gift, from the King of Light.' He waved it in front of Lu, who could feel the arms of light take hold of his shoulders once more. 'It was crafted for one purpose. To make you mortal.'

Lu frowned. Could the King of Light really undo a power granted by Tlephilisse, and therefore, the Watcher-creators? It was improbable, considering that even Morl-Majgyn could not detect or prevent Lu's resurrection.

'That'd be foolish to assume, young Tatael. Your master knows nothing of what keeps me from death.'

'Then you would not be afraid to eat it, Lusini-Su. Eat it!'

Tatael forced the seed between Lu's pursed lips and then grappled the Reikan's jaw to prevent him from spitting it out. Lu tried to struggle, but as soon as he showed any resistance, his arms began to burn in the clutch of the phantom's embrace. Reluctantly, he swallowed the King of Light's gift, while trying to reassure himself that it would not work.

As soon as Lu's gag reflex and stomach had settled from the initial poisonous taste of the thing, he began to feel extraordinarily drained. It was as if the seed now grew within him, erupting with roots and tendrils that latched upon his innards, sapping his energy and consuming his strength.

Was Tatael's claim true? Was it working?

Before Lu had even a moment to dwell on his gathering fears, he felt himself become hoisted from the ground by the unseeable arms, and then thrown gracelessly into the basket. He was numb and felt no pain as his body crumpled into the frame of the wet cage, though his nose was now filled with the smell of brine, for it had clearly been marinating in the Empryc's salty perfume for some time and stank of it.

Tatael closed the lid of the basket and appeared to lock the opening with some form of thin, white chains similar to the material of the mail he adorned. The whole cage then shuddered as the rope-system became taut. Lu adjusted his eyes to the frame, and recognised finally what his enclosure was made of - pieces of his boat, or rather Demja's boat. It seemed ironic then, that the densely packed reeds of his vessel –his first real *freedom*- had been repurposed as his prison.

Chapter Nine

LUMINARY

For the best part of two days, Tatael Ram of Awreia had tortured Lusini-Su. That miniscule seed, crafted by the absent King of Light, had somehow ruthlessly stripped Lu of his Reikan breath capacity, thus enabling Tatael to repeatedly near-drown the Walker in his malevolently devised sea-cage, each time to the point of loss of consciousness.

Though Lu was initially cynical of claims that the seed would render him mortal, his current aquatic breath deficiency was evidence enough for those claims to suggest true consequence.

Still, after hours of intermittent submergence, Lu had not spilt a single word regarding the Den of Dawns to his tormentor. He assumed, due to this classification of torture, that Tatael was forbidden from bringing real harm to Lu's body. Perhaps the King of Light wished to keep him alive and unspoiled.

Though he grew weaker by the hour, he endured each moment with solemnity. He hallucinated, or rather *dreamed* of days upon Lila, alongside Tlephilisse or the Lavender Fox. He thought of the marvellous food on which he had indulged in the Den of Dawns, among the most splendid and joyous new companions. He would very much like to see them again, though he understood why Fym could not come to his aid at risk of revealing herself to Tatael Ram, and thus the King of Light.

During his brief waking stints above the surface, he found comfort and company in the stirring wind and the light of sun or moon. Though Lu was unused to suffering of this ilk, there was no dearth of thoughts that could offset his hopelessness. He would be free again, somehow. Lu's captor, however, was becoming impatient. Ram shook his head of thick, auburn hair and signalled for his unseeable soldiers to hoist the imprisoned Reikan from his jail, and back onto the jetty.

Until now, the young and handsome Awreikan had been a perfervid oppressor, seemingly relishing every moment of suffering that he inflicted upon Lu. Whatever feverish delight he had derived from such sadism apparently had since worn thin. Ram had now adopted an almost comically austere expression as his victim coughed and vomited.

'I apologise, Lu. It seems you are too much a veteran of torment to capitulate to this manner of interrogation. I follow an order, to deliver you alive and unscathed to my master. T'would be interesting, I think, to discover how much pain I can inflict without disobeying that command.'

Tatael unsheathed a long, white blade that appeared almost new or unused. Lu stepped back, still dressed in his lightweight but impenetrable suit of shells, only to meet the embrace of the invisible force. Lu frowned and struggled, as Tatael Ram gave a nod, as if to signal his spectres to remove the shellsuit.

There was no time to think of another solution. Lu charged directly forward at Tatael, aiming his throat straight for the point of the Awreikan's bone-white sabre. But the youngster recoiled, and Lu missed the blade.

Straight after impact, Tatael whipped around and tried to pummel the back of the Walker's head, but instead caught his wrist on the shoulder of the shellsuit. Weakened by the intermittent water-inhalation and hunger, Lu stumbled forward.

Then, as Tatael struck again, Lu impulsively reached for the blade. The white steel bit deep into the Reikan's left hand, but he did not notice the pain, for he was now acting in a state of determination. Blood and skin falling either side of the weapon, Lu slowly wrenched the sword out of Tatael's hand and pushed the man off the landing with all his remaining strength. Tatael Ram collapsed into the water, shouting impotent words of command as he splashed into the waves of the harbour.

Without delay, Lu used his right hand to pull the sunken blade from the remains of his left and took one sharp breath before plunging the whiteblade deep into his own heart, crumpling to the floor.

As he lay there, seconds from death, he felt the caress of the invisible hands reach for him hopelessly, and he heard the cries of Tatael Ram, who still struggled to climb back upon the jetty.

By the time Tatael had found his way upon the land, the body of the Reikan and his shellsuit were nowhere to be seen.

~

Voices were calling, moaning, and screeching under the turbulent crush of the Empryc gulf. Lu could feel his body, or his soul, being towed through the undercurrents, slowly in the direction of Lila, as if he were thread being pulled through tough fabric by the hand of a god. Though amorphous shapes and light drifted all around him, he could not focus on anything that passed by. Despite his best efforts, Lu could not even see his own body amidst the throbbing aquamarine. To whom did these wailing voices belong? Could each voice match one of the floating lights that travelled here and there in this wash of water and colour? Lu stopped himself from speculating the fate of his aimless mystery companions, for he feared he might share that fate. He believed that whatever was happening to them now happened to him also.

There was no way of knowing how long he had drifted in this mess of sea and souls. This underwater realm had offered no recognisable sights so far on his journey. Occasionally they would pass through sea-caves, thronged by a patchwork audience of fish, who would happily bounce about their chambers, incognisant of their ethereal visitors. There came a point when Lu found his course differing from those he had travelled alongside. The other shapes, moaning and morose, were beginning to steer down towards the dark, while Lu's direction had not altered. And as a distance began to separate him from his companions, their voices became clearer, and Lu could hear them for what they were.

He heard the cries of Demja, and of Haln, and of Pernim. Though still the words were muffled, and the visions were abstract, the tone of those voices was distinct enough for Lu to recognise. They were dead, all three of them, passing on to the next life that awaited them.

With no body of his own, and no tears that he could cry, Lu screamed, and he called and he begged for his friends' return, but one by one they vanished into the Empryc depths. A futile, stifled groan was his last farewell to his brief, yet dearest friendships.

Then, there was a great swelling sound. A warbling, both deep and shrill, came from that same netherworld. In an explosive rush of colour and of *power,* a great, winged beast emerged from the shadows and raced towards the surface. In its beak, it towed the shapes of the Awreikan dead, as if they had been spared the abyss at a moment's notice by this gigantic bird. From the beckoning brine, their souls had been lifted by the beast, safely on to the next life. It was only as the creature, monstrous and multicoloured, escaped the waves of Empryc and broke the surface, did Lu realise he had seen it before.

By now, Lusini-Su was feeling a little more confident of the destination of his own current path. He had not transcended alongside his deceased loved ones. He carried on alone, through the Empryc. He was returning to Lila, after all. Soon, he was in among the teeth of the Empryc Crown, where corpses in the wreckage had attracted sea-creatures of a more bloodthirsty ilk, scouting for fresh meat impaled upon the rocks.

Lu drifted through the shallows, onto the white sands, and through plants that were once so dutifully tended to, now overgrown. Though he was no longer beneath the waves, an aqueous sound still swirled above the muffle of the Lila ambience. Lu was relieved. He did not long to hear the harrowing perish song of Tlephilisse echo between the Lilan passerines, only moments after witnessing the departure of his other friends. He felt as though he floated as she once did, between trees and bushes, never touching ground.

And there, through the clearing in the centre of the circle-stream, lay his naked, grey body. He continued to approach until he finally hovered above it. As was the case last time, Lu's vanity suffered immensely at the sight of his withered and fragile frame, though this time and from this angle, he felt a little less self-depreciative. He was grateful to return to life, regardless of the setbacks.

Head throbbing and eyes peeling open, the Reikan forced himself upright. He was sat upon the bed of teething darklilies, in the centre of the enchanted ring of water. A smile played across his tired, malnourished face. Though the King of Light's bewitched seed, forced upon him by Tatael, had been successful in temporarily stripping Lu of his old-world attributes, and even beguiled him through a peculiar dream or vision of his journey to the Lila, it had failed to do what Tatael had inferred. Perhaps this Luminary was not as much the sorcerer as they appeared. Perhaps the potency of Lu's immortal enrolment, bestowed by ones who were as much as Gods, was unrivalled. Or perhaps the King of Light did not wish for Lu to die at all. In truth, Lu had been quite curious to meet the infernal sorcerer. Now, however, he was curious only to see the King of Light die, preferably by his hand. The Reikan got to his feet and stretched his scrawny muscles, his chest aimed towards the sky. 'Hmm?'

As he contorted his body, he caught a glimpse behind him of his shellsuit. It was placed untidily among the lilies, alongside the undergarments he had died in. Furthermore, the Daleian jewellery he had been wearing was scattered above it. But it was not this that caught the Walker's attention most; lying flat among the flowers and grass was Umbra, sheathed in its unassuming scabbard, alongside what appeared to be a murdan - a small, round shield-like item used for parrying attacks. This murdan, however, was made of shell that matched the shellsuit, with some kind of horn protruding from either side of its diameter, presumably to be used as a dagger.

'How is it that you have come to me...?' Lu muttered to his effects, old and new, as he ran an investigative finger across the front of the murdan.

Once he had bathed in the strange water of the river-ring, Lusini-Su dressed himself in his undergarments and shellsuit, fixing his scabbard into his belt, before finally reintroducing his silver-pink jewellery to his flesh. After the Walker was fully clothed, he began to wander to his storeroom, his left hand slashing and stabbing tactfully with the glassblade into the air. With his right hand, the sailor-warrior attempted a handful of murdan manoeuvres that he'd seen before, but his execution was poor.

Upon his arrival at the Lila settlement, it occurred to Lu that if he were to return to Lila this regularly, it would be best to keep his stores plentifully supplied with food and liquid sustenance – dying and returning to his old, malnourished form caused him a great deal of hunger. Lu opened the hut to find that most of his ingredients had not kept, so he made his way for the south-beach.

Back and forth, the Walker trudged, bringing Umello and Buacoctin back to his lodgings, along with any other berries, nuts, or vegetables he discovered along the way. By now, Lu had expected to see the Lavender Fox, who would undoubtedly offer him passage off the Lila Isle. Regardless, he did not wait for the beast. He was already occupied enough to not mind a short pause in the conflict that was occurring elsewhere. His trawling was already a method of distraction, to keep his mind from mourning the drifting dead he had seen in his dream.

It had been over half a day since Lu's rebirth, and he was beginning to feel a little restless. He had been eating frequently, and training with Umbra and the mysterious murdan in whatever way he could, focussing his agility and his limited strength into the most effective blows, and learning ways to dodge and defend from imaginary adversaries. He was also wary of the forces that Tatael commanded, things that were unseeable, invincible. What magic begat them? How could such an opponent be undone?

The sailor-warrior stood beneath his gigantic likeness, as the moon rose to its peak in the reflective, marine expanse of night. He was not tired, but stillness had fallen upon him, causing him to delicately trace the inscription at the foot of the great sculpture.

'A Night of Superlunary Gazing', he whispered softly. 'And what a wonderful night it was, my friend.'

He allowed himself a moment of penitence and wept, though he questioned the sincerity of his guilt. Maybe a life upon Lila was the path he should have chosen, away from all that was deadly on Taromet. It certainly seemed idyllic to Lu when considering the current state of affairs, though he knew that it could not be. His eyes wandered from sand to coast to Empryc spine, until he was lost in the rippling blackness of the beyond. Morl-Majgyn would have come for him eventually, and he could not have stayed; this was the unfortunate truth.

Lu turned immediately, alerted by the sound of disturbed air, followed by a thump, and the laughter of clattering metal. It was the Lavender Fox, donning war gear of silver-green, and an expression that was not without strife. Beside the Fox stood two hooded figures, one smiling and one without expression. Lu was pleased to see all three of them.

'Lusini-Su!' smiled the Mistress of the Bhia, standing tall, blue, and majestic. 'I have been watching you, and I commend you for all you have done this far. We require your assistance.'

Beside her, Fym turned to calm the clearly disgruntled Lavender Fox, who seemed unhappy to be dressed in its mail.

'I am glad to see that our sorcery has worked, also' added the Daleian Azdinist, nodding towards the glassblade in Lu's hand.

Lu attempted to enquire about the murdan, but the Mistress spoke first.

'Indeed. Without wasting time on weary back and forth exchange, we will simply tell you all that you need to be told, Lusini-Su. Then, when we are finished, you may ask questions you believe to be relevant.'

Lu nodded, and noticed a grin on Fym Sallow's face, presumably due to the comical bluntness of the Mistress's statement.

Plunging deep into the cool night, the Mistress and her apprentice, Fym Sallow, elaborated on the current state of Awreia. The majority of the intercourse came from Sallow, with the occasional interjection from the towering, inhuman Sorceress, for whom Lu's fondness was rekindling.

'As you know, Awreia has been taken by the one called Tatael Ram' spoke Fym. 'I have been observing the Awreikan since first I learned of his interest in you, Lu.

He is an avid reader and theorist, himself twice rejected by the scholars of Daleia. It is not surprising that he should find himself aligned with the King of Light on his quest for answers.'

The Mistress nodded.

'He has been unable to convey much information to his superior regarding yourself thus far and knows nothing about your adopted role as River Sprite upon the Lila. He believes you to be dead, vanquished completely by the poison supplied by his master.'

'I'd have expected more suspicion from him, considering the bizarrely immediate disappearance of your body and armour, and the extent of his research. But perhaps he believes it to be the work of his master's sorcery; though he is well-read, Ram is young, and foolish, after all.'

The Mistress laughed in response to Fym's end comment.

'Indeed. As you've noticed, Walker, it took some effort but Fym and I have managed to align your possessions with the nature of your reincarnation. One of the reasons we came to meet you on the Lila was to ensure that your suit, murdan, and sabre had returned to you by command of death.'

Lu found himself pondering the meaning of her words, only to remember that his thoughts were free for the Mistress to spectate.

'And what we mean by that, Walker, is that if you are to return to Lila in death, we made it so that your more uncommon possessions could vanish - or "die" - with you, to prevent them from falling into other hands.'

Lu nodded, understanding the necessity of such a precaution.

'However, this is a sorcery that can be rewritten by someone such as Majgyn, or possibly even the King of Light, should they learn how' The Mistress continued. 'So, you would do well to avoid making a habit of dying in the presence of their allies; Umbra cannot come into their hands at any cost.'

But now Lu's mind was filled by the thought of Tatael's invisible henchmen.

'The living light... Fym, would you please explain to Lu how he should dispatch the Lightlingerers?'

Fym Sallow cast the Mistress an odd, unrewarded look, before turning back to face Lu.

'One day –when there's more time- I will explain the existence of the Lightlingerers to you, Lusini-Su. For now, all you need to know is that there are nineteen at Tatael's command and that you carry the one thing that can destroy them.' The Azdinist approached the Walker and carefully took the glassblade from his hand. She caressed the sharp side of the sabre as she continued to speak.

'As I understand, you're already familiar with the way that Umbra undoes the immortality of its victims?'

To which the Mistress nodded. 'He is familiar; we shan't forget that he has already slain Tlephilisse the Guiltless.'

Lu scowled a little at the Mistress's insensitive reminder and glanced at the beautiful Sailor-Likeness. The Mistress caught his eye, however, and offered him an apologetic smile, for she had heard the upset in his mind.

Fym began to speak again, almost oblivious to the silent exchange between the Walker and Mistress.

'The essence of the Lightlingerers is already known to Umbra. In fact, it's likely that, alongside that of Tlephilisse, the blade also transferred the secret of *their* undoing into your flesh when you performed your first ritual under the red shadow moon. Either way, it'd be safest for you to attack using Umbra, and not by hand. As it is, you are hardly skilled in combat, let alone in hand-to-hand affairs.'

But the Mistress appeared to disagree with her pupil and shook her head. 'Attack the Lightlingerers with Umbra - if you wish for Umbra to be seen by their master. We must disguise the blade first, Fym.' To which Fym Sallow nodded, grunting once in agreement.

Lu stared unblinkingly as Fym spoke more of these nineteen 'Lightlingerers' – beings sent by the King of Light, to be commanded by Tatael; beings that could sear his flesh, yet could not be seen.

Fym reached out and placed her hand on Lu's shoulder.

'I've already enacted a simple sorcery that will allow you to behold the King of Light's agents, Lu. You'll see them as I do – humanoid, yet reminiscent of the stars.'

Lu was sure that the Mistress would vanish as soon as this meeting concluded, but why couldn't Fym fight to defend Daleia-Dal? What was to be the role of the other Azdinists and sages in the Den of Dawns? He was not fit enough to fight these nineteen demons, even *with* the witch-blade at his side.

The many, broken songs of the Lila-chorus were seeping back into the silence as Lu concerned himself with his fears. Affectionately, the mail-clad Lavender Fox stepped towards Lu and brushed its great, armoured head against his shoulder, to which the Walker responded by wrapping his arms around its neck, pressing his forehead against an exposed patch of fur on the soft animal. He felt unwell, unskilled, and unfit for conflict.

Fym and the Mistress muttered among each other, sharing Umbra in their hands, but their words did not reach the ears of the sailor-warrior. Face buried in the fur of the fox, all was still and subdued. There was no time, or tension. The sound of the fox's breathing and its heartbeat were all that Lu could hear, and those sounds were so comforting that the Walker felt unable to pull away, at risk of falling back into the panic of reality.

'Lusini-Su, it is time now to depart' spoke the kind voice of the Mistress.

The sailor-warrior warily pulled his face from the fox's warm, lavender coat. The Mistress stood before him, in her both awesome and sobering radiance, a gleaming sword in her hand. But it was not Umbra that she held out to the Walker. It was – at least, in appearance - the short-sword he had carried before arriving in the Den of Dawns.

'Tonight, the Lavender Fox will fly you to Daleia-Dal, before Tatael Ram arrives – though it shall not be the same Daleia-Dal that Tatael expects. The acolytes have swapped it, by Azdinic illusion, with a duplicate of the cuthrealm of night, but this substitution can only be sustained for a few hours. Unlike the true cuthrealm of night, time in this illusion will pass in tandem with time on Kraj, whereas time will hardly pass at all for the villagers. The majority of which shall be sleeping, and those who work at night will be none the wiser to their shift between planes.'

The Lavender Fox lowered its rear end towards the Walker, who, sheathing his sword, instinctively climbed upon it. Fym stepped forward and handed the Walker a vial of blue liquid.

'Drink this, for strength and for focus' she smiled. 'Do not fear Ram, for he is mortal. Do not fear the living light, for they will not attack unless commanded. Besides, both your shellsuit and murdan should withstand any heat that the demons have to offer.'

Lu nodded firmly and threw his head back as he swallowed the contents of the vial. Throwing it back to Sallow, he urged the Lavender Fox to ascend and began to feel the familiar yet peculiar sorcery of Fym's potion flood through his muscles. He could see his limbs thicken, and his skin return to a healthier shade. As the Reikan and fox commenced their skyward drift, Lu felt renewed and ready for battle.

Chapter Ten

STARHEADS IN THE
REALM OF NIGHT

Though the Lavender Fox writhed so quickly through the Empryc night sky, Lu found himself stargazing in dreamlike wonder. "Humanoid and star-like" – that was how Fym described the phantoms Lu soon must face. Soldiers, but also prisoners, she had said. Soaring elegantly beneath so many piercing lights, Lu found it hard to imagine how creatures of servitude and captivity could even begin to resemble stars - distant, night-borne fires that seemed to twinkle with more freedom than all who scurried below them.

Through night-mist, the fox tilted down towards the treetops of the jungle that sat behind Awreia. Initially, Lu had tried to avert his eyes from the wreckage of the coastal town, but as they passed over to meet the jungle's dense canopy, he turned his head as if to make sure he did not dream the ruins before. He had not dreamed them, however. The sight of Awreia's scorched and battered remnants was now all that burned behind his orange eyes as he rushed on to meet the responsible force. If vengeances were all that inspired the sailor-warrior tonight, then they would suffice. Tatael Ram would be dead long before dawn returned.

And there was Daleia-Dal, under the glamour of darkness, beneath the veil of the cuthrealm of night. Even sat among the surrounding plains that were cloaked in nocturnally ordinary shadows, the cuthrealm of night seemed superlatively desolate. Much like a heavy petal being released by a retiring, exhausted wind, the Lavender Fox bobbed down until eventually landing lightly on the top of an array of connected buildings. For now, Tatael and the Lightlingerers were nowhere to be seen. Lu decided that his position atop the cuthrealm ruins would serve to be an optimal lookout point while he awaited their arrival. After dismounting, Lu was almost surprised to find that the Lavender Fox did not abandon him this time. Instead, the beast sulked quietly beside the Walker on the rooftop wreckage, keeping a low posture. Together, they maintained the comportment of thieves, cowering from visibility, without sound and without movement.

Shortly, the enemy arrived. Glowing behind the gates, on the verge of the false Daleia-Dal, marched nineteen bobbing orbs of fire. As the orbs entered the fallen city, Lu narrowed his reaching eyes, trying to grasp the form of these burning beings. The Lightlingerers moved with unusual, slithering steps. Once they had passed the gates, the Walker was able to discern their shape, and all at once he knew Fym's description to be accurate, if not a little generous in her suggestion of human qualities.

Their heads twinkled and flickered like miniature suns, with no features or expressions save for the various intensities at which each one's head seemed to burn. Some starheads flashed rapidly as they slipped through the dark, while others seemed quivering, thirsty, and unsettled. Some seemed almost reluctant to burn, as if lingering at the end of a wick, teasing extinguishment.

The starheads glowed with such brilliance that the light made it difficult to identify the colour of their bipedal yet foreign bodies. In fact, their torsos and all four of their limbs were still almost transparent save for the light that flowed down from the head, behaving like residual shine trapped in a body of glass or ice. The four limbs were identically slender and pointed, save for the lack of feet on the lower limbs, and the tendril wisps that flowed from their upper limbs in place of fingers

As the infernal horde dispersed throughout the ruined city, Lu crouched to his knees and shuffled uncomfortably in his shellsuit to the edge of the rooftop that was furthest from danger. To the left of the building's rear was a set of blackened and damaged balconies, onto which Lu descended. The Lavender Fox followed swiftly behind, to join the Reikan who was now spying intensely on Tatael Ram. Though a festoon of parasitic creepers, hanging from the ruin, obscured the Awreikan's face from Lu's vision, it was certain that the intruder had not anticipated Daleia-Dal to be in such foul condition. Confused, he had stopped in his tracks, while the lightlingerers continued to spread themselves out to each corner of the cuthrealm of night. This was precisely what Lu had hoped for. Though Ram certainly believed the starheads to be invincible, these supernatural opponents were at their most vulnerable when separated, for the Walker would be able to pick them off one by one.

With some difficulty, Lu dangled his armoured body off the broken balcony before releasing his grip and alighting upon a bed of uninhabited soil below.

His shellsuit, murdan, and disguised glassblade clattered somewhat upon the impact of his descent, threatening the silence of the realm. Lu frowned at his ageless, grey skin. Maintaining the quietness, and thus his anonymity, was sure to be a challenge. This did not appear to be an issue for the Lavender Fox, however. Despite the beast's cladding, it landed lightly and without a sound.

There, upon the distressed soils, the Reikan and his companion waited in silence for the approach of one of the starheads. Lu shivered as a cool wind licked at his skin and through his uncovered hair. Should he have worn a helmet, to protect himself from the lightlingerers? This would usually be an occasion in which Lu would wallow in self-doubt, unsure of his safety or his commands - or of the intentions of his commander. This time, however, his consumption of Fym's blue potion had evidently ridden him of his fears. He was not afraid of the lightlingerers or of Tatael.

A slow pattering muttered from the front-east corner of the building; Lu gripped his short-sword and his murdan as he awaited the first of his victims. With steps that slithered and lurched through the darkness, a glowing figure with a blinding head curled around the corner of the ruin. The demon's face, or lack thereof, flickered with a probable cognisance of the Walker and the fox, but Lu did not wait to find out if he had been noticed as the creature arrived. Holding his murdan close in front of his face for protection, he stabbed at the lightlingerer's burning visage without hesitation. The limbs of the phantom twitched convulsively, as a coarse but quiet shriek escaped its sizzling crown. Then, as the Walker retracted his blade, the body of the creature seemed to blow away on the wind, leaving only its radiant head behind, which slowly sank down to the ground.

For a handful of seconds, the orb of fire flickered and hissed on the floor but did not cease its glow. Lu began to doubt the power of Umbra.

These demons were not mortal. If Fym and the Mistress were wrong about the blade's pre-existing contact with the starheads, his enemy would be recovered before long. Another moment passed as Lu prepared to strike again at the sphere of light. Then, without warning, the starhead expanded violently. Thinning as it grew, the light stretched and dissipated into the cuthrealm before finally being engulfed by the darkness.

It was near black again in the cuthrealm of night, save for the illumination cast here and there by the movement of the wandering lightlingerers. Before Lu had fully processed the death of the first starhead, the Lavender Fox coiled around in response to something it had seen. Sure enough, there was an approaching glow from a nearby alleyway, and it was travelling fast.

Perhaps the starheads were linked as a hive of insects might be. The death of one had probably alerted the others to Lu's location. If so, the Walker would need to re-evaluate his strategies - he could be facing numerous phantoms at once. As the menacing shine drew near, Lu instinctively tried to hoist himself back up onto the ruin he had descended from, but to no avail.

Two mischievous silhouettes had become visible from across the damaged stone path, with the Lavender Fox standing bravely before them as if to defend the dazed Reikan. Lu hissed a quiet but cutting call for the fox to retreat, which the beast visibly discarded. The Walker was concerned for the fox's safety, despite its armour. Surely its exposed areas would be dangerously susceptible to the fire of the starheads? One of the demons raised a slender appendage, unleashing an unnervingly slow – but powerful - blast of white heat that wafted with aggression towards the Reikan. Lu raised his murdan to protect his face, stepping to the side. Despite not hearing a sound, he expected to see the Lavender Fox injured or possibly dead when he lowered the shield. But upon lowering the murdan, Lu was pleased, if not surprised to see that the fox was considerably more animated than before.

While there was no evidence of the starhead's flaming projectile from only a moment ago, a lilac mist had begun to form as the fox danced weightlessly around the lightlingerers. Had the Lavender Fox absorbed the blast, and converted it into power of its own?

As the fox danced, and the localised mist thickened, the creatures became increasingly incapable of movement. Soon, they were more or less immobilised. Lu saw his opportunity for attack. Though preoccupied by its own manoeuvres, the Lavender Fox managed to move aside, permitting the Walker to leap ahead and slash at the faces of the frozen fire-wraiths. One after the other, the lightlingerers hissed and deflated into the same throbbing, orb-like form that the first had assumed.

This time, the Walker did not watch or wait to spectate the success of Umbra's sorcery, for he knew that the blade's work was done. Without thinking, he was on top of the Lavender Fox, and the pair sailed silently back to the top of the central, connected ruins. From atop their lookout, Lu spied a new trio of approaching starheads and signalled towards them by pointing his blade in their direction. Immediately, the fox complied with Lu's instruction. Descending, swooping and swirling around the trio, the fox began a new mist-dance, with Lu still on its back.

As the Lavender Fox snaked and spiralled, around and between each lightlingerer, Lu felt a strange power emanating from the beast, and transferring into his body. As peculiar as it was, he paid it no mind for the moment, as he began slashing in at the starheads, stabbing two of them in the face as the lithe fox continued to summon its mysterious haze. Gradually, the third of the blazing trio fell subdued to the power of the fox's sorcery, but just as Lu raised the disguised glassblade and prepared to strike, he was himself struck by a blast of fire from behind.

Though his flesh was protected, the shellsuit took the impact in full, and the Reikan was sent hurtling forward towards the paralysed starhead.

Once Lu was back on his feet, he quickly made sure to stab the already-compromised phantom through the head, before turning to face an approaching line of four or five more lightlingerers, marching in a blazing column down a different decrepit alleyway.

Lu's left arm twitched, as a small shock rippled from the grip of the disguised glassblade. Then, the blade was still. But whatever had prompted the shock had been successful in inspiring Lu's next move, for the feeling was entirely reminiscent of another time, which seemed a life-age ago.

With all his self-doubt eliminated by the power of Fym's potion, Lu raised his sword in the direction of the queuing lightlingerers. A rush of extraordinary pleasure, accompanied by a freezing pain, shot from the Walker's core, and through his left arm.

In tricolour, a blistering energy of azure, fire orange, and pinkish purple beamed from the point of the short sword, and through the faces of every starhead in front. The ruins creaked too and began to collapse behind the starheads.

All sizzled and sulked as the Azdinic blast raged on. Then, Lu began to scream; a power began to drain from his body. It was a power of which he had no understanding, of how to use it, or of how much or how little remained. Eventually, he gripped his left wrist with his right hand and forced the arm down, and the trigon flood of intertwining blue, orange, and purple stopped abruptly.

Lu looked at the blade in disgust, before using his murdan-bearing right hand to wipe the sweat from his grey forehead. Though another five starheads were dead, the sound of his scream and the falling wreckage all seemed to echo through the cuthrealm of the night.

'WHERE ARE YOU?' bellowed a young, distressed man from afar. 'WHO ARE YOU?'

The Lavender Fox coiled around Lu, allowing him to climb aboard while the new rubble and dust were still settling. The two sailed up to the peak of another nearby ruin and cowered behind a chimney. Lu glanced around the broken brickwork and squinted through the dust and the dark to see Tatael Ram, dressed all in white armour and weaponry, standing nearby in the cuthrealm gardens. He seemed disturbed, and alert, but the arrogance in his stature had not changed at all, nor had his youthful handsomeness.

Before Ram had a chance to spot the Walker in the dark, the Lavender Fox nagged at Lu's right elbow, and Lu was forced to avert his eyes from the unnerved

Awreikan, to instead glance at whatever the beast had seen.

Four more lightlingerers were already on their way up the side of the ruin, strolling vertically up the wall as if they were weightless, not obeying the same laws as the land-bound. For a moment, Lu felt a great desire to stand before the approaching starheads and blast them with the same sorcery as before. Still, he had no control over this power - the surge would no doubt topple the entire building, hurling Reikan and Fox to their stone-crushed deaths.

The Lavender Fox had not hesitated to act, however. Lifting off from the ruin, it valiantly swooped in among the demons. Lu could do nothing but watch the fox, as it slowly appeared to exhaust its supply of magic. Each twist and turn seemed to summon little to no mist, while some movements almost seemed to clear the mist rather than gather it. It was then that Lu began to understand the fox's relationship with Azdin.

The Reikan made himself into a target, keeping some distance from the nearest starhead as he frantically waved his arms and beckoned for an attack. As expected, the phantom prepared to send its blaze towards Lu, who, anticipating the attack, hissed aggressively to catch the attention of the Lavender Fox. The fox appeared to become immediately aware of the Walker's plan and dived in front of the starhead, where it received the full force of the demon's flaming breath.

Though it seemed almost unbelievable to Lu, the idea had worked!

Immune to, if not *empowered* by the impact of the enchanted fire, the re-energised Lavender Fox whipped its body around and began the spiral dance once more, summoning floods of the paralysing haze to its aid.

Soon, the lightlingerers were all near frozen in their tracks. Two had made their way onto the horizontal of the rooftop; Lu cut through them with no problem at all, slashing through one fiery head after the other. The remaining two were still straddled mid-step up the side of the ruin, but Lu had already considered how he would handle them. Their heads were aligned, at least enough for his plan.

Standing at the edge of the building, the Walker launched the disguised witch-blade directly down and watched as the sword sailed consecutively through the heads of both of the stationary sentinels. Lu felt indestructible as he smiled at his efforts. Without thinking, he impulsively jumped off the edge of the building to collect his blade at the bottom. But the fall was far greater than the euphoric Reikan had expected.

As he landed, he felt the bones in his legs crunch and grind together, and he buckled into the mud in shock. With his left hand, he reached for Umbra, gripping it aggressively, as if to distract from the sensation of the broken bones. The Lavender Fox swooped down beside the Walker, and with a concerted effort, the injured sailor-warrior pulled himself up onto the shoulders of the armoured beast, trying his best to ignore the pain as he shifted his legs into a straddling position over the seat-shaped metalwork on the fox's back.

A pair of gleaming starheads slipped around the corner of another otherwise black avenue. Enraged, and impatient, Lu raised his sword and blasted the demons with ease, gladly accepting the freezing pain of the manoeuvre as a distraction from that in his legs. It was for this reason that, even once the starheads were hit, he felt reluctant to end his tri-coloured surge, twisting his body and obliterating every nearby building until eventually, the Lavender Fox began to yelp in distress, its legs struggling to brace against the force of the blast any longer.

Lu lowered his arm and again felt disgusted at his lack of control over his sorcery.

Every dark building in sight appeared to be crumbling from the blast, and soon the cuthrealm of ruin was nothing but a cuthrealm of dust. As the dust-cloud subsided, and the ringing of destruction had ceased, Lu's eyes and ears were able to focus on the few things left in the realm of night.

Only Tatael, accompanied by a single lightlingerer, appeared to have survived the onslaught.

'Lusini-Su...' whispered the armoured Awreikan. 'How can it be... how have you cheated death twice?'

Lu managed an expression somewhere between a grin and a grimace, before wiping what felt like more sweat from his forehead again. He looked at his right hand, which was now wet and stained not with his sweat, but with his blood. He had been so absorbed in the destruction that he had not felt the shards and scraps of the buildings flying into his face, slicing at his skin.

'How are you alive?' demanded Tatael.

Lu spotted a quiver in Ram's lips. The Awreikan was frightened.

The Lavender Fox began to approach Tatael, who instinctively raised his whiteblade for combat.

'Consider this an act of revenge' snarled Lu. 'For Haln, and Pernim! For Demja, and for the other sailors!'

The faces of Runil and Darathus flickered through Lu's mind, along with the rest of the kind sailors upon

Horral II who may have died in the scourge of Awreia, who Lu never had the chance to meet again.

Swallowing back the rising bile in his uneasy stomach, Lusini-Su, the Walker of the Bhia, aimed his short sword in line with Tatael Ram and allowed the deadly charge of his Azdin to flow forth once again.

Time seemed heavy, and reluctant to pass, as the intertwining colours of the surge flooded from blade to man. Lu roared until his voice became a broken, inhuman shriek. It was a cry forged half by victory's imminence, and half by the strain of the blast.

On impact, the colours of the surge reflected so violently that Lu could see very little at all. He felt as though a ring of magic had enveloped him; his body began to numb, and his vision began to fail. The last thing the Walker saw was the distant shape of the Lavender Fox fleeing into the sky.

Lu fluttered his eyelids furiously, in an attempt to awaken himself from his delirium. Eventually, his vision, along with the sensation in his limbs, began to return, but by then it was too late.

He was lying on his back, and Tatael Ram stood above him, readying his whiteblade for the kill.

'Impressive weapon! But it seems my armour, a gift from the King of Light, is truly indestructible!' panted the Awreikan. 'I'll gift your sorcerous blade to my master, along with your corpse!'

With both hands, Tatael Ram slammed the sharp of his blade down towards the Walker's throat. Lu raised his left arm to defend himself, and to his relief, Ram's weapon bounced vigorously off the shellsuit, though not without the impact shattering what felt like every bone in the Walker's forearm.

Nonetheless, this gave Lu a brief window of time to reach for his nearby murdan with his right arm while Tatael still staggered and recovered from the repercussion of his strike. Soon, however, Ram was ready to attack again, and Lu defended again, this time with the murdan. Lu was unable to stand, or attack, due to his injuries, but he refused to die tonight at the hands of Tatael.

If he *did* let Tatael slay him, the suit and the sabre would be safe – travelling back to the Lila along with his body, though any inclination to allow this result was dwarfed by an unstoppably fierce (and bestially unreasonable) desire to see Ram dead, tonight. But the Awreikan had already recovered from the blowback of his second strike and was certainly not going to make his next attack so easy to predict.

Ram swung his sword sideways, and it crashed into Lu's armoured torso, before slipping down and biting into an area of Lu's flesh that was less protected. The Reikan yelped, still managing to fling his murdan straight up into Tatael's jaw. The sharp of the murdan's horns sunk deep into Ram's cheek, causing him to cry out in shock. Then, Lu raised his now empty right hand and tried to channel the same sorcery he had forced through the short-sword. If he could manage another blast, even if it were smaller, then he would aim for Ram's helmless head.

But nothing came from Lu's trembling limb at all. No matter how much he strained, he could not will the Azdin from his body.

Though Tatael could tell that Lu had failed to conjure an attack, he was clearly afraid of the Reikan's abilities, and quickly sliced Lu's right hand clean off at the wrist. Lu screamed, recoiling his bleeding arm and curling into a position of agonic defeat. A mess of blood, Lu could do nothing now but wait for Tatael to kill him.

And he waited, and he oozed; his body throbbed, ready to be sated by the release of death. But there was no death to be had, for Tatael had frozen still, for reasons unknown to Lu. Though his eyelids were aching, Lu fought to keep them open. A shadow travelled over his body, before landing between Reikan and Awreikan.

It was a yellow-hooded, looming figure, astride the Lavender Fox. The yellow rider dismounted, raising a long arm to pull a great, shining sword from thin air. Sword in hand, the rider stood facing Tatael, awaiting his response. But it was not Tatael who responded.

Lu forced his eyes to remain open as the last lightlingerer, who had remained motionless at Ram's side until now, began to alter its appearance. In seconds, the starhead became an exact reflection of the yellow rider, mimicking all but the dazzling blade in the first rider's hand.

A long, awful silence fell over the cuthrealm of night, as the robed twins appeared to examine each other, only a short distance apart. Then, before the first yellow rider could react, the other wrapped its cloak around Tatael Ram and the pair vanished instantly. The original rider sheathed their blazing sword back into the empty air and turned to face Lu. A pair of hibiscus-red eyes peered from the darkness beneath her yellow hood.

She gazed pitifully at the broken body of the Reikan.

With slow, thoughtful steps, Fym Sallow approached. She kneeled beside him and kissed his bleeding brow. At that moment, Lu involuntarily relaxed, surrendering his body to his agonies, which caused him to faint.

~

Lusini-Su's ears were filled with the sound of a tremendous crack, promptly causing him to regain consciousness in a comfortable, but unfamiliar bed. Alert and prepared for danger, he opened his eyes. He was gowned, swathed in sheets and blankets, and alone. The room he was in felt warm, but a pleasant breeze visited his face now and again.

This was a building in the Den of Dawns.

As he slowly became more awake, Lu dragged his eyes from left to right across the room, to locate the source of the sound that had roused him. To his relief, his shellsuit, murdan, and Umbra were all neatly organised against the wall beside his bed, along with what appeared to be his old travelling attire. Wrapped in his peculiar black cloak (which he had missed the comfort of) was a small, quivering round lump.

Then, the lump cracked again thunderously, startling Lu. What was beneath his cloak?

The tired, grey man instinctively tried to reach towards the cloak, but his efforts were met with excruciating discomfort. His legs were still broken, and his left forearm still shattered. Upon lifting his right hand from beneath the blankets, Lu gasped in silent horror. He had not dreamed the injuries inflicted by Tatael Ram – his right hand was truly gone; his right forearm concluded abruptly, into a bandaged stump.

Before Lu could mourn his hand a moment longer, an odd crunching, scratching, hissing sound came from beneath his black cloak on the floor. No sooner had the Walker realised what the lump was, it began to contort and writhe under the cover of the fabric until it was no longer a lump at all.

A white-blue flurry of teeth, scales, and whiskers erupted from the onyx-black fabric. Immobilised, and unable to defend himself, the Walker clenched his eyes shut as something the size of a hare landed lightly upon his lap, squirming and squawking like no creature he had ever heard before.

He dared not look while the monster wriggled on top of him. Gradually the beast seemed to exhaust itself, before coming to a standstill. After a moment of no movement, Lu relaxed his tightened eyelids and opened them. Curled up on top of his blanketed, broken legs was a small, light-blue dragon! It was wingless, with a pair of forelegs and a pair of back legs all tucked under its snake-like belly. Its slender, whiskered head, dressed in a white-blue mane, was nuzzled into the fabric of Lu's sheets, and its long, similarly white-blue haired tail dangled just over the edge of the bed.

For a while, Lu could do nothing but watch this extraordinary creature purr and breathe in its sleep. *This* was what had been in the Mistress's egg that he had been guarding? The more he pondered the peculiarity of the Mistress's egg, and his role of caring for it, the less sense anything made.

Footsteps sounded in the hall outside of Lu's room. The door opened, and Fym Sallow walked in.

'It hatched!' she whispered. 'The egg has hatched! And you are awake!' She turned to look at Lu, thinly veiling a smirk that was perhaps induced by Lu's confusion and distress.

'Fym... What is this creature? And what has happened since last we spoke?'

Lu's voice was painfully hoarse.

The Azdinist walked closer to the Walker and elegantly, but sturdily, crouched beside him.

'The dragon? I know nothing of her parents – or her purpose, for that matter.' Fym smiled softly, stroking an ink-painted, bejewelled hand across the sleeping serpent's scaled body. 'I know little more than you. Between us, we must protect her, and raise her as if we were mothers. Ljubi has entrusted us with this role, for she ever-passes between realms and gateways through which the child cannot follow.'

'Ljubi?' Even more so than usual, Lusini-Su felt out of his depth in conversation with Fym Sallow.

'Ljubi. That is the name of the one that we call Mistress. A name I did not learn until I had been her apprentice for nearly a thousand years. But do not address her by this name until she grants you permission – I don't think I should have told you, but I have done it, regardless.'

The Walker nodded graciously, resisting his desire to pursue the matter. He raised his incomplete arm from the sheets.

'I'm wounded, Fym. Why didn't you let me die, and return to Lila? Why did the final starhead become your twin?'

Sallow turned her head away from the Reikan.

'There is much you don't understand, Lusini-Su.'

Lu was becoming irritated with Sallow's mysterious replies.

'Fym, I'm sorry if I seem impatient, but you appear to be avoiding my questions. Maybe I would understand more if you were to tell me more? We share a destiny, do we not?'

'You failed your mission, Lusini-Su. Not only were you unsuccessful in killing Ram - you also lost control of your power. The moment you unleashed an Azdinic attack from the blade, the Lightlingerers alerted Morl-Majgyn to your survival. Though he is uninformed of your allegiance, the Apprentice God believes you to be a powerful Azdinist - and thus a threat to his growing dominion.'

'Morl-Majgyn...' Nightmarish visions of the impossibly vast, shimmering dragon flashed through Lu's mind.

'His forces await you upon the Lila Isle. If you had simply wielded the short-sword as you were instructed, I would have gladly killed you in order to renew your broken body upon the Lila. If you had wielded the sword as you were instructed, Tatael's armour would not have deflected the Azdinic blast, and you would have defeated him in regular combat!'

As Fym spoke, Lu began to notice the stress in the Azdinist's face. She looked as though she had not slept in days.

'Fym... I'm sorry. I'm sorry that I failed you – I didn't know how to command my Azdin. I was hoping you would teach me.'

Fym cleared her throat and returned her attention to the dragon on Lu's lap. Her raised voice has roused the creature. Agitated, it had lifted its head to spectate the conversation, but as the Azdinist stroked its face, the pacified dragon nuzzled its snout back into the blankets of the bed.

'And I will, Lusini-Su. But for now, I must conserve and grow my own power; we will need as much Azdin as our bodies can carry before we dare to challenge Majgyn's forces and reclaim the Lila. The Brown Acolytes will mend your legs, and regrow your hand, but the process will be slow, as we must still spend our combined Azdin on keeping the Den of Dawns veiled from enemy eyes.'

'Majgyn's servant, the King of Light...' whispered Lu. 'Tatael will have returned to the King of Light, telling tales of my weapon and my magic. Of the Lavender Fox, and of you!'

But Fym seemed unperturbed by such thoughts.

'The King of Light is already very much aware of the Lavender Fox and I. Apart from the Den of Dawns' defence system, you were the only secret we had left to keep from the sorcerer. But now they have seen you in the flesh, though they chose not to attack you. I am unsure as to why.'

'There was only one other in the cuthrealm of the night...' Lu trawled through his memories – when else could he have encountered the King of Light?

'As I said earlier – there is much you have yet to learn. While we wait for my power to grow, and your body to heal, I would very much like you to help me record my own history in the same way you have documented your own. It will be essential if you are to understand your destiny, the identity of the King of Light, the nature of our blades, and how we must use them to defeat Majgyn...' The Azdinist's voice began to trail off; she seemed disturbed by something, as she continued to massage the scales of the sleeping serpent.

'Again, I must apologise for my impatience' said Lu, firmly. 'But I cannot wait until I have finished documenting your adventures to learn the sorcerer's identity.'

Fym inhaled slowly and returned her eyes to meet with Lu's.

'If I tell you now, you must accept it without question. You must promise to write my story.'

The Walker frowned at Fym's awkward request, before agreeing to it.

'I promise I will write your story, Fym. Now tell me, who is the King of Light? I am entitled to know, after all he has taken from me.'

'The nineteenth lightlingerer' muttered Sallow.

'The hooded figure... I'm afraid I don't understand. Why would the King of Light steal your identity?'

'She didn't. She was, and *is* my identity. An identity I created, and an identity I intend to destroy.'

– END OF PART THREE –

EPILOGUE

And the Walker did not speak another word to the Azdinist, who claimed to be the 'King of Light' for the rest of the week. It seemed to him that, while he had held Tatael accountable, he should have blamed the Awreikan's master, the King of Light, for the deaths of Haln, Pernim, Demja, and the rest of Awreia.

If Fym Sallow was the King of Light, then she was not Lu's ally. If the Mistress was Fym's mentor, then she was not Lu's ally.

Rejecting most hospitality and all visits from the other Acolytes, Lusini-Su became withdrawn in his confusion, finding a single comfort in the company of a small, blue dragon that often visited his chambers.

Occasionally, he caught fragments of conversations from passing occupants. The defences of the Den of Dawns were strengthened, and the city of Daleia-Dal was still safe. There had been no sightings of either Tatael or his master since Lu had faced them in the cuthrealm of night.

Lu continued to wallow in the comfort of his depression for nearly a month, before finally succumbing to boredom. His mind grew tired of revisiting his anguish, and his body was becoming increasingly stiff and useless with every day that it went untreated. In some ways, he felt himself becoming the very same husk that once traipsed the Bhia floor.

It was this realisation that pained him most of all. He would not let himself return to dormancy after everything he had seen, done, and lost on his quest for freedom.

One morning, the Walker called for the aid of the brown acolytes. As healers came rushing to his bedside, he relaxed his tired, grey forehead.

As promised, he would listen to what Fym had to say.

He would document her story.

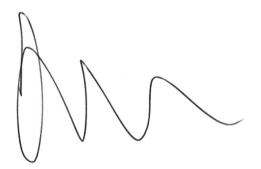

Milton Keynes UK
Ingram Content Group UK Ltd.
UKHW012143151223
434414UK00005B/24

9 781803 816722